DEADLY VIRTUES

Also by Jo Bannister

Perfect Sins

Death in High Places

Liars All

Closer Still

Flawed

Requiem for a Dealer

Breaking Faith

The Depths of Solitude

Reflections

True Witness

Echoes of Lies

DEADLY VIRTUES

JO BANNISTER

MINOTAUR BOOKS NEW YORK

This is a work of fiction. All of the characters, organizations, and events portrayed in this novel are either products of the author's imagination or are used fictitiously.

DEADLY VIRTUES. Copyright © 2013 by Jo Bannister. All rights reserved. Printed in the United States of America. For information, address St. Martin's Press, 175 Fifth Avenue, New York, N.Y. 10010.

www.minotaurbooks.com

The Library of Congress has cataloged the hardcover edition as follows:

Bannister, Jo.
Deadly Virtues / Jo Bannister.—1st ed.
p. cm.
ISBN 978-1-250-02344-5 (hardcover)
ISBN 978-1-250-02345-2 (e-book)
1. Police—England—Fiction. 2. Mystery fiction. I. Title.
PR6052.A497D37 2013
823'.914—dc23
2012042105

ISBN 978-1-250-07177-4 (trade paperback)

Minotaur books may be purchased for educational, business, or promotional use. For information on bulk purchases, please contact the Macmillan Corporate and Premium Sales Department at 1-800-221-7945, extension 5442, or write to specialmarkets@macmillan.com.

First Minotaur Books Paperback Edition: November 2014

10 9 8 7 6 5 4 3 2 1

DEADLY VIRTUES

CHAPTER 1

JEROME CARDY KNEW he was going to die the moment he saw the other car in his rearview mirror. He knew it wasn't going to stop: it was already too close, if it was braking at all it was too little too late, and he had nowhere left to go. As soon as the lights changed, a milk tanker the size of Rutland had moved into the junction. With enough milk to protect a generation from rickets in front and the big silver hatchback coming up fast behind, all Jerome could do was brace himself for the inevitable. He knew what was going to happen. He'd known for weeks.

He could have got out while there was still time. But he'd had too much to lose. He'd told himself that it might never happen. That the future isn't set in stone. That if he was careful, if he kept out of trouble, no one could touch him. If he played it cool, stayed out of reach, he might never have to choose between the love of his life and, well, his life. . . .

And now it was too late to choose. The choice had been made for him. All Jerome could do was close his eyes, make himself small behind the wheel, and wait.

The impact, when it came, was less than he'd been expecting. Jerome's car stayed where it was, held by its own handbrake;

the milk tanker found the gap it had been waiting for and moved off; Jerome rocked for a moment in his seat belt, then settled back, still waiting.

When nothing else happened, cautiously he opened one eye.

It hadn't been enough of an accident to stop the rush-hour traffic. The cars that had been in line behind him were now carefully edging past and on their way home. Not so much an accident as a shunt: if nobody's hurt, you exchange details and you, too, get on your way. Jerome wasn't hurt. He turned slowly in his seat to look behind him.

The other driver was a middle-aged woman, her mouth shocked to a dark round O. She made no move, nor did her expression change, as he slowly got out of his car and walked back to her. "Are you all right?"

She blinked, and went from total paralysis to frantic hyperactivity without passing through normal. She didn't answer him but dived into the well of the passenger seat, scrabbling for her handbag. "We have to call the police! Have you got a phone? I have a phone—in here somewhere. I can't find it! Have you got a phone? We have to call the police."

"Well, actually," said Jerome gently, "we don't. Unless you're hurt. I'm not hurt, and nobody else was involved. We can just exchange details and let the insurance sort it out."

Her eyes stretched almost as wide as her mouth. She was a well-dressed, middle-aged, middle-class woman who might never have been in an accident before. The little card from her insurers that told her what to do in the event of an incident hadn't warned her how distressed she'd be, how difficult she'd find it to act logically or even to make sense.

Jerome said again, "*Are* you hurt? Do we need an ambulance?"

After a moment she shook her head. "No. You?"

"I'm fine," he assured her. "Listen, why don't we park your car, I'll drive you home, and we'll swap details over a cup of tea?"

It was as if she was drowning and he'd thrown her a lifeline, but she didn't like to grab it because she didn't know where it had been. "Can we? Don't we have to call the police?"

He shook his head. "It's a minor traffic accident. Nobody's hurt—nobody's drunk—nobody's committed an offense. We pass it over to the insurers. I'll park your car if you don't want to." He opened her door and extended a courteous hand.

Her name was Evelyn Wiltshire. She was a middle-aged, middle-class Englishwoman, and she was also shocked, which may have been part of it, but mainly she just wasn't used to young black men trying to take her by the hand. She recoiled instinctively. "Police! We need to call the police. I have a phone, somewhere. . . ."

Jerome fought to keep calm. If he snapped at her, if he frightened her, the opportunity to sort this out in a civilized fashion would be gone. And he had much more to lose than she did. "My name is Jerome. I'm a second-year law student. Really, I wouldn't tell you this was all right if it wasn't. Why would I? The accident wasn't my fault. It's not me the police will accuse of driving carelessly."

Mrs. Wiltshire had finally found the phone. She stared at it as if it might bite. She stared at Jerome, ditto. His future hung by a thread.

She'd been brought up to do the right thing, even if it wasn't in her own best interests. She started to dial.

Jerome felt himself grow desperate. "If you're worried about the cost, why don't we just fix our own dents? We don't even have to involve the insurers, if you don't want to. There really isn't that much damage. Is that all right? Can we do that?"

"But . . . I ran into you. . . ."

"Yes. That's okay. My father owns a garage—he'll sort me out. There's no need to involve the police. Is that all right?"

For a moment longer it hung in the balance. Then Mrs. Wiltshire swallowed. Fifty years of middle-class morality weighed more with her than her own immediate wishes. "No, I'm sorry. I'm going to call the police."

Jerome was backing away before she'd finished dialing. "I'm sorry, too. I really am sorry. But I can't wait." He ran back to his car and drove off without knowing or even caring where he was driving to, only that he was putting distance between himself and the scene of the accident. Such a little accident. Such a trivial reason to die.

I see you took my advice." The woman had a nose meant for pince-nez: sharp as a blade, with a pair of diamond gray eyes above. Everything about her—the nose, the glasses, the tailored suit she wore, the way she scraped her dark hair away from her face and pinned it into a ruthless bun—said *severe*. But as she glanced at the dog curled up on her rug, she smiled, and the smile knocked ten years off her age and softened her face in unexpected ways. Her name was Laura Fry, and she was a trauma therapist.

The man looked at the dog, too. As if he couldn't quite remember where it had come from. "Yes."

"Is it helping?"

He considered. "I'm not sure."

"It's a nice dog. I'd have thought you'd enjoy the company."

"I do."

"Being alone can become a habit that's hard to break."

"Yes."

Laura Fry smiled again. "Gabriel, this process would be more useful if you didn't spend words as if they were fifty-pound notes."

The man blinked, managed a pale flicker of a grin. "Sorry." Then, as if he was trying to cooperate, to enter into the spirit of the thing: "I talk to the dog."

"Good." Laura nodded reassuringly. "Talking to the dog is good."

A faint, fragile frown. "Is it?"

"Of course. She likes you talking to her, doesn't she?"

"Yes."

"And you feel better for talking to her?"

Again, he had to think. "I suppose so."

"Then where's the downside? Unless you start thinking she's talking back." He didn't return her sly grin, so she pressed on. "Gabriel, this was always going to be hard. We both knew that. Getting a dog isn't going to turn your life around—make you forget what happened, or make it hurt any less. It's a dog, not a magician.

"But it will help. You need to find ways of relating to the world again, and looking after something that needs you is a start. It doesn't actually matter whether you like dogs or not. She's your responsibility now. She was a stray dog with nothing, not even much time left, until you came along. Now she has a home and someone to love. You don't even have to love her in return. A square meal every day and she'll *think* you love her, and that's what counts."

"Then what's the point?" His brow was creased, as if he was genuinely trying to understand. He was a man in his late thirties with rather a lot of dark curly hair and creases that looked like laughter lines around his deep-set brown eyes. They'd been there a long time. He hadn't laughed much recently.

Laura elevated a pencil-sharp eyebrow. "Apart from the fact that because of you she lives instead of dying? Looking after things is good for us. It makes us feel needed. It makes us think about something beyond our own hurts. It forces us into some kind of routine, and routine is good, too. You're eating better, aren't you? I can see. You make her meal, and then you get something for yourself. She needs walking, so you walk her—fresh air, exercise, nod an acknowledgment at other people doing the same thing. You were hardly leaving the house, and now you are. That's the point."

She looked down at the dog again, all nose and legs, curled on the rug as if posing for an illuminated manuscript. "What do you call her?"

"Patience."

"Ah." Just that.

Gabriel Ash looked at her warily. "That's significant?"

"Possibly. Do you know why people talk to dogs?" He waited. "Because they feel silly talking to themselves. It isn't always easy to find a human confidant. The dog is an uncritical listener"—the diamond gray eyes twinkled mischievously—"a bit like a therapist. Talking to a dog is like holding a conversation with yourself—with another aspect of yourself. The fact that you call your dog Patience suggests to me that, somewhere inside yourself, you recognize the fact that patience is what you need. To be gentle with yourself, to give yourself time to come to terms with what happened. You could have called her Spotty, or Snowball."

He almost flinched as he looked down at the animal at his feet. "If I'd called her Snowball, she'd never have spoken to me again."

"Ah."

He darted a furtive sideways look, as if he'd let something slip, something that would cause him trouble. But then, he always looked as if he was afraid of causing trouble. "Again with the 'ah'?"

"You think she wouldn't like it because it's an animal's name?"

"Because it's not a name at all—it's a thing. Like a chair, or a tablecloth. If we want animals as companions, why would we name them after inanimate objects? It's not . . . respectful. Giving them a proper name—a person's name—makes you think of them as some*one* rather than some*thing*. Encourages you to treat them decently."

He saw the way Laura Fry was looking at him and rocked back in his chair, his gaunt face catching the light from the window. "And now you think that because I chose a bitch and gave her a woman's name, I'm thinking of her as a wife substitute."

The therapist shook her head. "Not at all. Gabriel, there's nothing wrong with you. There's nothing wrong with how you're feeling or what you're doing. Something terrible happened in your life, and you're struggling to deal with it, and anything that helps, even a little bit, is a good thing. Getting a dog is a good thing. Caring about her is a good thing.

"You're not mad. You're not even slightly unhinged. In the normal way of things you and I would never have met. All I'm trying to do, all these conversations are about, is to help you find a way of managing what happened without it destroying you. Whatever you call her, if the dog gets you out of your chair and makes you go into the kitchen, and then makes you walk as far as the park, she's already had a positive influence." She leaned down and patted the white dog.

"She doesn't . . ." He bit his lip.

"What?" He wasn't going to answer; she pressed him. "What, Gabriel?"

"I'm not sure she likes being patted."

"No? Well, in that case you chose her name well—she's very patient." But she had the grace to leave the dog alone.

She saw the pair of them out. Her office looked over Norbold's Jubilee Park, a view she enjoyed, even if most of her clients were too wrapped up in their own troubles to appreciate it. "Next Wednesday, yes?"

"Yes."

Behind the pince-nez Laura Fry's sharp eyes were concerned and almost affectionate. "I'm always afraid that you won't come. That you'll decide therapy is for wimps and you can manage without. That you'd rather manage without. You've thought about it, haven't you?"

He wouldn't lie. "I was never much good at sharing. Even . . . before."

"I know that. I know these sessions are a trial to you. All I can tell you is, you are getting better. Stronger. I can see you getting stronger."

"Yes? Then why—" He stopped.

"Why what?"

He looked across the expanse of the park, the trees in their fresh spring livery, so he wouldn't have to look at her. "Then why do I feel afraid all the time?"

He was a client, and Laura Fry didn't weep for clients. She helped them instead. She said softly, "Because the wounds are still raw. Because the situation is unresolved. Because not knowing is worse than knowing the worst. Because not enough time has passed yet for you to pack the hurt and the uncertainty away where you can get on with your life without constantly tripping over them. Because you need"—she looked at the dog, now tugging with gentle insistence at her lead—"patience. You won't always feel how you feel today."

He nodded, and walked away and didn't look back. Not until he judged she'd have gone back inside did he wipe his sleeve across his eyes.

Jerome Cardy was heading for the motorway. From there, all England was before him. He should have done this before. He could call, explain. She could join him. They'd be safe. Anywhere but Norbold, they'd be safe.

He almost made it. He could actually see high-sided vehicles on the motorway overpass, to his right and maybe a mile ahead, when the police car swung out of a side street and into line behind him, and his heart shot into his throat.

For ten or fifteen seconds, driving with infinite care and watching it in his rearview mirror, Jerome tried to tell himself it was a coincidence. A patrol car, patrolling. That everyone experiences a momentary anxiety when a police car comes up behind them, but ninety-nine times out of a hundred it's just doing what it does, showing the flag and deterring people from dropping litter and murdering their neighbors.

But at the end of those ten or fifteen seconds the police car didn't turn away and vanish as mysteriously as it had appeared. It turned on its siren and flashing blue light, and when Jerome looked back in dread, he saw the officer in the left-hand seat signaling him to pull over.

There was no time to think. Either he did as he was told or he made a run for it. No one who knew him, no one who knew what had happened at the junction, would have thought there was any question about what he would do. But then, almost none of them knew what he was facing. What falling into the hands of Norbold's police would mean. And the motorway was less than a mile away. All England waiting . . .

Like the woman in the silver hatchback, Jerome was a law-abiding citizen. It went against every tenet to run from the police. If there's been a misunderstanding, you stop and sort it out. Running only makes you look guilty. He swallowed. He passed a hand across his mouth. And then, acting on purest instinct, the instinct for self-preservation, he floored the accelerator.

Once again luck was not with him, so the escape attempt was over almost before it had begun. It was the middle of the evening—people heading out formed a bottleneck at the approach to the motorway. Traffic slowed to fifteen miles an hour. You can't make a dash for freedom at fifteen miles an hour, but neither was he prepared to risk lives by driving up onto the pavement or against the traffic flow. Jerome Cardy clenched his fists on the wheel, wiped the sweat off his brow with his cuff, and, feeling sick, pulled over.

CHAPTER 2

HALF A MILE AWAY, in a shady corner of Jubilee Park where the steps of the war memorial provided the youth of Norbold with a convenient stage to drink themselves stupid, a small gang of teenagers was indulging in a bit of dummy baiting.

It wasn't that they nurtured any particular dislike for the man with the white dog. They didn't even know his name. They saw him most days, but he didn't bother them. He didn't seem to bother anybody. All they knew of him was that he walked his dog in the park every morning and every evening, rain or shine, and muttered to himself as he went.

It was enough. They were between about fifteen and nineteen years old, they'd given up on school not because—as they'd told friends and family—it was stupid but because they'd come to believe that they were, and they didn't see any way that their lives were ever going to improve. On top of that they'd run out of cider. One of them grinned a vacuous grin and nodded at the man with the dog, and the others hauled themselves off the stone steps and followed. Partly to see what happened, partly to make sure that something did.

Gabriel Ash didn't so much mutter to himself as talk to his

dog. If this was indeed a sign of madness, a great many of us would be eating our meals with plastic cutlery, but in fact it's nothing of the kind. It can be a sign of loneliness. Or just that your social circle is such that there's more satisfaction in talking to a dog.

Patience saw the group approaching before Ash did. She turned toward them with a low growl. She wasn't a big dog, but there was a lean athleticism to her that emphasized those features hounds have always been bred for: speed and bite. The boys broke stride before they came within range of the long muzzle, which was nothing more than teeth covered by a curtain of lip, currently lifting at one corner.

"Hey, dummy—your dog's growling at me!"

Gabriel kept walking and didn't look around. He didn't want trouble. He'd already had all the trouble one man could cope with.

"Hey, dummy, I'm talking to you! Your dog's growling at me. What you going do about it?"

He still didn't look around. "Take her home," he said quietly. "Right now."

"Shouldn't have brought it out in public, a dangerous dog like that."

"She isn't dangerous, and she's on a lead."

"That's a pit bull terrier, that is. Them's illegal."

Another voice, oddly reasonable: "No, it's a lurcher."

The boy who had spoken first turned on the one who'd joined in. "Who asked your opinion? Anyway, what's a lurcher?"

"It's a sporting dog. Gypsies use them to chase rabbits. Mostly got a bit of greyhound and a bit of terrier in them."

At least he'd diverted attention away from Ash. His friends were staring at him as if they thought that knowledge, any knowledge, was a dangerous thing. "What makes you such a frigging expert?"

"My granddad used to breed lurchers. That one's got a bit of pointer in it. He'd have called it a 'gentleman's lurcher.'"

The older youth was shaking his head darkly, perplexed and disapproving in equal measure. "You're a constant frigging wonder to me, Saturday. Mostly, that I've known you for nine months without punching your frigging lights out. Now, find me a stick. I'll teach this dummy to bring his dangerous dog into our park."

The boy called, apparently, Saturday took a step back, shoving his fists deep into the pockets of his battered jeans. "You don't need a stick. Just thump him. Like you usually do."

"I need a stick," said the older boy with a kind of heavy insistence, "because before I thump him I need to put that thing out of action. Get it?"

Saturday's eyes flared unhappily. "My granddad says, 'Only a coward takes a stick to a dog.'"

"Yeah? Well, I'll thump your granddad as well, then, all right? Now find me a stick."

"No!" But before his rebellion cost him too much, he added hurriedly, "But I'll hold the dog while you thump him. That do?"

The older boy looked at Patience, looked at Saturday, looked at Ash. "You'll hold the dog? That dog?"

"Yeah."

"While we thump him?"

"Yeah."

"What if you let it go?"

"I won't."

"What if it bites you?"

Saturday considered. "Thump him quickly. If it bites me, Trucker, damn sure I'm letting go."

"Oh, for frig's sake!"

But Saturday was already moving toward Ash, one hand out for the lead. "Give me your dog, mister," he said softly. "Otherwise she's going to get hurt."

Ash held his gaze for a moment. He looked like the rest of them—maybe sixteen years old, thin, and none too clean—but there was something in his eyes, a spark of humanity, that made Ash think maybe he could trust him. After a moment he proferred the lead.

Saturday nodded and took it. "Come on, girl, you come with me. Your dad's going to be . . . busy . . . for a minute or two." He led her—growling and whining her protests, digging in her long paws and leaning all her weight into her collar—behind the group as it split and then gathered around the man.

He'd told Laura Fry that he was afraid all the time. But perhaps this wasn't what he was afraid of. Or perhaps he'd lived with the fear long enough to learn a kind of fatalism. He made no attempt to evade what was coming, either to escape or to fight back. He stood with his head bowed and his hands spread slightly from his body, and he waited.

He was a grown man; even now he was probably the match of any of these youths. But they were eight, and they hemmed him in so tightly that no one passing on the road or on foot through the park would have seen what was happening.

So there really was no need for the first blow to come from behind. That was Trucker, of course. Though Saturday couldn't actually see him through the press of backs, it was always Trucker who struck the first blow, and usually from behind. He winced, bracing himself against the dog's urgent efforts to free herself.

Ash thought he was ready. He knew he was going to take a

beating. But a lot worse things had happened to him, and part of him didn't even care.

But he was wrong. He wasn't ready for the direction the assault came from, the lack of any warning, or the sheer vicious force of the blow. It took him in the small of the back and dropped him, gasping, to his knees, and down there it was only a matter of moments before they started using him as a football. He curled up tight, trying to take the worst of the assault on his arms and legs, but eight is a lot of people. Sixteen fists and sixteen feet. Half a minute of it and he couldn't have risen to save his life. A minute more and there might have been nothing left to save.

Even Saturday, who'd seen it before, was startled by the mindless violence of the attack. He knew Trucker had a nasty temper and the others would follow where he led, but he hadn't known they were capable of murder. In his head, in one of the long, terrible seconds while he watched, he amended that to *we*. If he hadn't been holding this dog, he'd have been in there, too, doing what the rest of them were doing. Beating a man senseless. And then, if nothing came to stop them, beating him to death. For nothing. No reason, except that they were bored.

He looked about him, for once in his life hoping that a police patrol might cruise by. There were more of them than there used to be—it was called "zero-tolerance policing," and apparently it went down well with the tax-payers—but not here, not now. The only other person in the park was an old lady walking a Westie, and she was shuffling away in the opposite direction as quickly as her lisle stockings would carry her.

Which left him and the dog. He thought about it for another crippling second; then he shrugged. "See what you can do," he whispered, and dropped the lead.

Then, with a flash of foresight, he let out a yell. "Ow! You . . . bitch! Sorry, Trucker, she got away from me. . . ."

Impossible to judge if this attempt to cover himself had been registered, because before he had the last words out the loosed dog struck into the melee like an Exocet missile with teeth.

These are civilized days. Even the wolves around our hearths are for the most part pretty well behaved, with the result that most people have never seen a real, serious, mean-it dog attack and have no idea the destructive force of the canine mouth. Tacticians who talk about bringing power to a point could hardly find a better example than in the dentistry of the domestic dog. The canines, up front, sharp and penetrating to wound and grip; the serried ranks of the carnassials, farther back, where the shearing power of the jaw is greater, angled and honed to strip flesh off bone and then to splinter the bone. Two or three times a year, due to bad breeding, bad handling, or maybe just badness, somebody's dog leaves the reservation—stops begging for biscuits, running after Frisbees, and Dying for England—and rips a child's throat out. And everyone expresses horrified astonishment. But that's what a dog is: a killing machine. You only have to look at the anatomy. The wonder is not that once in a blue moon it fulfills its potential, but that it happens so incredibly seldom. That an animal that could quite literally take your hand off almost always chooses to lick it instead.

The lurcher bitch Patience made the transition from faithful pet to apex predator in the time it took her to cross ten meters, which was about a second, and she arrived fangs-first at the wall of vicious aggression surrounding her owner.

A human backside is only soft flesh lightly upholstered. Her teeth met in the middle.

In another second the accompanying sound track, which had been grunts of effort and hoots of derision, turned to howls of pain and frantic yells of "Gerritoffame!" A space opened up as the gang abandoned its murderous sport and redirected its energies to self-defense. A few of the braver ones swung a leg at the flashing dog, but they were far too slow, presenting only another target for her to snap at in passing. The space widened, the little mob lost focus and organization, and then suddenly they were fleeing, overtaking one another in the desire to put distance between themselves and the furious animal. Saturday ran with them. A few seconds more and there was only Gabriel Ash, lying on the ground, bloody and unmoving, and Patience, prowling a defensive circle around him, long jaws panting wide, the white hairs still erect between her shoulder blades.

From the edge of the park, the two-tone of a fast-approaching police car. The old lady with the Westie had had a mobile phone in her handbag. Ignoring the signs, the driver came the direct route across the grass and his companion got out, edging cautiously toward the injured man while keeping her eyes constantly on the dog. But Patience, as if she understood, sat down and let her come.

Her name was Hazel Best, and she hadn't been in Norbold long. In fact, she hadn't been a police officer for very long. She was still on probation and this was her first posting.

The men and women she'd trained with had commiserated, thinking she'd drawn the short straw. Norbold wasn't the sort of place where careers were made. For that you needed one of the big cities, where crime stalked the streets and some of the people it stalked were rich and famous. You needed the opportunity to disarm an ax maniac or foil a bank robbery from time to time. You needed the possibility of saving a celebrity's toddler from kidnapping, or to be the thinnest of thin blue lines between a terrorist wearing the ultimate in hi-viz vests and his intended targets. Of course, you also needed to survive these experiences, but if you did, you could expect promotion, fast-tracking, maybe even a medal.

And all these things were more likely to happen on the streets of London, or Glasgow, or Birmingham or Manchester, than in a small West Midlands town where the biggest employer was a manufacturer of flowered tea sets and the average age of the population was fifty-three. Indeed, Norbold was famous—infamous, among Hazel Best's fellow probationers—for its low crime rate. The general feeling was that, in order to build up some kind of an arrest record there, she'd have to stop people for being old and disorganized, and wielding a walker without due care and attention.

Hazel let them enjoy their joke. In fact, she was curious to learn how you policed a town so as to keep the level of almost all crimes consistently below the national average. And she'd been told the answer the first day she reported for duty. The answer was Johnny Fountain.

But Norbold's charismatic chief superintendent and his signature brand of zero-tolerance policing had not been enough to save the man at her feet from the kind of beating that leaves people deaf, blind, or brain-damaged. While he was unconscious and masked in his own blood, there was no knowing how serious his injuries were. Hazel shouted, "Ambulance!" to her colleague in the car, then—still keeping one eye on the dog—reached down to touch the man's shoulder. "It's all right," she said, using the calm of her voice to cut through the terror that had been his last conscious thought. "You're safe now. We'll look after you."

Constable Wayne Budgen, having made the call, came over to help. He winced. "They fairly laid into him this time."

Hazel looked up in surprise. "You mean this has happened before?"

"Not like this. But yes, he's been roughed up a time or two. Local kids, mostly."

"Why? Who is he?"

"I don't know his name. Everyone calls him 'Rambles.'" The frank incredulity in her stare made him flush. "'Rambles With Dogs.' You know—like *Dances with Wolves*? I think he's a bit . . ." He made a spiral movement with one finger about his ear. "He wanders around the place talking to that dog."

"You're telling me that he's suffering from a mental disability, and therefore the local youth make a hobby of kicking him up and down the park."

Hazel's voice was level, but Wayne Budgen knew perfectly well when he was being told off. And he wasn't sure how to deal with it. Theoretically, he was senior to Hazel Best—he'd been on the job longer; that's why he'd been given the task of showing her around. But she was a couple of years older than he was—twenty-five, twenty-six. She'd done something else before joining the police. He wasn't sure what, but from the way she was looking at him, it might have been teaching.

He spread a defensive hand. "What can we do? We can't lock him up."

"No. Perhaps we should try locking *them* up."

"It's different ones each time. Look, I'm not saying it's right. I'm saying it happens. Vulnerable people get bullied. We stop it when we see it." He saw the skepticism in her gaze. "If you don't believe me, look at the crime returns. Common assault—eight percent below the national average. Eight percent. That's a lot of people—people like him—that get home safe in Norbold who'd be in Accidents & Emergency in most other towns."

Hazel sighed. "Yes. Yes, I know, Wayne. I'm not blaming you. Like you say, some things are always going to happen. It's just, if you're one of the people it always happens to, it won't seem that important that people somewhere else have it even worse."

Across the park they heard the sound of the ambulance. It seemed to mean something to the man on the ground, too, because finally he started to uncurl and make vague gestures toward getting up. Hazel knelt beside him.

"How are you feeling? I'm Hazel, by the way. Maybe you shouldn't move around too much until the paramedics have had a look at you."

"I'm all right," he mumbled. She wasn't sure how much of his lack of clarity was due to his broken lip, how much to concussion, how much to his mental condition. He looked around for his dog, and then, having located her, looked at Hazel. "Really. I don't need the paramedics."

"Well, they're here now," said Hazel reasonably, "so they might as well check you over. You've got some nasty cuts there. They'll probably take you to the Royal to get a few stitches put in."

"No." Ash shook his head with infinite caution. "I'm not going to the hospital. They can slap on some of those butterfly plasters, they'll do just as well."

Which rather surprised Hazel Best. He didn't talk like a man with psychiatric problems. He talked the way she talked—the way normal people talk.

Guided by the old mantra that no head injury is so trivial it can safely be ignored nor so serious it should be despaired of, the paramedics wanted to take him in for X-rays. Ash refused. "I'm not going to the hospital," he said again. "I don't want to be rude. I'm grateful for your help, but you can't make me."

Constable Budgen frowned. "What's the problem? You one of these religious nuts . . . people?"

Gabriel Ash gave a little snort that seemed closer to laughter than anything else. "No, just an ordinary nut."

"You're worried about your dog, aren't you?" Hazel realized. "Because you can't take it into the hospital. I'll look after it for you, if you like."

He smiled. A bloody, beaten thing it was, too, but the warmth was genuine. "Thank you. But I don't need to go to the hospital. If you want to help, help me up."

It was a bit of a dilemma. People are entitled to refuse offers of assistance, however well intentioned and indeed well advised. On the other hand, if there was some doubt about his mental capacity . . .

"How do you feel about police stations?" asked Hazel. "Ours is just around the corner. The police surgeon can have a look at you, we'll have a cup of coffee—I don't know about you, but I need one, and Wayne here's desperate for a fag break—and you and your dog can have a quiet sit-down for an hour. If you still seem all right then, I'll take you home. Deal?"

He thought about it. "Deal."

She helped him up. She gave him the dog's lead. "I don't know your name."

"Gabriel Ash. And this is Patience."

CHAPTER 3

CHIEF SUPERINTENDENT John Fountain regarded the reflection in the mirror with fond solemnity. Not his own face, which had been a thing of no great beauty when he was young and now showed the effects of too many late nights and pie and chip suppers, but that of his wife behind him, the tip of her tongue protruding between her lips as she concentrated on the bow tie he himself had given up on. Her name was Denise, and he supposed that by conventional standards she wasn't a thing of any great beauty, either; but she was to him. She was the only woman he'd ever loved, and he loved her more now than when they were twenty.

Which is why he went on sitting at the dressing-table mirror while she fiddled with the stupid strip of fabric instead of groping around in his chest of drawers for the ready-made one. Denis—he called her Denis: it had been their joke for so long it didn't even seem like a joke anymore—insisted that an occasion like tonight demanded the real thing. Fountain doubted that anyone in the Town Hall would care or even notice whether his bow tie was elasticized or not; and if the speeches went on long enough for someone to pay that much attention to his attire, he knew they'd know he wasn't the one who had tied it. Johnny Fountain wasn't the kind of man who spent time prettifying himself. He was the kind of man who rugby-tackled football hooligans and arm-wrestled them into the backs of Land Rovers while younger, more cautious officers were leafing through the police manual.

In a way, that was what tonight was about. Norbold's great and good were gathering under the Town Hall candelabra to pay tribute to the vision, determination, and application of one man, and that man was Johnny Fountain.

He caught his wife's eye in the mirror. His voice was a low Yorkshire rumble. "You're not going to embarrass me tonight, are you?"

She pretended not to know what he meant. "Embarrass you?"

Fountain sighed. "Well, saying 'Hear! Hear!' loudly every time someone says something nice about me would qualify. So would asking the mayor, the assistant chief constable, and Her Grace the Duchess to pose with me for a photograph."

From the disappointment he glimpsed in her reflection, he thought he'd already hit pay dirt, and the list was hardly exhaustive. Nor had he any confidence in his ability, or the time frame available, to expand it to include every way she might find to make the evening memorable for all the wrong reasons.

"But I'm proud of you, dear," Denis said fondly.

"Well, that's nice to know. But can we settle for the occasional smug smile rather than blasts on a feathered whoopee whistle?"

Behind him her smile was distinctly smug. "I'll do my best."

"No one can do more," Fountain acknowledged graciously.

* * *

She did try. To some extent she succeeded. But her husband, and everyone else who knew her, was aware of how sorely the evening in the Town Hall tested her resolve. Denis Fountain was a woman who had always embraced life, who had no talent for—and saw no point in—playing it cool. She was bursting with pride and didn't care who knew it. Wanted people to know it. And everyone who stood up to add to the litany of praise heaped upon the head of Norbold's senior police office only stoked the fires, until his wife was glowing like a small sun with a new hairdo. If only there'd been room in her tiny evening bag for a feathered whoopee whistle!

And the best thing about it, the very best, was that every word was true. All these people weren't here simply because it was Fountain's turn: they'd done the mayor last month and the Paralympic archer who'd come in second at the European championships the month before, and now it was time to do the chief superintendent. The speeches were such music to Denis's ears because they were an honest acknowledgment of a plain and simple truth: that, like pushing water uphill, and in the first instance with precious little help and no expectation of success, her husband had turned Norbold from a crime black spot into one of the safest places to live in the whole country. Crime was low because people who wanted to make a career of it found better prospects elsewhere. The clear-up rate as a proportion of reported crime was impressively high. As a consequence, the fear of crime in and around Norbold, from the middle-class suburb of Sedgewick to the council estates of Hollybush and the Flying Horse, ran at the sort of levels usually associated with pastoral communities in Dorset. People no longer expected to be the victims of crime, and they knew who they had to thank for that. It had taken him ten years, but ten years wasn't too long for people to remember what Norbold was like before Johnny Fountain.

And because this was essentially a testimonial, people were kind enough not to mention his one failure, the one facet of local crime he had yet to make inroads against. In part this was because the people who attend gala testimonials for important local figures are themselves important local figures and tend not to live or work in the kind of areas where drug dealing and drug taking have a major impact on people's daily lives. So they see it as somebody else's problem.

Fountain had slashed the rates of burglary, mugging, damage to and thefts from cars, dangerous driving, and attacks against the person that were not drug-related—all the crimes that respectable, responsible people could imagine themselves and their families falling victim to. For the most part they saw drugs as something other people's families got involved in; unless of course they knew better, when their focus shifted to hoping the police *wouldn't* find out. In short, if Chief Superintendent Fountain had to have a blot on his copybook, drugs was the best page to have it. The great and good of Norbold avoided referring to it because they knew how, to a man conspicuously successful in every other aspect of his work, it must rankle.

No one had ever counted Nye Jackson of the *Norbold News* among the great and good, and this was to his credit. There's something seriously wrong with a reporter who isn't getting under people's skin. After the meal and the speeches, as the diners circulated, he made sure a little eddy washed him up against the guest of honor.

Johnny Fountain was a big man. Nye Jackson wasn't. He was a wiry red-haired Welshman with a chip on his shoulder because he was still working on a provincial weekly at the age of forty-three: too old to be working his way up to *Panorama*, too young to be coasting toward retirement. He'd been in Norbold for eight years. People serve less time for murder.

He fought to keep his drink safe from passersby who hadn't noticed him and inquired of the chief superintendent's shoulder, "Any progress with that van business, Mr. Fountain?"

Fountain looked around before looking down for him, smiling like a genial adult pestered by a child. "Hello, Scoop. You clean up nicely. I hope you got all the flattering things people were saying about me?" The North of England accent was matched by a craggy face and lion's mane of white hair. He was in his mid-fifties now.

"Pretty much." Jackson nodded offhandedly. "At least, I got the first speech on tape. I can do the rest with Copy and Paste."

Fountain gave a broad, avuncular grin. "And they say the Welsh have no sense of humor."

"Oh, we have a sense of humor, Mr. Fountain," said Jackson, deadpan. "I can laugh myself silly watching what passes for rugby round here. No, I was asking about that business up at the Flying Horse. Burned-out van containing a small portable chemical plant, the charred remains of wannabe drug dealer Sonny Pruitt, and enough party poppers that pigeons flying through the ash cloud were landing in the town square and looking for cats to fight. I was wondering if you'd come up with any leads yet."

Fountain nodded amiably. His bow tie had come undone and he made a desultory effort to fix it. "It's not really me you should be talking to. Can I get DI Gorman to give you a call? It's his case."

"Fine. I left him a message this morning, but I don't think he must have got it." He met Fountain's eye, and both of them knew exactly what had happened to the reporter's message, and also that Detective Inspector Gorman would now have to respond to it. Maybe Nye Jackson wasn't a world-class journalist, but he was persistent, and sometimes that's as good.

Fountain looked around as politely as he could for someone else to talk to. It was sod's law that there was no one within hailing distance.

Jackson looked the way the chief superintendent was looking and saw what he saw, and also knew what he was thinking. He didn't take it personally; or only to the extent that it seemed to him more like a compliment than anything else. He might, out of kindness, have made an excuse and moved on himself. But kindness wasn't one of his weaknesses. He helped himself to another drink from a circulating tray and observed mildly, "Funny about the drugs, Mr. Fountain, isn't it?"

Fountain sought him out again as if looking from much farther away and much higher up. "Funny? In what way?"

"Sorry," said Jackson, insincerely, "I don't mean to be a wet blanket, especially tonight. You've worked wonders in this town. I've covered the courts here for eight years, I've seen the crime rate go down, month on month. And right across the board, except for that. Wouldn't you think that, by now, the way law-abiding citizens have been reclaiming Norbold would have worked its way through every aspect of life here? Even that one. What makes the drugs scene so different?"

Johnny Fountain gave a long-suffering sigh. "Who knows, Mr. Jackson? Maybe it's just going to take a little longer."

"I expect so. And after all," added the reporter, just a little pointedly, "it's not like Sonny Pruitt's any great loss to anyone. I mean, no one deserves to get murdered. But some people deserve it even less than others, yes?"

The chief superintendent knew better than to either agree or argue with that, on the record or off it. He did his police-issue noncommittal smile.

At which point rescue loomed, in the form—always beloved

but never more than now—of Denis, aglow in peach satin and a perm that would have protected her from small projectiles or a modest avalanche. "Johnny? *Look* at your tie! Oh." The happiness fell out of her face. "You're busy."

"Not at all," insisted Fountain, gathering her in the crook of his arm. "We were just discussing the vagaries of crime. You'll excuse me, Mr. Jackson?" And he swept her off toward the dance floor like a man who has just discovered there are worse ways to spend an evening. A brief but perfectly timed hiatus from the band allowed Denis Fountain's voice to drift back: ". . . Perfectly *dreadful* little ginger hack . . ." Jackson grinned to himself.

CHAPTER 4

THEY SAID THERE was a problem with his insurance. They said his account didn't tally with that of the complainant. He said he wanted his solicitor present during questioning. They said fine, they'd find him somewhere to wait while they contacted him. No one seemed to have any particular instructions regarding him. Jerome Cardy tried to tell himself that maybe he'd misread the situation, that the worst he was facing was a fine.

It was a nice modern police station with nice modern cells that were not in a damp basement but up on the first floor, light and airy. The custody sergeant took his details, and his shoes ("Look, no laces! I can't hang myself with elastic gussets!" "Can't help that, son, rules is rules.") and then pulled a face. "Ah."

The arresting officer raised his eyebrows. "What?"

"Got the painters in one to three. Got a woman in five." He looked at Jerome. "How do you feel about dogs?"

Was this it? Was this how it was going to happen? His voice was hollow. "What kind of dogs?"

"Oh, it's a nice dog—clean, well behaved. Its owner's in

there with it, sleeping off a thumping. You'd be helping me out if you'd wait in there with them."

Jerome was past arguing. "Sure. Whatever."

Sergeant Murchison gave a relieved nod and conducted him to cell number four. "You won't have any trouble here. Look, it's not even locked. But try not to disturb him. He's had a rough day."

"Do my best," agreed Jerome weakly.

"Good lad." He closed the door but still didn't lock it, leaving Jerome and the white dog weighing each other up.

But gradually reality caught up with him. The dog and its sleeping owner might be the perfect companions for an hour in the police cells while his solicitor was summoned, but Jerome Cardy was still in the last place on earth that he wanted to be. The fact that nothing had happened to him yet was no proof that nothing was going to happen. He sat down and considered his options.

The door wasn't locked. He could make a run for it.

He wouldn't get far, and then they'd have an excuse to treat him as a different kind of offender. Right now all he'd done was leave the scene of a minor accident that he hadn't even caused. Jerome was pretty sure it was in his own best interests to keep it that way.

He could ask to see someone who wasn't a police officer.

He was too old to need an appropriate adult, too fit to need a doctor, and he'd already asked for his solicitor. If his solicitor arrived, all would be well; if he didn't, there was no reason to suppose that a message would reach anyone else, either.

Or he could wake the man snoring gently on the other bunk and explain the situation. Get himself a witness.

* * *

Gabriel Ash woke to a gentle but insistent hand shaking his shoulder.

In spite of what he'd told the police surgeon, he wasn't all right. His head hurt and every bone in his body ached. His split lip and one cheekbone had swelled up, and there was an unpleasant buzzing in his ears. He had no medical background, but given the circumstances, concussion seemed—to coin a phrase—a bit of a no-brainer. He knew he should be in a hospital; he also knew he wasn't going to a hospital, and not only because of Patience. If he went into a hospital, they might not settle for stitching his lip. He might be dealing with well-meaning young men called Simon for months.

Sleep seemed the best alternative. He had laid his aching head on the bunk's pillow, pulled the blanket over him, and let his eyes shut and his mind empty.

He had no idea how much time had passed before he was wakened, except that it wasn't enough to mend his hurts. You only know how many muscles it takes to sit up after each one has lodged a separate protest. Also, he was still dizzy and struggled to make his eyes focus. Patience was sitting quietly, watching him. He raked up a reassuring smile for her, which somehow—her lips never moved—she managed to return.

They were no longer alone in the cell. A tall young black man was bending over him, his hand still on Ash's shoulder. His lips *were* moving, but Ash could make no sense of the quiet, urgent flow of words. He held a hand up as if to deflect a blow, hoping it would work better this time than last. "Slow down. I'm not firing on all cylinders right now. Say it all again, in words of two syllables or less." Even concussed, Gabriel Ash was an articulate man.

Jerome was talking fast because he didn't know how long

he had, and quietly because he didn't want to be overheard. But he was smart enough to recognize that what he managed to say wasn't nearly as important as what his companion managed to understand. Jerome wondered if he'd be better talking to the dog.

He might have been. Ash was doing his best, but it didn't make any sense. He wasn't sure it would have made sense if he *hadn't* been concussed. Britain didn't execute convicts any more, and when it had, it didn't do it for traffic misdemeanors. "I'm sure you've got this wrong . . ." he began.

"No, *listen,*" insisted the young man. "This isn't about the shunt with the car. It's about getting me in here. Any excuse would have done. Now they've got me, they won't let me go."

Ash was pretty sure you couldn't get a life sentence for careless driving, either. Agitation, paranoia, the sheen of sweat on the young man's face . . . "Have you taken something? Do you need to see a doctor?"

Jerome would have slapped him if he hadn't been afraid of scattering what was left of the man's wits. "No! I think I'm going to die in here. And God help me, you are my only chance that it won't be written off as an accident. Remember what I'm telling you. When you get out and I don't, find someone to tell."

"But why . . . ?"

The shutter in the cell door opened and a face glanced in. Then the door opened. "Come on, Jerome, we've freed you up a comfy little bed-sit all of your own."

Whatever he'd been trying to say to Ash, he wasn't prepared to say it in front of the policeman. He made one last desperate attempt to stay where he felt safe. "I like dogs. . . ."

The officer remained where he was in the corridor, waiting patiently. "Mr. Ash and his dog aren't actually supposed to be here. There'd be hell to pay if you got bitten. Or fleas."

Ash began indignantly, "My dog doesn't—"

But Jerome interrupted. His lips smiled, but his eyes were focused intently on Ash's and there was the sense that he was saying, or trying to say, more than the actual words. "I never asked you. What's its name?"

"Patience," said Ash, surprised.

"I had a dog once. Othello. That was its name. Othello."

"Really?" Ash didn't know what else to say. "What sort of dog?"

"A sniffer dog. Like you see at airports."

Ash frowned. There was something very odd about this conversation. It wasn't often, these days, that Gabriel Ash felt to be in the company of someone less in contact with reality than himself. "A spaniel?"

"Yes."

The policeman was growing restless. "Come on, Jerome. You can talk to your new friend and his dog after you've finished here. Your solicitor will be here soon. Till then, let's leave Mr. Ash in peace, yes?"

There seemed nothing else for it. Jerome Cardy went with the officer, who closed Ash's door behind him. A moment later Ash heard another cell door close, and this time also lock.

He sat on the edge of his bunk for some minutes, puzzling over the encounter. Patience had no suggestions to offer, and finally he came back to his first conclusion, which was that Jerome Cardy had been indulging in illegal substances. Satisfied with that, at least mostly, he pulled the blanket over him again and went back to sleep.

* * *

Again, he had no idea how long he'd slept, but he stirred to the urgent entreaties of the dog, which was whining and scratching at the door and butting his hanging hand with her nose. He blinked himself awake. "Do you need to go out?"

But Patience was—when not dealing with thugs—a civilized dog, discreet about her personal requirements. This was different. Something had alarmed her.

Ten seconds later, the whole of the cell block was in an uproar.

Every police station has a supporting cast of regulars who shouldn't really be part of the criminal justice system, who wouldn't be if there was any other agency to take responsibility for them, and Meadowvale was no exception. Old ladies who shoplifted because, having outlived their families, being arrested for theft gave them a brief respite from the crushing loneliness. Old men who weren't so much drunk and disorderly as confused and still fighting battles they'd won sixty years before. Heroin addicts who, when they asked for help with their addiction, were put on a waiting list eighteen months long. People like Gabriel Ash, wandering around the town, mumbling to his dog, until he annoyed someone enough to take a swing at him. And people like Barking Mad Barclay.

Barking Mad was not, of course, the name on his birth certificate. That was a much more prosaic, much less descriptive Robert.

The other thing Barking Mad isn't is a diagnosis. In fact, though he'd been arrested numerous times, committed twice, and examined by every psychiatrist within a fifty-mile radius, no one had ever come up with a convincing diagnosis. He wasn't a psychopath or a sociopath; he understood absolutely the difference between right and wrong, and the effect his behavior had on others. He didn't hear voices telling him what to do. He did what he wanted to do.

As far as could be established, he hadn't been either abused or overindulged as a child, nor was his father also his grandfather and his uncle. If life had been harsh to him, it was only acting in self-defense. Unless there was something amiss deep within his brain, where it would only be discovered by cutting it into thin slivers and putting it under a microscope—and don't think that didn't seem an excellent idea to those who knew him best—he was just a very angry man who responded with uninhibited aggression to anything that irked him.

As luck would have it, he was also a very large and powerful man, known at Meadowvale as a "three-hander." You didn't even try to arrest him until there were at least three of you to do it.

Hazel Best was new to Norbold. She didn't know this.

After seeing Gabriel Ash and his dog settled in the Meadowvale cells, she and Constable Budgen had gone back on patrol. They'd overseen chucking-out time at the local hostelries, hushing the noisier revelers and steering others away from the car parks and toward the taxi rank. By one in the morning the town was quiet, but there remained hours of their shift still to serve. Wayne Budgen suggested checking the all-night café for criminal masterminds. When none was immediately apparent, they took a corner table and—as cover—ordered a pot of coffee and some sticky buns.

They were still waiting for the criminal masterminds to show up when the call came in. Another disturbance at the park, this time involving vandalism at the war memorial. As they hurried out to the car, Hazel mumbled around the last of her bun,

"It'll be those same yobbos again, bet you anything. The ones who kicked nine bells out of . . . um . . ."

"Rambles," Budgen reminded her. "Let's hope so."

Hazel looked at him in surprise. "You can think of someone you'd be less happy to meet on a dark night in an empty park than half a dozen young thugs who six hours ago were trying to beat a man to death?"

"Oh yeah," said Wayne fervently. "Barking Mad Barclay."

In primitive societies, you never speak of fairies for fear they might appear. Primitive societies know a thing or two.

Norbold's war memorial was a simple, dignified affair—a four-step plinth topped by a stone obelisk engraved with the names of the fallen, in two world wars and all the campaigns since. There were a lot of them.

Barking Mad Barclay was head-butting the obelisk.

If that had been all, they might have taken the view that twelve tons of granite could stand up to anything the human head could throw it, and waited until either boredom or brain damage intervened. Unfortunately, before he started on the obelisk, he'd overturned three of the four stone urns located around the plinth and rolled them into the Garden of Remembrance, scattering the faded remnants of wreaths. This is the kind of thing that upsets people, and it left them with no option but to make an arrest. Or at least try to.

"Gonna need backup," predicted Wayne Budgen.

Hazel elevated an eyebrow. "Really?" They were both young, fit, robust, and well trained, and the suspect—which hardly seems an appropriate term when actually you've seen him head-butting a war memorial—had blood pouring down his face and a glazed expression in his eyes. "We can take him. Can't we?"

"That's . . ." But before he'd got more than one word into the explanation, something unexpected happened to Constable Budgen. He blushed. She was a woman—all right, a couple of years older than he was, and maybe a shade more substantial and capable-looking than the girls he usually went for, but still an attractive young woman with green eyes and a lot of wavy fair hair that she tied back for work but which tended not to stay tied back—and she was looking to him, expecting him, to help her subdue Barking Mad Barclay. And Wayne Budgen was too embarrassed to tell her he was afraid. Of course they should have waited for backup. Budgen knew that; every police officer in Norbold should have known that. It was just Budgen's luck to be patrolling with the one exception when it became an issue.

He'd been thumped before. What was going through his mind now was that it would be better to be thumped again than let Hazel Best raise that eyebrow any higher at him. He amended what he'd been about to say. "If he flattens me, call for backup."

But Hazel hadn't joined the police in order to watch other people do the difficult bits. "He probably *would* flatten you," she admitted, adding with hasty tact, "if he could. He might not flatten me." She pinned her most amiable smile in place, climbed the stone steps, and tapped Barking Mad Barclay on the shoulder. "Excuse me. Hello?"

It had the desired effect, in that he stopped what he was doing and peered around at her. He had a Zapata mustache that was the height of fashion around 1975, currently clotted with blood, and tiny, bleary eyes looking in slightly different directions. "What the footling hell do you want?" He did not say *footling.* And he spoke with a Glasgow accent that he affected only when he'd been drinking. Budgen knew for a fact that he'd been born in Kidderminster.

Hazel proffered a tissue. "Do you know you've cut your forehead?"

He looked at the tissue. He looked at Hazel. He looked at the floodlit obelisk, which had a bloodstain the size of a football on it. "No! Really?"

"We ought to get that looked at for you. You don't want it to scar."

Budgen was watching with amazement, admiration, and deep disquiet. She was talking to Barking Mad Barclay as if he was normal—as if he'd tripped on the steps of the war memorial and hurt himself on the obelisk. The constable had no idea what would happen next. Probably what usually happened when a police officer approached Barclay armed with anything less than rocket-propelled grenades. But he thought there was just a chance that it might work. That Barclay would accept the offer of her hankie and go with her to see the police surgeon. If that happened, Hazel Best would be the toast of Meadowvale Police Station. Even Wayne Budgen might get a little reflected glory.

Alas, the remarkable doesn't happen nearly as often as the blindingly obvious. Barclay slurred, "Go footle yersel'," and swatted Hazel as if swatting a fly. She landed in the middle of the Garden of Remembrance with a ringing in her ears and no clear idea of which way was up.

After which they did it Constable Budgen's way and got backup. Hazel took no further part in the arrest. Back at Meadowvale, Sergeant Murchison made her a cup of tea—well, fetched her one from the machine in the corridor—had the police surgeon look at her, took a photograph of her bruises for the report, then sent her home.

CHAPTER 5

BARKING MAD Barclay was known in Meadowvale as a three-hander. Except when he was worked up, like now, when you tried to round up the front row of the Division rugby team in order to tackle him.

Except like *right* now, when there was someone in there with him, taking the brunt of all that anger, when the first officer on the scene hit the alarm in passing, threw open the cell door, and threw himself at the big man without waiting for anything. It happened to be Sergeant Murchison. It could have been any of them. He knew he'd get hurt. He knew he could get injured quite badly. It didn't have to matter. If he waited, even a few seconds, he was going to have a dead man in his cells. Already, in the time it had taken him to run here from his desk in the outer office, the shrill yells of terror and the bubbling ones of pain had been cut off, leaving only the deep animal grunts of effort.

Donald Murchison had seen a lot in twenty years of police work. He thought he was ready for what he was going to see when he went through the cell door. But he wasn't. The place was an abattoir.

He was lucky that, by and large, the police station was

staffed by people just like him. They grumbled and whinged, they gossiped, they backbit, they clock-watched and counted off the days to their pension; but when the shit hit the fan, without pausing to think of the cost, they supported one another with everything they had. Murchison had barely got a hand on the berserker in his cell before four colleagues were piling through the door behind him, grabbing anything that moved and hanging on to it for grim death. One of them grabbed Murchison, and apologized breathlessly before shifting his grasp.

With five of them hanging on to him like bulldogs locked onto a raging bull, at last even Barclay's manic strength began to wane. The thick limbs, each now dragging a policeman, slowed and submitted to restraint. After another moment the big man allowed himself to be dragged down, tumbling with a kind of monstrous grace into the wreckage of his victim.

Finally there was time to take stock. No one was shouting anymore. The only sound in the cell was of aching lungs being replenished. Then Wayne Budgen whispered a thunderstruck, "Bloody hell!"

Murchison's hands looked as if he'd dipped them in blood. And he didn't think any of it was his. He dragged in a long breath and tried to think.

"Okay. Ambulance. Dr. Wellington was here earlier—see if he's still on the premises. Send Rambles home and put this . . . animal . . . in there. Find the straitjacket. I'm going to want SOCO, Forensics, and the Home Office pathologist. And somebody had better call Mr. Fountain."

Johnny Fountain was still wearing his dinner jacket when he arrived to take command of the situation. The first thing he did was to pull off the hated bow tie. The second was to call Sergeant Murchison to his office. “What happened, Donald?”

If there’d been anyone else present, Donald Murchison would have stayed on his feet. But these two had respected each other for ten years, and he sank into the chair on the other side of Fountain’s desk as if only willpower had kept him upright this long. He vented a sigh of utter despair. “I don’t know what to tell you. A misunderstanding? Somebody misheard? I thought I’d got Cardy in four and Barclay in five. Cardy was certainly in four earlier—I looked in on them.”

“Them?”

“Rambles . . . sorry, Gabriel Ash. You know who I mean—goes everywhere with a white dog on a lead? He’d got himself duffed up earlier, and Hazel Best put him in there so someone would notice if his brain started leaking out of his ear. I had Mary Watson in five—DIC and driving while disqualified. We got her processed and sent her home, which left five free. When Barclay came in, that’s where I allocated him. Only sometime in the previous quarter of an hour someone must have noticed five was free and moved Cardy in there, and never got around to telling me.”

“Who?”

“I don’t know. I haven’t even asked.” He swallowed. “A boy just died in my cells—I’m not going to keep the class back until someone puts their hand up. We’ll find out who did what and why, but we don’t have to do it while the blood’s still wet on the floor. For now, sir, all that matters is that we know who’s responsible. I am. I was the custody officer. It was my job to allocate cells in such a way that a mild-mannered black law student wasn’t put in with a violent racist. Jerome Cardy is dead because I slipped up. And I’m more sorry than I can say.”

For a long time Chief Superintendent Fountain said nothing. But it wasn't the silence of censure: Fountain understood as well as anyone how little mistakes can mount up until all at once in the middle of the night there's a full-fledged disaster. He'd served in pretty well every position in the police service—he was never a dog handler—on his way to where he was now. He knew that sometimes even the best intentions, coupled with years of experience, aren't enough to avert a tragedy.

Murchison sucked in a deep breath. "You'll be calling the IPCC." He knew that when the Independent Police Complaints Commission took over, his career would be effectively over.

"I suppose so," Fountain said slowly.

Murchison blinked. There really wasn't a choice and Fountain had to know that. "Sir?"

"The bloke with the dog. Ash?" Murchison nodded. "*Why* was he in the cells again?"

"Hazel Best thought he was concussed. She wanted to take him to the hospital, but he wouldn't go because they wouldn't let his dog in. He's a bit . . ." A tap of the forefinger to his temple. "So she put the pair of them in number four, where we could keep an eye on him for a couple of hours. He was asleep every time I checked on him."

"Hm." Another of those little departures from procedure that aren't supposed to happen but happen all the time and usually do more good than harm but just occasionally introduce the spark to the box of fireworks. "So he wasn't locked in?"

Murchison shook his head.

"Did you lock the door after you put Cardy in there?"

"No. Ash wasn't under arrest—I didn't want to lock him in. And Cardy wasn't the type to make trouble."

Fountain was nodding slowly. "And after Mary Watson was released, five probably wasn't locked, either."

The sergeant had no idea where he was going with this. All he could do was answer honestly. "No, sir."

Fountain leaned forward very slightly in his chair. "Donald, maybe nobody moved Jerome Cardy. Maybe he moved himself. What if he got tired bunking with a snoring idiot and his flea-ridden dog? He saw that the cell opposite was empty, both doors were unlocked, so he just ambled across the corridor and made himself comfortable. He wouldn't have thought he was doing anything very wrong, let alone dangerous. Then when Barclay was brought in, you and everyone else thought number five was empty.

"I've been there when we've been wrestling Barking Mad Barclay into a cell," he recalled warmly. "There isn't a lot of spare time for checking under the blankets. If he went through the door without somebody's ear in his teeth, you'd just slam the door and shoot the bolt before he had time to turn on you. Do you suppose that's what happened?"

If you fall off a ship in the middle of an ocean, you're pretty sure you're going to drown. It's not exactly that the fear passes, but an element of resignation creeps in. If there's no hope, if there's only one way it can end, there's no point fighting. Despair drives out panic.

But if someone throws you a life preserver, everything changes. You might still drown, but you might survive. And the hopeless calm of waiting for the inevitable gives way in an instant to terror. That you might not reach the life preserver, that the rope will break. That was what was in Sergeant Murchison's eyes now: the recognition that there was a way he might come out of this. And the hope, and the fear, that recognition engendered.

"I . . . I suppose . . . it hadn't occurred to me. But maybe that's what happened."

Fountain was nodding again. "Well, we can't ask Cardy, poor chap. We could ask Ash, though I doubt he could tell us much—and I doubt we could put much faith in anything he *did* tell us. We can ask the guys if any of them moved Cardy. But if no one owns up, that's probably why. No one did move him. He moved himself."

The sergeant was thinking fast. "If that's what happened, there should be footage on the CCTV."

"You haven't looked yet?"

Murchison shook his head. "I didn't want . . . I wanted to give one of the guys time to say it was his idea to move Cardy before I checked the tape."

Fountain could understand that. "Let's have a look at it now. It might let everyone off the hook."

But it didn't. The two men gazed impassively at the screen as the image of the row of cells pixilated and broke up at some point between Jerome Cardy's being brought in and Robert Barclay's rather more dramatic arrival.

Chief Superintendent Fountain said with commendable restraint, "It's doing that again, is it?"

Sergeant Murchison felt as if the Coast Guard cutter had thrown him an anchor. "The technician said he'd sorted it out."

"All right," said Fountain wearily, "so there's no CCTV. So we have a theory but no supporting evidence. I think we have to be frank with the IPCC—tell them we think we know what happened but we can't prove it. If they think something else may have happened, it's up to them to establish what."

Murchison swallowed. "They're going to think we're covering for one another."

Fountain shrugged expansively. "They won't like it, I know that much. I wouldn't like it if it was my investigation. It's always more satisfying to know what actually happened than to be left by default with what probably happened. But they're realists. They know there isn't always forensics, you can't always find an impeccable witness. Sometimes, the likeliest explanation is the best you're going to do. And unless someone comes forward to say different, the likeliest explanation is that Jerome Cardy was the author of his own misfortune. That the only one to blame for his death is Robert Barclay." The chief superintendent looked his custody sergeant in the eye. "Do you suppose anyone *will* want to say something different?"

Murchison stood up. Thoughts were racing through his head like getaway cars. "I doubt it, sir. If no one's looking for another explanation, it doesn't seem too likely that anyone will offer one."

Fountain gave a little grunt. It might have been agreement, sympathy, or just dismissal. "I think you should go home now, Donald. Try to get some sleep. Things'll seem brighter in the morning."

"Yes. And—thank you, sir."

Fountain gave him a puzzled look. "What for?"

Most people would have turned on the television, looking for a local news bulletin. Gabriel Ash no longer owned a television. Or they might have asked around at work, or called a friend. Ash hadn't worked for four years—was not so much unemployed as unemployable—and didn't have any friends. There was a newsagent opposite the park. He and Patience went out as soon as it opened and bought the local paper.

There was nothing in it. At least, there were lots of things in it, but nothing that interested Ash. Events at Meadowvale Police Station had occurred after the *Norbold News* went to press.

He wasn't sure what to do. He could wait for the evening papers, but none of them published in Norbold and might relegate the story to a couple of paragraphs on an inside page. He could wait for the next edition of the *News*, but it only published twice a week, and the Monday issue was mostly full of sport reports.

Or he could do nothing. This was in many ways his default option. These days, not many things struck Ash as important enough to disturb the routine he wore like a suit of armor but still trivial enough that he might be able to do anything useful about them. The death of Jerome Cardy certainly qualified on the first count and failed on the second. If there was no point exposing himself to scrutiny, interrogation, and derision, he would rather not do it. He had never courted attention. These days he'd do almost anything to avoid it.

But a man had died. At least, Ash thought he had. Something terrible had happened—he knew that from the silence that had descended on the police station, which even the hurried footsteps, the clipped commands, and, soon afterward, the nearby wail of an ambulance siren somehow did nothing to dispel. A somber-faced officer had asked him to leave, and there seemed to be some urgency, because he was collecting Ash's scant belongings while Ash was still fumbling to tie his shoes.

And even if he was right and the young man he'd briefly shared his cell with was dead, the tragedy would hardly have disturbed the isolation he'd crafted around himself, except for one thing. Jerome Cardy had known he was going to die. Had asked for Ash's help, not even to protect him but simply to remember. To bear witness.

Memory was one of the things that gave Ash problems these days. Remembering when he needed to, and forgetting when he should.

He looked at the dog. "What do you think? We should leave well enough alone?"

She didn't need to reply. The severity of her expression—nobody can look down their nose at you like a lurcher—was answer enough.

"Oh, all right." Ash sighed. "I suppose . . ." Inspiration struck. "I know. Let's find . . . thingy. . . ." The search for the young policewoman who'd helped him the previous night wasn't going to be made easier by the fact that he'd forgotten her name.

CHAPTER 6

Alone among Norbold's police, Hazel Best had no idea what had happened after she'd been sent home. Groggier than she'd been willing to admit, she'd gone straight to bed and slept through until ten on Thursday morning, when she woke with a headache and a black eye.

She regarded her battered reflection in the bathroom mirror. "Memo to self," she told it wryly. "Many potentially violent situations can be defused by taking a casual and friendly approach. But not all of them."

She made coffee, found there was no bread for toast, had the coffee anyway, then headed for the shops.

As she emerged, a bag in each hand, she saw them: as distinctive a pairing as Laurel and Hardy, Gabriel Ash and his white dog wandering across the road, apparently oblivious to the traffic maneuvering around them. Fortunately Patience was on a lead. It ensured that Ash reached the curb safely.

Hazel dropped her shopping onto the backseat of her car, then moved to intercept them. She pinned a reassuring smile in place in case he didn't recognize her without her uniform. "Hello. How are you this morning?"

He stared as if she'd grown an extra head overnight. She remembered the black eye. "Don't worry about that. A little misunderstanding." She was searching his face for some sign that he knew who she was. "Constable Best—Hazel. We were talking yesterday evening, after you were attacked in the park. I went back later, but there was no sign of the little thugs who did it. How about you? Any ill effects?"

He was still staring at her, his face pale against the shock of dark hair. "You don't know, do you?"

"Know what, Mr. Ash?"

"Someone died in the police station last night. Killed—murdered. I was there. I was talking to him half an hour before."

Hazel felt the blood drain from her face and her eyes, or at least one of them, saucer. She reminded herself that this was Gabriel Ash, Rambles with Dogs—in less politically correct times he'd have been described as the village idiot. She didn't think he was lying. But just because he believed it, that didn't make it true. She started groping for her phone. "I'd better call in. See if they need me . . ."

If they'd needed her, they'd have called her. But if they were dealing with that ultimate disaster, a death in custody, they might have forgotten she even existed. She wasn't part of the Meadowvale furniture yet. Whether she was needed or not, she ought to offer her help, if only to man the phones and free up people who would be of more use.

Assuming there was any kind of truth in any of this.

She put the phone back in her bag. "Mr. Ash, do you know who it was who died? Do you know who killed him?"

"He was just a boy. Nineteen, twenty." Ash's deep-set eyes had gone distant. "I never saw the man who killed him. But I heard him. He was so . . . *angry.* Mad with rage. The boy was yelling for help and I was yelling, and Patience was barking, and the police were there in just a couple of minutes, but it was already too late. By the time they got the cell open and the crazy man off him, the boy was dead.

"I think," he added carefully. "That's what's someone said. But they sent me home, so I never heard for sure. I came out for a paper, hoping they'd have it, but they haven't. And I need to know, you see." There was a catch in his voice and his eyes were deeply troubled. "If he's getting better in hospital, then it was probably just a coincidence. But if he's dead . . ."

His voice petered out, drained by emotion. Hazel thought he'd finished. But a moment later it came back stronger and he finished the sentence. "If he's dead, there are things I know about it that I have to tell someone." He was looking at her as if he thought that she might do.

Hazel swallowed. If she wasn't careful, she was going to be the laughingstock of Meadowvale—the probationer who believed Rambles With Dogs when he told her he'd witnessed a murder.

But what could she do? Even a stopped clock tells the right time twice a day. Maybe there was something in what he was trying to say. She couldn't dismiss it as a figment of a deranged imagination without at least checking with Sergeant Murchison. "Tell you what, Mr. Ash," she said. "Let's go to the police station right now. You and Patience get in the car, and we'll go and find out exactly what's happened to who. Yes?"

After a moment he nodded. "Yes. Thank you." And then, as a kind of postscript: "Ash."

Hazel smiled. "Yes, I know, Mr. Ash."

He shook his head. "Not 'mister.' Just Ash. Most people call me just Ash."

Not at Meadowvale they don't, thought Hazel as she let him into the car. "Is that what I should call you?"

"Most people do," he repeated. "Except my therapist and, of course, Patience."

Hazel Best froze, an ice sculpture of a woman halfway into a car. Everything he'd said to her in the last five minutes, all the fears that had raced through her mind, came back to mock her. Rambles With Dogs. They didn't call him that just to be unkind.

She got herself unlocked and finished climbing into the driver's seat, though no longer with the same sense of urgency. "What does Patience call you?"

"Gabriel. Or sometimes," he confided with a tiny, rueful grin, "*you hapless idiot*."

He hadn't imagined everything. Jerome Cardy was dead. Dr. Wellington, the police surgeon, who saw him first, was pretty sure, but that didn't stop the paramedics who arrived soon afterward from throwing him into the back of the ambulance and taking off with lights flashing and sirens wailing, because sometimes you can be sure and still wrong. But none of the high-tech equipment in A&E was able to detect any signs of continuing existence.

The doctor who signed the death certificate checked with Sergeant Murchison before completing it. "A man did this? You're sure? An unarmed man? The last time I saw anything like it, it was a farmer who'd lost an argument with his bull."

All the time the sergeant was talking, quietly, in the corridor, where they could have a little privacy, Hazel Best was turning a papery shade of pale. "And this was the guy who knocked me into the flower bed?"

Sergeant Murchison—who shouldn't still have been at

Meadowvale but was and showed no signs of leaving—nodded grimly. "Robert Barclay. The man you tried to arrest armed with nothing more than a winning smile while Wayne Budgen watched from behind the squad car. He could have killed you, Hazel. And that is not a figure of speech."

She swallowed. "I know. Wayne said we should wait. Just for the record, though," she added in a spirit of fair play, "I asked him to stay back. Wayne. He wasn't hiding, he was trying to avoid making things worse."

"Yes?" grunted the sergeant. "That worked a treat."

He'd had a bad night, and things weren't going to get better for a while, and the last thing Hazel wanted to do was add to his woes. There remained the question of Gabriel Ash. "You remember the guy I brought in earlier? Who got beaten up in the park?"

"Rambles? What about him?"

"He's outside in my car. He says he was there when it happened."

"He was. Till I needed his cell for Barclay."

"He says the boy knew something was going to happen to him."

"I imagine he did. He'd been arrested for leaving the scene of an accident and trying to give us the slip."

"I mean something terrible."

Murchison frowned. "That's silly. Hazel, something like last night happens once in a career. If you're unlucky. There was no reason for Jerome Cardy to think anything bad was going to happen to him. Except . . ." He considered a moment. "He was a law student, wasn't he? Well, that's it, then. If he'd ended up with a record, his career would have been over before it started."

"I suppose," she said, a little doubtful but still mainly relieved. "Ash must have got it wrong. He was pretty shaken up."

"Yes," agreed Sergeant Murchison kindly. "I dare say being as dotty as a dalmatian doesn't help, either."

She asked if there was anything useful she could do, but he couldn't think of anything. "Mr. Fountain's called Division. They're organizing a Fatal Incident Inquiry. They'll want to ask how you came to bring Barclay in, and his demeanor at the time."

"Yes, of course," said Hazel, a shade absently.

When she said no more and her brow creased in a troubled frown, Murchison prompted her. "What?"

"Sarge—was this my fault? If I'd done as Wayne said and waited for backup, and we'd brought him in without getting him all riled up first, would Jerome Cardy still be alive?"

He stared at her in astonishment. "No. Hazel, no. You did nothing wrong. Hen, this is what we do. We pick up the pieces. Which means, something was smashed before we got involved. We try to keep the broken glass off the streets, but we can't glue it back together again. I've known Robert Barclay since he was a nipper. All that time I've known, and everyone here has known, that sooner or later he'd kill someone. It was that inevitable. Don't fret yourself. This would have happened regardless of anything you did or didn't do. It would probably have happened regardless of anything *I* did or didn't do."

So he was feeling guilty, too. Perhaps they all were—everyone at Meadowvale. Perhaps it was right, or at least healthy, that they should.

Hazel made an effort to pull herself together. She gave him a grateful smile. "Okay. Well, I'll leave you in peace. I'll be in this evening. If you need me before then, you have my number."

When he saw her returning, Gabriel Ash went to get out of the car. But she waved him back. "Let's go somewhere quiet and I'll tell you what I know."

Her first thought was to take him to the park, to talk in the leafy quiet and paradoxical privacy of an open space with members of the public constantly passing. Then it occurred to her that he might not feel the same way about parks, at least this one, as she did. Instead she turned down toward the canal, found a tiny lay-by with a picnic bench and a view over the still brown water to spring green willows growing along the far bank.

"Okay," she said, turning the engine off. "It's not good news."

She told him what had happened. She told him that everyone had done their damnedest to save Jerome Cardy's life but that it had been in vain. He'd suffered too much damage.

Ash heard her out in silence. She could almost see his mind churning behind the deep-set dark brown eyes, but he didn't interrupt her, neither to confirm what she'd been told nor to contradict. Even after she'd finished he went on thinking about what she'd said for several minutes.

She waited patiently, using the time to study him. Hard to put an age on him, she thought. Late thirties? Tidied up—the thick black curls trimmed neatly, the battered jeans and sweater replaced by something smarter—he might have looked younger. Or he might be older than she thought: that look of earnest concentration gave him a slightly childlike air that made it hard to get a handle on him. Also he looked underfed. He had the bone structure to carry a certain amount of bulk, but nothing hung off his frame except the rough clothes. If he didn't look quite like a tramp, at least he looked like someone understudying the role.

Finally he said, "This isn't right." He sounded worried and slightly offended—like, Hazel thought, someone from a culture where they don't have jokes watching someone do stand-up. As if all the words were familiar but the meaning eluded him. Perhaps, she realized with a flash of insight, that was exactly what having psychological problems was like: turning up at a party where everyone but you knew all the latest slang.

"This isn't right," Ash said again, insistently. "What happened wasn't an accident. He *knew* it was going to happen—the boy, Jerome. He knew he was going to die—long before he was put in the other cell, before this other man was even brought in. How could that be?"

"It couldn't," agreed Hazel gently. "Ash, you were hurt. You were concussed and asleep, then all this happened. You must have some of the details wrong."

"No." He seemed absolutely sure at first, and then, as he thought about it, less so. "I don't think so. He knew something bad was going to happen to him. He wanted me to remember."

"What exactly did he say?"

But she was right—a lot of the details were lost in the fog. Ash ran a distracted hand through his thick hair. "I . . . I'm not sure. He said it wasn't about the car crash. That was just an excuse. He said I had to tell someone when I got out and he didn't." His eyes found Hazel's. "That's what I'm doing. I'm telling you."

She smiled reassuringly. "Yes, you are. And we're going to make sense of it. Did he say anything else?"

Ash screwed his face up in the effort to remember. "Something about Shakespeare."

She wasn't expecting that. "*What* about Shakespeare?"

"Something about a dog. He had a dog. He called the dog after . . ." He lost the thread, shook his head helplessly.

"He called his dog after a character from Shakespeare?" suggested Hazel. "Macbeth? Caesar?" She gave a tiny grin. "Bottom?"

But Ash wasn't ready to see the funny side of any of this. "I don't know. And I don't know why he told me."

"Because you had your dog with you. He was just making conversation."

But that wasn't how Ash remembered it. "He woke me up. To tell me this stuff. To tell me to remember. And to mention the fact that he used to have a dog called Bottom?"

It didn't seem very likely. But then, none of it did. And the most probable explanation was that an unquantifiable amount of it was a by-product of the man's troubled mind. Some of it happened, some of it didn't; some of it he was remembering just wrongly enough to put a completely different slant on it.

There was no more Hazel could do but take him to wherever he called home, put the kettle on—if he owned a kettle—bid him good day, and draw a line under the whole regrettable incident. There was nothing to be gained by trying to reconcile what Gabriel Ash thought he remembered with what she'd been told by Sergeant Murchison.

It wasn't just that Ash would make a terrible witness. There are, as every police officer knows, plenty of people who see something happen, remember what they've seen, report it accurately, and still make terrible witnesses in court because they fall apart under the most rudimentary cross-examination. You nurse people like that, help them as much as you can, hope a jury will recognize the difference between a nervous witness and an unreliable one; and if the worse comes to the worst, remind yourself that their evidence enabled the investigating officer to understand what had happened even if he couldn't always prove it.

But Ash wasn't like that. His mind was fundamentally disordered. Even if he had heard something significant, how could anyone hope to sieve it out from the noodle soup simmering away in his brain? The sensible thing to do—the only thing to do—was to dismiss him as a witness in the same way that she'd dismissed the dog. They might both have seen or heard something useful, but there was no way of accessing the knowledge.

"Let's get you home," she suggested. "If I find out anything more, I'll let you know."

CHAPTER 7

THE HOUSE CAME as a surprise. At first Hazel thought he'd brought her to the wrong place—that he'd forgotten where he lived. Then she thought the house must have been divided and maybe he had a bed-sit in the basement. But no. Gabriel Ash—Rambles With Dogs—lived in a double-fronted stone-built Victorian house at the pricey end of Highfield Road. Even after the bottom fell out of the housing market, it must have been worth a small fortune.

"You'll come in?"

She'd had no intentions of doing so, but nothing nobler than curiosity made Hazel follow him up the front steps and into the hall.

It had been built as a family house, but it wasn't one anymore. As soon as she stepped inside she knew he lived here alone, unless you counted the dog. Not because he'd lapsed into a kind of squalor that no woman would have tolerated—the place was both clean and tidy. But there was an essential grayness in every room, a lack of warmth or color—not so much the decor as the very air itself. It was a sad house, a house that had known better times.

There was a kettle on the Aga. "I don't think I've got any biscuits." He gave her a thin smile. "Only dog biscuits."

He'd taken Patience's lead off as they came in, and she'd led the way into the kitchen. This seemed to be the main living-space, furnished with an ancient brown leather sofa and a chair, a bookcase full to bursting, a television set that had been state-of-the-art a decade earlier, and a dog bed. In spite of which, Patience appropriated the sofa. Ash didn't even try to move her. He waved Hazel to the chair, and when the tea was made, he sat down beside his dog, stroking her ticked white fur absently.

Hazel was trying to fit what she knew about the man with where and how he lived. "Have you lived here long?"

"Three years." He didn't elaborate.

"On your own?"

"Yes."

She didn't pursue a line of questioning that was in danger of becoming impertinent. Partly because she thought she knew the answers. His wife had left him and he'd fallen apart. There had been no shortage of money at one point, but the good job that had enabled him to buy this property had been a casualty of the split and now he went on living in a house that was too big for him and that he couldn't afford because he was clinging to the shreds of a happier past. One day soon the bank would give him the choice between selling up and foreclosure; until that happened, unable to make the move on his own, his occupation of it would contract into fewer and fewer rooms. Hazel thought that if she came back here in six months, she'd find he was sleeping in the kitchen as well.

No wonder the house seemed mournful. She wondered if they'd had children. If, for Ash, the rooms still echoed with the shrieks and laughter of excited children who now made only an occasional phone call and sent *Love you, Daddy* cards for Christmas and his birthday. If there was a shoe box somewhere with every one of them carefully preserved.

It wasn't just morbid curiosity on Hazel's part. It was significant that Gabriel Ash hadn't always been as he was now. He hadn't been born a sandwich short of a picnic. Once, not very long ago, he'd been an intelligent man with a good job. Maybe he'd always carried the seeds of breakdown within him, as many people do who are driven to achieve. But he'd held his life together with conspicuous success until not very long ago. His mental difficulties didn't go back far, so perhaps they didn't go down very deep.

So maybe she shouldn't dismiss quite so lightly what he was telling her. She sipped her tea and said, "Tell me again what Jerome Cardy said."

Ash's eyes flew wide. They were the color of bitter chocolate, and, with the thick black hair and olive-tinted skin, gave him a slightly Mediterranean air. They had an expression in Norbold for someone with roots elsewhere: "A granny missing from the graveyard." Hazel thought Gabriel Ash had at least one granny buried a long way from Norbold.

"Othello!" he exclaimed, startled by the way the memory had returned. As if it had bitten him.

"Come again?" Hazel Best's mother had thought it was a terribly common expression, but she'd never quite cured her daughter of using it.

"The Shakespeare reference—what he called his dog. He called it Othello."

"Did he?" she said levelly. "Okay."

Ash seemed to think it mattered. "Why did he want me to know that? That's not casual conversation. He was being taken to another cell, but he hung back long enough to tell me that he once had a dog called Othello. Why?"

If he was remembering correctly, it *was* odd. "Did he say anything else about it?"

"He said it was a sniffer dog."

Hazel frowned. "That's not a breed. You can't go out and buy one. Could he have had a security-trained dog?"

"I don't think he had. I didn't think so at the time. He didn't talk like someone who had dogs. If you know what breed it is, you say so—if you don't, you say it's a mongrel or a crossbreed, or a Heinz fifty-seven. Or a lurcher." He looked down at his own dog with a smile. "That boy didn't know what kind of dog Othello was. I asked if it was a spaniel and he said it was, but he didn't sound as if he'd ever thought about it. I don't think it was a real dog. I think it was a piece of information he wanted me to have."

"You mean like a secret message?" It was as improbable as the house.

Ash nodded. "I think so. He wanted to give me some information without the policeman realizing what he was doing."

"What policeman?"

"The one who came for him."

"But . . ." There was no point. She tried another tack. "Why?"

"I don't know."

Hazel thought, worrying the idea like a terrier, but nothing came to mind. "Othello. Othello the sniffer dog."

"Sniffer dogs look for drugs."

"Or explosives. Or dead bodies. Or various other things, actually. You can train them to associate just about any smell with a reward."

"Othello strangled his wife."

"Jerome Cardy wasn't married."

"But he was black."

"You think that's relevant?" It wasn't a criticism—she genuinely wondered.

"I have no idea," confessed Ash. "But it wasn't an off-the-cuff remark. It meant something to him, and he thought it might mean something to me." He rolled his eyes to the ceiling in a gesture of despair. "God help him."

"All right," said Hazel. "So what do we know about Othello?"

Gabriel Ash had had a good education once. But it was getting to be a long time since he'd studied English literature. "He was a Moor. Wasn't he the governor of Cyprus? He killed his wife after his sidekick convinced him she was having an affair. She wasn't. She loved Othello, and he loved her. But he killed her just the same." His eyes had gone distant again and there was a hint of bitterness in his voice.

"It was jealousy that killed Desdemona," Hazel recalled. "Is that what Jerome was trying to tell you? That someone was jealous of him?"

"Maybe. I don't know."

"And why tie it up in ribbons? If he thought someone was going to hurt him, why not tell you who, and why?"

"Because we weren't alone. He wanted *me* to know. He didn't want the policeman to understand."

The mysterious policeman again. "Ash, are you sure about that? That someone took Jerome to the other cell? That he didn't just wander off by himself?"

He looked momentarily offended. But he did her the courtesy of running through it in his mind once more. He reached the same conclusion. "Someone came to the door. He told the boy he'd freed up a cell for him. He seemed to think Patience might bite him, or"—he glanced apologetically at the dog—"worse." He mouthed the word *fleas* at Hazel, as if it would cause offense if overheard.

Every time she was tempted to put some credence to what he thought he remembered, he did this. Behaved like a lunatic. She asked the question because asking questions put her in control, made her comfortable. "Would you know him again? This policeman."

Ash shrugged. "I didn't see his face. He was in uniform, but I didn't get his number, if that's what you mean. I heard his voice. An older man rather than a younger one."

Against her better instincts, Hazel found herself toying with the information. Sergeant Murchison was not a young man. If there had been any shifting of prisoners to be done, as custody officer that night he was the one likeliest to have done it. But Sergeant Murchison said Jerome Cardy had shifted himself.

People get forgetful as they get older. If a cell had become vacant, he would have transferred Cardy to it; and if he had forgotten—if something had distracted him before he got it logged—when Barclay was brought in amid a flurry of fists and oaths, it would have been the easiest thing in the world for him to fling open the cell door and have the wild man shoved inside. Perhaps he never remembered that Cardy was in there, and a young black law student was the last person that Barclay, the rabid racist, should have been in with. Or perhaps he remembered just too late, at which point it was only a question of whether he owned up to his error or not.

If he did, no possible good could be served, but his own career would suddenly be in jeopardy. People would start wondering if he was still up to the job. Retirement would be proposed as a way of avoiding repercussions. If that wasn't what he wanted—and Sergeant Murchison had not struck Hazel as a man counting the weeks to his pension—perhaps even an honorable man could be forgiven for failing to volunteer the information that made sense of everything that had happened.

If, she reminded herself forcibly, what Gabriel Ash thought he remembered bore any relationship to the truth. This was a man who'd lost everything, including a large portion of his wits. He avoided saying the word *fleas* in front of his dog, for God's sake! He'd been sleeping off a concussion when he was wakened by assorted comings and goings and finally by all hell breaking loose. In such circumstances anyone might have got some of the details wrong. In such circumstances it would be amazing if Gabriel Ash had got any of the details right.

"Mr. Ash, do you remember when we went into the police station after you were hurt?" Ash nodded. "Do you remember meeting the sergeant who was in charge?"

"Yes."

"We spoke to him, didn't we? Then he showed us where you and Patience could get a bit of rest."

"He put us in a cell." Which was another way of saying the same thing.

"Do you think that's what you're thinking of? That the concussion made you confuse the two memories? That you *did* see the police officer at the door, but it was earlier, when he was showing you to the cell. That he wasn't actually there later, when Jerome went for a look around."

For several seconds he made no attempt to answer. She couldn't be sure if he was offended or thinking about it. Then he said, "What about the things Jerome said to me?"

Hazel shrugged sympathetically. "You took quite a beating. Bad dreams were probably the mildest aftereffect to be expected."

Still that ambivalent, almost unwinking gaze from his deep,

dark eyes. "You think I dreamed it. Everything the boy said. Everything that happened."

"Not everything," she protested. "He was certainly in with you for a time, and maybe you were talking. And later he left the cell, and later still all hell broke loose next door. You didn't imagine any of that. But the mind has a way of trying to make sense of unconnected bits of information. I'm just wondering if that's what's happened. That after you knew something awful had happened to Jerome Cardy, your brain—which was also having a bad day—drew together things it had heard and seen in different contexts, including dreams, and made them into a plausible narrative. I don't think you're making any of this up. I think your brain, also from the best of motives, may have been playing tricks on you."

"And Othello, the sniffer dog?"

Hazel gave a sympathetic smile. "Does it seem likely? Because most things that don't, didn't happen. Or didn't happen the way we remember. It's not just you. Every time we talk to a witness we have to consider what other factors might have affected what they think they saw. Most people try to tell the truth. But it's very easy to get it wrong."

He had nothing to say to that and she had nothing to add. She stood up, putting down her cup. "Try not to worry about it. The people who'll investigate what happened are very experienced. They'll get to the bottom of it. Thanks for the tea. I'll see you again."

Ash stood up, too, and showed her to the door. "I don't think I thanked you. For last night. For looking after me."

"All part of the service," she said brightly—too brightly. It must have been obvious to him that she'd satisfied herself as to what had happened and exactly what his testimony was worth. She hoped he wouldn't think she was being rude. But probably, she reckoned, by the time she was back in her car he'd have forgotten what it was they were discussing.

But she was wrong about that.

After Constable Best had gone, Ash went back to the leather sofa in the kitchen and sat down beside his dog again, his right arm slipping automatically and naturally across her back. She gazed at him with expectant amber eyes.

"She didn't believe me. She thinks I imagined it."

The dog said nothing.

"*I* don't think I imagined it," Ash said stubbornly. He poured more tea, sipped it reflectively. "I *think* that boy asked me for help. *Would* I have dreamed something like that? In so much detail?" He simply didn't know. "But if it wasn't a dream, then I owe him . . . something. To do as he asked—to find someone who might believe me. Someone who might understand what he was trying to say."

Still the dog said nothing.

"He was only twenty years old. He must have parents in the town. And it's not a common name. Someone who wanted to find them probably could."

Patience raised a back foot and delicately scratched her ear.

"Maybe I should talk to Laura first." It had taken the therapist a year to get him to use her first name. "She'll think it's a bad idea. Maybe it *is* a bad idea. She'll say it's more about my feelings of guilt than anything the boy said. That I'm making a mystery of it because you can hope to solve a mystery, where you can't hope to put right a tragedy."

He looked sidelong at his dog as if waiting for a response, but there was none.

"I know what you're thinking. That this is displacement activity. That I *want* there to be something going on that no one else knows about. Because I used to be good at this. When there was space in my head to think. That I'm never going to pick up where I left off, but I could do if I had to. And maybe then there wouldn't be enough space left in my head for . . . Or at least, not every minute of every damned day."

He sighed. "And you're probably right. What happened at Meadowvale Police Station is most probably what appears to have happened—a monstrous, horrible thing, but not a mystery. Robert Barclay killed Jerome Cardy because he is a bad man; Jerome died because he was unlucky."

He stood up and walked to the window. The view was more pleasant than remarkable; but then, he didn't look out much. "But just suppose for a moment that you're wrong. Suppose Jerome meant exactly what he said when he told me he was going to die in that police station, and something quite different when he talked about Othello. If he was trying to alert someone to what was happening to him. No one at the police station is going to ask these questions. Either they don't know there's a puzzle to solve or it's in their best interests to leave well enough alone."

Gabriel Ash thought a little longer; then he made up his mind. "I'll go tomorrow. To express my condolences to his parents, and ask if any of this makes sense to them."

What he didn't say, aloud or even in the privacy of his own head, was, "Maybe if I can get to the bottom of this mystery, the other one—the old one, the big one—might seem slightly less unbearable."

Be careful, said Patience.

CHAPTER 8

YOU NEED TO make yourself presentable.

Ash ignored the voice in his head, which is something he didn't often do, at least when they were alone. So the dog said it again. You need to make yourself presentable before we go and see them.

"Who?" His furtive glance showed that he knew exactly who.

The Cardy family. I know you're going to see them. I saw you looking up their address in the phone book.

Phone books are something the average dog knows very little about, unless it's how quickly you can shred one if you're left alone in the house. So Ash was probably right when he rationalized these conversations he had with Patience as being something that took place inside his head. Undoubtedly Laura Fry would have agreed, if he'd told her that he didn't just talk to the dog but also heard her reply.

She said that talking to animals was a way of holding a debate with other viewpoints within your own mind. He wasn't sure how she would react if he was honest with her—if he admitted that he seemed to hear the dog respond exactly as he heard other people speak, except that she didn't move her lips. He didn't hear other animals talk, just Patience. Laura had said he wasn't mad. He wondered if she'd want to review that diagnosis if he reported, word for word, the conversation he was now having. And all the others that he'd had in the last three months, since discovering that the stray dog he'd adopted to give him something to think about beyond his own misery spoke better English than most teenagers.

His first thought was that the therapist was wrong and he was indeed mad. He was terrified, precisely because it didn't come out of left field. Things had happened in his life that would have driven anyone mad. But he'd thought the crisis had passed. He'd come as close to a mental breakdown as you can without slipping irrevocably over the edge, but somehow he'd clawed his way back. Or, to be fair, been dragged back by talented and dedicated people who'd convinced him he could learn to live in the world again, even though everything about it had changed.

Perhaps it helped that he hadn't had much choice in the matter. Ash hadn't so much separated himself from his former life as had it taken from him. But isolation can become a habit, too, and after he left London he'd withdrawn into himself much as a crab does, for protection. He'd turned his back on everyone he once knew, all the support he might have had, excepting only Laura Fry, who was imposed on him almost as a condition of remaining at large. He'd returned to live alone in this empty house, the house where he'd grown up, wrapped himself in his most comfortable old clothes, existed for months at a time only on those foods that could be delivered. He knew people—neighbors, tradesmen, the local police—thought he was strange, but until he got the dog he'd agreed with Laura, that underneath all that, the essential core of him had survived more or less intact.

The first time the dog spoke to him, he thought it had finally happened: that his ravaged personality had splintered and his brain was now leaking out of his left ear. He thought he should probably get himself committed. Again. That would be the end of everything—especially those last dregs of hope that made him pay the phone bill religiously even though he never made calls.

When he'd calmed down a bit, and Patience was quietly washing her paws and there was no gray goo on his shoulder, he tried to make sense of it. And this was what he came up with: that the words that seemed to come from the dog were actually emanating from part of his own mind. It was talking to him like a friend, helping him to see things clearly, and he only credited its input to the dog because that seemed marginally less peculiar than debating with a semidetached bit of your own brain.

A few times he'd been close to putting this theory to Laura Fry. She might concur immediately. She might say it was a common phenomenon, a recognized part of a traumatized individual's coping strategy, that it didn't mean he was mad at all. Or, of course, she might regard him in a silence that became less reassuring the longer it lasted, put her letter opener where he couldn't reach it, and pick up the phone. That was what kept him from confiding in her. He'd rather think he might be finally, permanently, irrevocably mad than have it confirmed.

So now he dealt with the phenomenon—that was a fairly safe word—by accepting it. If it was a less traumatized portion of his own brain inviting him to hold an internal debate about things—things that had happened, things he might do next—then it made sense to join in. If it was a psychosis, it was best not to draw attention to it. And if it really was that he'd come home from the pound with a talking dog, he'd be wise to take her advice seriously. The aliens had landed, obviously they were smarter than people, but since they walked on four legs and flashed fangs when they smiled, they'd been misunderstood and taken not to any of the world's leaders but to Battersea Dogs' Home.

He did as he was told and went to look in the wardrobe.

In spite of how they'd parted, Hazel Best harbored a faint unease about discounting what Gabriel Ash had told her. It made no sense, and it came from a man who was clearly unreliable, and yet . . .

Almost more than anything else, she was puzzled by her own reluctance to let it go. She could shed no light on the death of Jerome Cardy, and she was pretty sure Ash couldn't, either. She hadn't been there; he'd been there in body but probably not in mind; and that should have been the end of it. Hazel was annoyed with herself that she kept thinking about it, taking the pieces apart and trying to get them to fit together better.

At least she'd had the sense not to discuss the matter with people at work. Just imagining the response made her wince. If she told anyone there that the man known throughout Meadowvale as Rambles With Dogs had given her tea and no biscuits and a version of events that varied slightly but significantly from Sergeant Murchison's, and that if Ash was remembering right then the custody sergeant responsible for Jerome Cardy's safety had made an elementary mistake that resulted in his death, they'd laugh in her face. If they were feeling generous. They'd tell her all the other things they'd been vouchsafed by village idiots, perhaps even by this village idiot, and how difficult it was to climb the promotion ladder if you couldn't tell the difference between the probable, the possible, and the downright ludicrous.

She might have risked it. She might have told herself that if Ash had got any part of his story right, the least a police officer owed to a murdered boy was to try to get at the truth. If there was nothing to find, if Ash's fears were entirely baseless, she could dismiss him and them with a clear conscience. At which point, giving her colleagues a laugh would seem a small-enough price to pay.

What stopped her was the danger that being the office joke for a week mightn't be the end of it. Donald Murchison had been a pillar of the police community—and they *were* a community, even a family, in the way they bickered and grumbled and picked fault with one another, right up to the point that something threatened any one of them, at which point they instantly closed ranks—longer than Hazel had been alive. He'd been at Meadowvale longer than anyone else. He was both liked and respected.

If she suggested—however tactfully—that an honorable man, tired and losing concentration halfway through the graveyard shift, had forgotten where he'd put his prisoners and a twenty-year-old boy had died because of it, the laughing would stop. Whether her colleagues believed her or not wouldn't be the issue. Forced to take sides, to a man they'd back Sergeant Murchison. Of course they would. They trusted him, and they hardly knew her. And after this, most of them wouldn't want to. They'd end their conversations when she sat down with them, discuss with her nothing but the weather, keep her at arm's length. Lock her out.

And for what? A suspicion cast by an idiot. *She* didn't believe him—why should anyone else?

And yet . . . a man had died. If he died because an honest officer had made a mistake, decent people everywhere would recognize that as an accident. A deeply regrettable accident, but an accident nonetheless. But if, a few months down the line, someone else died because the same officer got tired enough to make another mistake, that wouldn't be an accident—it would be Hazel Best's fault. Because, having been aware of the problem, she'd shied away from tackling it.

She wished she wasn't the new girl in Norbold. She wished she'd had time to make the kind of friends you can talk things through with, even difficult things, who'll listen without judging and help you find your way to your own heart. But she hadn't. She was on her own.

If she'd been sure there was a problem, she'd have gone to Fountain whatever the personal cost to herself. But all she had was this niggling doubt, raised by the most unreliable of witnesses, and she wasn't ready to throw either her career or Sergeant Murchison's into the trash can for a fishnet stocking of a notion, more holes than substance.

Because almost certainly it was a phantasm, a night terror with no basis in fact. Finally, that—the danger that she could be accusing a decent man of something he hadn't done—mattered more to her than any backlash against herself. It wouldn't just be unwise to make an allegation on the word of Gabriel Ash; it would be wrong. He was a damaged individual, not to blame for the wild inventions of his troubled mind. But she was an intelligent woman in a responsible job, and she had a duty not to allow his fantasies to harm a good police officer. Her instinct had been right. Nothing Gabriel Ash thought he'd seen or heard could be counted on, and without his witness there was nothing to pursue.

It was a long time since Gabriel Ash had made anything resembling a social call. He had no social life. He had no friends left: not because they'd abandoned him but because he'd abandoned them. Some of them had tried very hard to stay in his life, to offer ongoing sympathy and support. But there's a limit to how much you can help someone who refuses to see you, won't take your calls, cuts himself off from the world you inhabit. Even the most dogged of them had given up after two years.

These days, the nearest thing he had to human companionship came from Laura Fry. He saw her once a week, for forty minutes at a time, and she was paid to listen to his troubles. But if one day he looked left when he should have looked right and got flattened by the Coventry bus, it would fall to her to identify his body because there was no one closer.

To visit Mr. and Mrs. Cardy, at first he dressed as he did for his appointments with his therapist. But when he looked in the mirror, it was all wrong. He was clean and tidy enough—though he'd always been one of those men who only have to put on a new suit for it to immediately start looking shabby—but he didn't look . . . he didn't look . . .

Responsible. That was what he didn't look. He didn't look like someone grieving parents would talk to because it might help them discover what had happened to their son. If they saw him coming up their drive they'd think he was delivering the local freesheet.

He went back to his wardrobe, pushed aside the three or four things he wore all the time—cords and sweatshirts, and rugby shirts for teams he couldn't have named let alone played for—and knocked the cobwebs off some of the things behind them. A good white shirt that he hadn't worn since the last time his wife ironed it. A suit that hung off his bones now, even after he'd punched fresh holes in the belt. A dark tie. He could do nothing about the unruly black hair—a ponytail, a hairband, an impromptu haircut with the kitchen scissors—that wouldn't actually make things worse, but when he checked the hall mirror again, the man who gazed out at him at least looked like someone you might open the door to. And something else. He looked just a little familiar. Like someone Ash had known once.

He thought about phoning ahead, decided against. He'd have to tell them who he was and explain his purpose, and they might refuse to see him. He thought if he turned up on their doorstep, wearing his suit, they might take him for someone official and let him in.

It was a good reason, but it wasn't the only one. He hated using the phone these days. He made virtually no calls, and most of those he received were wrong numbers. He always answered, just in case, but it was almost never for him.

And then, once he made the call he'd be committed. If he went in person, he could change his mind at any point up to knocking on the Cardys' door. He thought he probably would. These days, he was a lot better at planning a course of action than carrying it out.

But, despite her clear expectations, he didn't want to take the dog. Just in case he got as far as their front door. Just in case they asked him in. "Nothing personal," he assured her. "They might have a cat."

Yes? said Patience politely.

He could never lie to her. "Okay. The real reason is, it's pretty hard to look official when you've got a dog on a lead. Unless it's a police dog. I don't suppose you can do an impression of a German shepherd?"

Not really, said the white lurcher.

* * *

Melvin Green was arguably the most important person at Meadowvale Police Station, and he wasn't even a police officer. But all those who were knew they would be easier to replace than Melvin. If a routine checkpoint turned bloody one day because it stopped a car containing not laundered diesel or a suitcase of cocaine but fifty kilos of improvised explosives, whoever had stepped forward to ask for ID, and the officers standing either side of him, and behind him, and back at the car ordering elevenses, would somehow be replaced by close of play. If CID, following up a lead that finally got them within collaring distance of Norbold's only serious godfather, Mickey Argyle, found themselves on the wrong end of an ambush, there would be a flurry of phone calls between Meadowvale and Division, and between Division and Scotland Yard, but by the end of the day there would again be detectives in the upstairs offices.

But if Melvin Green were to meet a sudden and unexpected end involving damp socks and a high-voltage power source, no one would have any idea how, or even if, the world would keep turning. Melvin was the Man Who Knew About Computers. Every enterprise needs one these days, and having an IT qualification is better than having a fast car, a time-share in the Algarve, and a season ticket for Wolverhampton Wanderers. It makes you everyone's friend. Men who would otherwise be stuck with the pretty girls' fat friends could take their pick in an office where a month's work could disappear at the press of the wrong button *but be found again by someone who knew about computers.*

This morning the new hottie from Uniform was standing next to him in the canteen queue. She smiled at him. What, want me to explain how Restore System works? thought Melvin with a secret smile. Forgot to back up your files at appropriate intervals, did you? She seemed a nice-enough girl; he'd probably help her out, though he'd be putting down markers for the Christmas party.

But despite the smile, as she lifted her tray she gave no indication that she knew even who he was. Melvin was taken aback and a little offended. It was getting to be a long time since he'd had to dust off a chat-up line.

She was new. She didn't know any better. He carried his tray to the table where she'd sat down, and sat down across from her with a smile. "Hello. I'm Melvin. I'm the computer geek."

Hazel gave him a friendly nod. "Good to meet you, Melvin. Hazel Best—I'm a bit of a computer geek myself. I used to teach IT at a Birmingham high school."

Melvin felt the confidence sliding off his face. It was as if someone had come into his office and said, "We're scrapping all the computers, Melvin. We've come up with something better." It was his only edge. Without computers he was just a geek. And the new hottie in Uniform used to teach IT. "Oh—er . . ." He hunted around desperately for something to brighten his tarnished appeal. "Anything electronic, really. MP3s, sat nav, cameras—anything like that. Anything electronic that you want a hand with, you come to me."

"Cameras?" She was just making conversation. She had nothing more in mind than being on good terms with all at Meadowvale, even the spotty youth with the see-through mustache. "I used to do a bit of photography. Wouldn't mind taking it up again."

"Tell me what you want to do and I'll recommend something," Melvin offered importantly. "Anything from high res to Happy Snappers. Or if you want something to shoot movies, I know just the thing. Mr. Fountain's got me sussing out a new CCTV system. After . . . you know. I told him six months ago it needed replacing, but the money wasn't there. The money'll be there now, bet you anything."

Hazel didn't have to ask. Nothing Melvin the computer geek could tell her would change anything. And yet . . . The imp on her shoulder was niggling away again. "Has it been on the blink for a while?" she asked innocently. "The CCTV."

"On and off," he said, nodding. "Not my fault. The whole system's reached the end of its useful life. But what with the recession and everything, I was told to keep it ticking over, that maybe next year we could think of replacing it. I did what I was told. I worked out what the problem was and how to avoid it crashing again. I told everybody, from Mr. Fountain down to the cleaning ladies. I told them what made it crash, and what not to do if they didn't want it to crash again. But do they listen? Do they hell. Then it's, 'Oh Melvin, the CCTV's down again. Can you sort it out?'"

Hazel made herself take a slow drink of her coffee before replying. She knew the abyss was beckoning. She knew she shouldn't be tap-dancing along the edge. Somehow she couldn't stop herself. "It's a recurring problem, then, is it? What happened yesterday was the same thing that happened before?"

"Exactly the same," said Melvin bitterly. "Someone had done *exactly* what I told them not to. I might as well talk Swahili for all the notice anybody pays."

They finished their coffee in a thoughtful silence.

Hazel went to the women's locker room, found it empty, and sat down to think it through again. Because what Melvin Green had told her *did* change things—or at least put a different complexion on them. The CCTV system had a history of failing. The fault had been tracked down, and everyone had been told how to prevent its happening again. But someone had done what everyone knew not to do and in consequence there was no record of how Jerome Cardy came to be in Robert Barclay's cell.

Jerome Cardy had told Gabriel Ash he was going to die in Meadowvale Police Station, and he had done. The systems set up to protect him had not only failed to keep him safe, they'd failed to record how the tragedy had occurred and who was responsible. If the custody officer knew how to scupper the CCTV, and if he'd recognized his culpability quickly enough, it would have been a good way to stop anyone else from finding out.

Hazel felt her options—as a responsible police officer, as a worthwhile human being—starting to narrow.

CHAPTER 9

One of the many difficult things about losing someone in suspicious circumstances is that you can't go ahead with a funeral. There are investigations, postmortems, inquests may be opened and adjourned, and though it makes sense that the body be preserved for further examination, it leaves the immediate family in a limbo world of grief without knowledge, mere onlookers to activities they have no part in.

If Geoff and Adelaide Cardy had lost their son to a road accident, a victim of the lethal combination of inexperience and self-confidence, one or both of them would have had to rein in their grieving while the immediate practicalities were dealt with: registering the death, informing friends and relatives, sorting out the paperwork, arranging the funeral, and contacting those who would want to attend.

It feels terribly difficult at the time, but in an odd way it's exactly what you need. Things that have to be done, that can't wait while your life falls apart in a million bitter shards. You do what you have to. You cry on your own time. And all the things that need doing, all the people who need seeing and talking to, are what get you through the first few days when shock and despair threaten to overwhelm you. By the time the funeral is over, so is that first tidal wave of shock. Even the exhaustion helps.

There could be no funeral for Jerome Cardy, not yet. There were people to notify, but a lot of them had already heard. A families liaison officer from the police station told his parents what had happened, and what would happen next, and then everything went quiet. They sat—sometimes in their front room, sometimes in their kitchen—together but hardly looking at each other as the slow hours passed. Sometimes Adelaide sobbed into a handkerchief. When Geoff Cardy felt the ache in his throat that presaged tears, he went into the bathroom. So passed the first thirty-six hours.

On the Friday morning there was a knock at the door. A man in a dark suit was standing on the porch. His shoes were newly polished. Geoff Cardy, who'd been in the army, noticed such things.

"My name is Gabriel Ash. I was in the police station the night your son died. I was talking to him not long before. I thought I should come and say how very sorry I am about what happened."

All the way over here, and the walk had taken twenty minutes, he'd been practicing what to say in his head. If he got it wrong, blushed and mumbled inarticulately, it would be awful for him, but it would also be awful for them, wondering what it was he was trying to say. Three months ago Gabriel Ash had had trouble talking to the grocer. The fear that he could mess this up had almost kept him from coming. He felt a genuine relief at having managed to introduce himself without stumbling.

Geoff Cardy, who was of course unaware of this, wasn't ready to ask him into the house. They talked in the doorway. "Are you a policeman, Mr. Ash?"

"No. I got mugged earlier in the evening. I was sleeping it

off in a spare cell. They put Jerome in with me until they could find him a cell of his own."

Cardy bridled. "But they didn't, did they? If they had, he'd be alive today. Instead they put him in with a psycho."

Ash shook his head, awkward and embarrassed. "I'm not sure what happened, Mr. Cardy. I was concussed—my memory isn't as clear as it might be. But he said some things to me that I'm hoping will make sense to you, because they don't to me."

Cardy frowned. He was a tall man, like his son. "What things?"

Behind him the door of the sitting room opened and Adelaide Cardy came into the hall. "Geoffrey? What's going on? Who is this gentleman?"

Cardy cast her a glance that said he wasn't entirely sure. "His name is Ash. He says he was with Jerome before he was killed. He says Jerome gave him a message."

"Not that exactly," said Ash quickly, but hope had already lit a candle in Mrs. Cardy's eyes. She'd thought she would never hear from her son again; now it seemed she might. It wasn't much—a message from someone he'd been in a police cell with—but when there's nothing else, and there's never going to be anything else, anything seems like everything.

"Don't keep him on the doorstep," she chided. "Bring him inside, sit him down. Let's hear what he has to say."

If Ash had felt uneasy about coming here, now he felt worse. This poor woman thought he had something meaningful to tell her—that her son's last thoughts had been of his family, something like that. And he hadn't. There were two things Jerome had said to him—at least, that Ash thought he'd said—and one was as trivial as it was peculiar, and the other he mustn't on any account share with the boy's parents. Even if his memory was accurate;

especially if his memory was accurate. Whatever he told them, he couldn't tell them that Jerome had known he was going to die. They didn't need to know how deeply afraid he'd been.

"I'm sorry there isn't more I can tell you. I was groggy—most of the time he let me sleep. Only, before he left, he said something that I haven't been able to make any sense of and I suppose I'm hoping it'll mean something to you. Anyway, I thought I should see you and pass it on."

He heard himself and winced. It didn't just sound lame; it sounded as if he was trying to find an excuse for being here, as if his real purpose was to weevil his way into someone else's tragedy for whatever satisfaction that might afford. He knew this happened.

"Mr. Ash," said Adelaide Cardy quietly, "will you take a seat? In a moment I'll make us some tea. But first, I would very much like to hear what my son said to you. I don't mind if it doesn't make any sense. If he thought it was worth saying, it's worth hearing. I'm never going to hear his voice again. Every word he left me is precious."

Chastened, Ash nodded and took the chair she indicated, and kept his eyes on his knees while he tried to shape his offering into a form she could find some comfort in. Knowing as he did that he was bound to fail, doomed to confuse and disappoint her. "You see, I had my dog with me. Jerome said he liked dogs. He said"—he looked up, watching the effect of his words on her face—"he used to have a dog called Othello."

He said nothing more. Neither did the Cardys. They seemed to be waiting for him to explain. When he didn't, Geoff Cardy's strong face started to fold into a frown, and Adelaide glanced up at him as if she thought she was being slow, that her husband must have understood even if she had not. When she saw his brow beetling, she looked back at Ash, her eyes perplexed. "That can't be right, Mr. Ash. You must have got it wrong."

"Jerome never had a dog," said Cardy shortly. "We can't have animals in the house—I'm allergic to the fur. You must have misunderstood."

Which was what Hazel Best thought. That he'd dreamed some of it, misremembered the rest. Perhaps she was right. Perhaps he should have known better than to credit anything that went on inside his head. Quite apart from the concussion, he knew his faculties were no longer entirely trustworthy. Maybe his aching head had made a hash of the filing and he was remembering these events just sufficiently off-kilter to create a mystery where none existed.

He had no way of knowing, no yardstick against which to judge. He thought that what he remembered, what seemed to have happened, what he thought he'd heard, was essentially accurate. But then, he would think that, whether or not. "Could it have been someone else's dog? Someone he knew. I'm sure he called it Othello."

Adelaide looked up at her husband, who had remained standing. "Was he thinking of a friend's dog? Do you remember him walking a dog for a friend?"

Cardy shook his head. "Not that he said to me. I'd have remembered. I'd have worried about him bringing its hairs home on his clothes."

Ash glanced down guiltily at his dark suit. But it had been in the back of the wardrobe since before he had Patience—he didn't think he was going to leave Geoff Cardy in a state of anaphylactic shock.

"Anyway," added Jerome's father roughly, "what kind of a name for a dog is Othello?"

A faint sweet smile stole across Adelaide's face. "It's a very *literary* name," she said with satisfaction. "Most children these days have no idea who Shakespeare is." The smile turned apologetic. "Comes of having an English teacher for a mother, I suppose."

"Was *Othello* his favorite play?" asked Ash, grasping for the straws of understanding.

She raised an eyebrow at him. "The story of a black man who murders his white wife because he can't believe she truly loves him? What do you think?"

Ash winced again. By now he was wishing he hadn't come. He was never going to understand what Jerome Cardy had wanted to tell him, not least because he couldn't be sure what Jerome had said. "Probably not."

Geoff Cardy owned a garage. He did not share in his wife's love of literature, had always felt a little excluded because their son did. Now Jerome was dead and she was sharing it with a stranger. Resentment rose in his throat like bile. "Mr. Ash, I thought you had something to tell us about how our son died. Or why. Or *something.* I'm sorry, but I'm not finding this particularly helpful."

"No, I'm sorry," said Ash, contrite. "I shouldn't have troubled you. I just thought . . . I thought he wanted to put something on record, something he didn't want to put into words, and I didn't understand what it was and I wondered if you might. I'm sorry if I've upset you."

Adelaide touched the back of his hand with a soft finger, startling him. He had grown unused to human contact. "Don't be sorry. My son had a bad death. He was afraid, and helpless, and much, much too young. But there's this. Shortly before he died he was with someone he trusted enough to talk to, and who cared enough about what happened to try to pass the message on. Maybe we'll never know what he wanted to say, or even if there was something. But you tried, Mr. Ash, and I appreciate that."

There was nothing more he could tell them and nothing he could learn. It had been a fool's errand. The effort of will it had taken to get him here, to make him talk to these people, had been wasted, as had their time. "Thank you for seeing me. I won't trouble you again."

But at the door he hesitated. "*Othello.* It's about jealousy, isn't it? About a man destroyed by his own jealousy."

"Jealousy, yes," agreed Mrs. Cardy, "and love. Iago is jealous of his commander's success and sets about ruining him. He sows the seeds of jealousy in Othello by hinting that his new wife is betraying him. Even more than jealousy, the play is about love running out of control, and the fear that comes with all love—that it will not last forever. Othello accepts Iago's lies because he can't believe that someone he loves that much loves him in return. Othello is as much a victim as Desdemona is. But who cries for him?" Perhaps she was unaware of the tears streaking her cheeks.

Ash hesitated, aware of how much pain he was causing and afraid of twisting the knife. But he thought he needed to know. "Was Jerome in love?"

With a quick, concerned glance at his wife, Cardy fielded that one. "Jerome was twenty years old. He was halfway through a law degree at Durham University. He didn't have time to be in love."

"Then, was there anyone he was afraid of?"

The boy's father bristled. "I'm guessing he was a *bit* worried about the man who beat him to death!"

"But he didn't know Robert Barclay. Even if he had, he'd have had no reason to suppose they'd meet in Meadowvale Police

Station. But when he was talking to me, he was already afraid. He knew something awful was going to happen."

He hadn't meant to say that. But it was out now. Not for the first time he hated himself for the loss of that ordinary self-control that normal people take for granted, that tells them when it's appropriate to talk and when things are better left unsaid. For months at a time Gabriel Ash had hardly spoken to anyone except his therapist and his dog. Now, when it mattered, he couldn't keep his mouth shut.

Mrs. Cardy rocked gently to this new revelation, blinking back her tears. "He'd been in an accident. He'd been arrested. He must have known he was in trouble."

"The accident wasn't his fault. But he left the scene, then he tried to evade the police. Why would he do that? Why didn't he just do what was required of him—report the accident and stay with the vehicles? Why did he run?"

But they couldn't tell him. They didn't know.

CHAPTER 10

WITH RELUCTANCE, with trepidation, fervently wishing she could turn a blind eye as easily as everyone else at Meadowvale seemed able to, Hazel decided she couldn't sit on the fence any longer. She had to speak to Fountain, whatever the cost to Donald Murchison and to herself. She went in on Friday morning. It seemed better to her to do this on her own time than during the hours she was being paid for.

She didn't make an appointment, for the same reason Ash hadn't phoned the Cardys. She tapped on the chief superintendent's door and asked his secretary if he was free.

The location of Johnny Fountain's office said a lot about the man and explained much of his success. His predecessor had made his office on the top floor, with panoramic views over the park and the canal and out to the Shropshire hills. Fountain had relocated the canteen to the top floor, putting himself at the hub of Meadowvale Police Station, on the first floor, at the top of the main staircase. Anyone going anywhere had to pass his door. He didn't have the views, or the peace and quiet, that his predecessor had enjoyed, but it was much easier for him to keep a finger on the station's pulse.

And it was easy for people to stop by on the off chance of seeing him. Hazel was pretty sure that if she'd had to climb three stories, nodding a greeting to everyone she passed on the way, she'd have changed her mind before she got there.

She was dreading having to put her suspicions into words. Part of her hoped he'd be busy, or not in his office, and she'd have to go away again. But coming back would be even harder, so she steeled herself to knock, smile politely at Miss Patel, his secretary—a fine-boned woman in her late thirties who protected her boss with a devotion that earned her the nickname "the Pitbull"—and ask if Mr. Fountain would see her.

To her deep dismay, he would.

"As a matter of fact," he said, waving her to the chair across his desk, "I've been wanting a word with you."

"Sir?" She couldn't think what else to say.

"That business in the cells. Horrible business. It's been hard to think about much else since it happened. I suppose you're the same."

"Well . . . yes, sir."

"We all are. Something like that affects everyone, even those who weren't involved. All the same," and he gave her a craggy smile, "we have other duties, other obligations, and I can't let everything else go to pot while IPCC tries to make sense of a few chaotic minutes in our cells. I should have had you in here before this."

Hazel felt her heart turn over and begin to sink. "Yes, sir?"

Fountain smiled. He was still a good-looking man, tall and broad, with a leonine presence that rendered the whiteness of his hair and mustache entirely irrelevant. "Cheer up," he said, "I haven't pulled you in here to sack you. I wanted to ask how it's going for you—if you're getting the support you need."

She was taken aback. "Yes—indeed, sir. People have been great. Helpful, and welcoming. Up to two days ago, I was really enjoying the job."

He nodded grimly. "And then you met Robert Barclay. I'm afraid the Barclays of this world are part of the job. No one joins for the privilege of dealing with them, but deal with them we must."

She sucked in a deep breath and asked the question that had been racking her. At least one of them. "Was it my fault, sir? If I'd handled it better—kept my distance, waited for back-up as Constable Budgen wanted to do—would things have worked out better?"

Johnny Fountain gazed at her with compassion. His voice was a soft growl. "You mean, would Jerome Cardy be alive today?"

Silent, Hazel nodded.

Fountain shook his head. "No, he wouldn't. That's not where it went wrong. There were two points where events could have taken a different path, and you weren't involved in either of them. Whatever got Barclay spitting tacks, that was one of them. We don't know what set him off and we probably never will. But once he was out of control, somebody was always going to call us, we were always going to have to arrest him, and he was always going to end up in the cells. If he'd come with you quietly, he'd have ended up there; if we'd gone in mob-handed, he'd still have ended up there.

"The other thing that went wrong was that Jerome Cardy was kipping in a cell where he wasn't supposed to be. That wasn't your fault, either. I don't think it was anybody's fault. Donald Murchison thinks it was his, because he was custody officer and should have known where his prisoners were, but what are you going to do—crucify him for not locking the door on a quiet law student and a sleeping tramp? It was a reasonable thing to do. That's what I expect IPCC to conclude: that nobody did anything wrong. Except Barclay, and what can you expect of a man known to one and all as Barking Mad?"

When he put it that way, Hazel found herself mentally backpedaling. He was right. What happened wasn't Sergeant Murchison's fault—the man risked serious injury to get Cardy away from his attacker, and was almost quick enough to save him. If he'd succeeded, he'd have been a hero to one and all, herself included. The fact that it took him just a few seconds too long to reach the cells didn't make him a villain. And if the sergeant had done nothing wrong, he had nothing to hide. In all probability the CCTV just crashed, as it had done before and probably would again.

"Gabriel Ash . . ." she began uncertainly.

"Ah yes. Rambles With Dogs." Fountain leaned back in his chair and steepled his fingers contemplatively. "Another deeply unfortunate case. He was quite a highflier at one time, you know. Worked for the government. Then he had a breakdown, and these days it's as much as he can manage to get his shoes on the right feet. Lives in a little world all his own. About all we can do for Rambles is try to keep the kids from tormenting him."

And that was it in a nutshell. The reason Hazel had felt uneasy about what happened when no one else did was that she'd listened to what Gabriel Ash had said about that night, when everyone else had had more sense. Nothing Ash said, nothing he thought he remembered, could be trusted. He was concussed, he'd been sleeping, but even wide awake he couldn't be considered a reliable witness. She felt moved to apologize. "I thought someone ought to hear him out. Just in case he had something useful to contribute."

"I dare say IPCC will feel the same way," said Fountain understandingly. "And get as much sense out of him, too. It's not your fault, Hazel. He's an intelligent, well-educated man and he can be quite plausible. Until you catch him discussing the political situation with that dog of his and realize his elevator no longer serves all floors."

Hazel nodded wryly. "I know what you mean. I took him home to Highfield Road. He calls her Patience. They're like an old married couple."

Fountain chuckled. "That was his mother's house. He inherited it after she died, but he only came back here to live after his breakdown. I suppose after he lost his job there was no point staying in London."

"Wasn't he married at one time?" She was remembering the sad house.

I think she'd disappeared," said Fountain pensively. "I think that's when the train jumped the tracks. Like I say, all very unfortunate. Well." He stood up. The interview was over. "It was good talking to you. I want you to remember I'm here—if there's anything you need to discuss, anything I can help with. I want you to enjoy your time in Norbold, and learn everything you can. I think you're going to be a good police officer, Hazel. I think you could go far."

There's a saying in journalistic circles: If you want to keep a secret, tell it to the police press office. But some things even they couldn't keep a lid on, and a death in custody was pretty well top of the list. So the *Norbold News* had a statement of the bare facts two hours after Jerome Cardy was pronounced dead. The following morning it received follow-up statements expressing the regrets of the senior station officer and an outline of how an investigation into the tragedy would be conducted.

What senior reporter Nye Jackson couldn't get was someone to talk to him about what had happened. Chief Superintendent Fountain declined on the grounds that the matter was now in the hands of the Independent Police Complaints Commission, while the IPCC cited the danger of prejudicing the inquiry. He tried hanging around the back way in to Meadowvale, in the hope that someone on the way home after the night shift would give him a throwaway because he was standing between them and their bed, but it didn't happen. The matter was too serious, and much too close to home.

Contrary to the impression given by popular television, most newspapers enjoy a good working relationship with their local police, because it works better for both parties than being constantly at loggerheads. Whatever Mrs. Fountain thought about him, Nye Jackson was a regular and well-tolerated visitor to Meadowvale Police Station, and could usually count on getting what he needed, officially or otherwise.

By the same token, the *Norbold News* was the main point of contact between the local police and the population it served, and Fountain knew how to use a cooperative newspaper to serve his own ends. It was a symbiotic relationship in which each party benefited, and also recognized the benefits conferred on the other.

But not this week. This week men and women Jackson had known for years—people he'd been drinking with, whose children's achievements he'd chronicled and whose parents' centenaries he'd recorded—pretended not to know him and hurried past to their parked cars, leaving him standing in a soft April mizzle with his collar turned up and his ginger hair plastered to his head. He felt like a beggar. *Can you spare a fact, gov? Nothing big, just a little loose-change fact from your back pocket? I've got a hungry newspaper to support. . . .*

Which left the boy's family. Jackson hated interviewing the newly bereaved, but it was part of the job, and you just had to get on with it. What surprised him, when he was younger and easier to surprise, was that usually they were glad to see him. They wanted to tell their story. They didn't want a death that had devastated their family to pass unnoticed in the wider world. They wanted to answer his questions and they felt better, just a little, when they had.

Not that their feelings, or indeed his own, were that important. There's an unspoken deal that a journalist makes with the readership of his newspaper. They'll buy—in both senses of the word—what he's selling them, but it has to be worth what they're paying. If it's the sort of newspaper that promises the truth, the whole truth, and nothing but the truth—there are still one or two around—then that's what the customers expect. If it's tits and bums, *that's* what they expect. And if it's "Aliens Ate My Mother-in-Law (says Luscious Linda, aged 19)," then Linda had better be both luscious and not a day over twenty, and shrinking her to two columns at the bottom of page four because some boffin somewhere has found the answer to world hunger will never be forgiven.

The *Norbold News* didn't do tits and bums. It only did Luscious Linda if she'd actually achieved something—runner-up in Miss West Midlands, perhaps, or a wobble-on part in *The East End of Coronation Farm*. It reckoned on doing the truth, as much of the truth as it could prize out of the lying bastards who ran the Town Hall, and nothing but the truth unless it was really entertaining. The denizens of Norbold and environs knew pretty much what to expect when they put their money on the counter, and would not have been happy if they'd got only those stories that the subjects wanted told, that the reporters wanted to cover, and that the editor knew he could print without getting his tires slashed.

So when he gave up on calling in some of the favors he was owed at Meadowvale, Jackson went back to his car, wiped the rain off his face with his handkerchief, and headed for Windermere Close, where the Cardys lived.

He was turning the car—journalists, like bank robbers, know the value of a smooth getaway—when a man emerged from the house he was heading for. His first thought was that it was Geoff Cardy on his way out, and he wondered whether to hurry and buttonhole him, and risk his being annoyed or too short of time to give a meaningful interview, or let him go and come back later. But it wasn't Cardy. As he turned, Jackson saw that the curly black hair masked not only a white face but one that he recognized. He gave a muted whistle. "Now, what are *you* doing here?"

It was a puzzle anyone might have set themselves. But reporters don't pose rhetorical questions; they collar someone who ought to know the answer and stand there until they get it.

Nye Jackson had his car door open when the black 4x4 with the tinted windows passed him, close enough that he had to jerk back inside. He scowled, and had a few choice comments ready to hurl after it, when he noticed what it was doing. It was turning at the end of the street and coming back. Like a journalist; like a bank robber. But it wasn't him it was stalking. Jackson went very still, watching.

Gabriel Ash reached the pavement and turned down Windermere Close, back toward town. His shoulders were hunched and his expression remote. Impossible to judge what might be going on behind the sunken, distant eyes. He didn't notice

Jackson waiting in his car. He didn't notice the big black 4x4 cruising up quietly behind him.

The first Ash knew, two men were getting out beside him—neither of them the driver: the car was still moving slowly forward—taking an arm each and very calmly, very professionally heaving him onto the backseat before he could raise a word of protest.

His first thought was that it was the police. He needed to make another statement about the last hours of Jerome Cardy—or rather, to repeat the first because someone had judged it not worth space in a filing cabinet and dropped it in the bin instead. But a quick survey of the men either side of him dashed that notion. These were not police officers. They were big enough, he already knew they were strong enough, and they were plainly accustomed to manhandling people who didn't want to go with them. But they wouldn't look at him. They stared straight ahead, and when he turned to look at the one on his left, the one on his right jabbed him sharply in the ribs with his elbow. Ash was still bruised from the encounter in the park, and maybe a man who cared more about the impression he created wouldn't have gasped and doubled up like that. But it was meant to hurt, and a policeman would at least have warned him first.

His second thought, which arrived a split second after the elbow, was that the same thing that had brought him to Windermere Close had brought the black car and its occupants, that they were somehow tied into events that had already cost a young man his life.

But there was no time to dwell on that, because Ash's third thought, which drove everything else out of his head, was that this was what had happened before. *This* was how people disappeared in broad daylight, and were never seen again, and nobody saw or heard anything. Only now, finally, he was going to find out what happened. Where the disappeared disappear to.

Nye Jackson wasn't sure what he was looking at, except that it was nothing good. It was odd enough coming here to speak to the Cardys, only to see Gabriel Ash leaving the house as he approached it. Watching him lifted bodily off the street by what he had no difficulty in recognizing as Mickey Argyle's rent-a-thugs kicked it into a whole extra dimension. Which was what, unless his reporter's instincts were starting to slip, they proposed to do to Gabriel Ash. Jackson had no idea why, but perhaps it didn't matter why. What mattered—perhaps the only thing that mattered—was what Jackson was going to do about it.

He could have stayed in his car, kept his head down, and called 999 after the big black car had passed. That's what most responsible, law-abiding citizens would have done. It's what law-abiding citizens were advised to do. And Jackson was one of those, even though it sometimes suited him to forget. But he was also a reporter, and that gave him a proprietary interest in events that normal people consider somebody else's problem.

He'd never been a front-line war correspondent, never donned a flak jacket—or a burka—and been waiting at the presidential palace when the NATO troops arrived. But certain obligations go with the job wherever you do it, and one is lifting your head above the parapet to see what's happening on the other side. Jackson knew well enough that in these precise circumstances it was dangerous lunacy to draw attention to himself. But his reporter's pride wouldn't let him duck down behind his dashboard until the danger had passed, like an ordinary civilian.

He threw the car door open, oblivious now of his paintwork, bounded into the street as the 4x4 wiggled to avoid him, and had his phone out before both feet had hit the tarmac. "Smile for the paper!" he yelled as the car surged past, and nothing in his demeanor gave away his deep suspicion that he'd let the battery get too low for taking photographs.

When the brake lights came on, the import of what he was doing hit him like a train and the expression of reckless exhilaration fell off his face, leaving his mouth open and his eyes wide with alarm. But only for a second, and there was no one to see. Then the back door of the black car opened and Gabriel Ash rolled off the seat and into the gutter.

For a moment, struck dumb by amazement and pride, Nye Jackson thought he'd probably managed to prevent a murder. He didn't know what to think when Ash, road dirt staining his best clothes, hauled himself to his feet and tried to run after the accelerating vehicle, yelling, "Don't Go! Don't Go! Come back!" as if his heart was breaking.

CHAPTER 11

BY THE TIME Jackson reached him, Ash had ground to a hopeless halt, bent over, hands on his knees, great sobs racking the gaunt frame somewhere inside his good suit. Jackson thought it was shock, but it wasn't; it was grief. His dark eyes were vast with it, the tears washing tracks through the grit on his face.

When Jackson reached out an uncertain hand, Ash turned on him like a tormented dog. "Why? Why would you do that? Four years I've waited. Four years I haven't known if they were alive or dead. Finally they come for me, too, and . . . you . . ." He ran out of words, overwhelmed by emotion. His body shook and sagged, and he leaned against a lamppost and very slowly slid down it until he was sitting on the pavement again.

There weren't many people in Norbold who'd have been able to make any sense of what Gabriel Ash was saying, why he was distraught instead of relieved, and hurling bitter accusations at the man whose quick thinking had saved him. Nye Jackson was one of those few, and even he didn't know much. He knew Ash had been a government adviser in one of the less well-publicized departments, that four years ago he'd lost his family, and that that wasn't a euphemism.

He bent down, forcing Ash to look at him. "Listen to me," he said, the Welsh accent harsh in his voice. "This is nothing to do with what happened before. Those men didn't have any news for you. They work for Mickey Argyle. I don't know what they wanted with you, but take my word, it was nothing good. Nobody wants Mickey Argyle taking an interest in them. If you'd gone with them, they'd have hurt you. Or killed you. Do you understand? They would not have taken you to your family. They don't know anything about your family. If you'd gone with them, they'd have killed you."

Finally a little intelligence seemed to creep back into Ash's eyes. He swallowed, looked down the road in the wake of the vanished car. "Who's Mickey Argyle?"

Jackson let loose his breath in a gusty, impatient sigh. "Jesus, don't you know *anything*?" Then, remembering who he was talking to, his tone softened. "No, I don't suppose you do know much about Norbold's criminal underworld. You haven't been getting out much since you came back, have you?"

Ash looked puzzled. "Do you know me?"

Jackson straightened up, offered his hand. "I know who you are." He introduced himself. "I work for the local paper."

"Then you know . . ." Jackson nodded. "It was in the paper?"

"Mr. Ash," said Jackson patiently, "it was in every paper in the country, for about ten days. Since then . . . well, there really hasn't been anything to add, has there?"

"No." Gabriel Ash took the proffered hand and stumbled to his feet. He looked again in the direction that the car had sped away. "Then . . . what did they want?"

Jackson shook his ginger head. "I can't begin to imagine. But then, I can't imagine what you were doing at the Cardys' house, either."

Ash told him. He saw no reason not to.

Jackson felt himself staring, and blinked. "*You* were the—" And there he stopped, mentally editing. In its next edition his paper would use the expression "learning disabled itinerant," which was ugly to the nth degree but more politic than "thicko tramp," which is what Jackson wrote when he got the story first thing on Thursday morning, just too late for a stop-press. "The other guy in the cells that night. The police press office didn't give us a name. They just said Cardy was originally in with someone else before he wandered off."

He looked across the road at the house he'd come to visit. "Well, I suppose that had better wait. We'll get you down to the cop shop, tell them what happened."

As they were walking up to the front door at Meadowvale, Hazel Best was walking down. She stopped at the sight of Ash's muddy clothes. "Whatever's happened to you *now*?"

"I'm not quite sure," Ash said honestly. "I think someone tried to kidnap me."

"*What?*"

"Who's Mickey Argyle?"

Hazel had heard the name, though it wasn't engraved on her heart as it might have been if she'd been stationed here for longer. "He's involved in the drugs trade in Norbold, I think. Why, what have you done to annoy him?"

Ash shrugged, bemused.

"Mickey Argyle *is* the drugs trade in Norbold," explained Jackson. "He was before Johnny Fountain rode into town, and he will be after he rides out. He's the one stain on your chief's escutcheon."

"And he tried to kidnap Ash?" Any more doubt in her voice would have called him a liar.

"Well, they weren't driving his car with the personalized number plates, but I'm pretty sure they were Argyle's gorillas. One of them I've seen before—his name's Fletcher—and the others came in the same boxed set."

"What did they want?" She was asking Ash.

"They didn't say."

Hazel clung on to her patience. "Gabriel, tell me what happened."

Jackson gestured at the door. "We're just going inside to report it. Come with us if you want. It's going to be a matter of public knowledge soon enough."

"Not that soon," said Hazel, turning and following them back up the walkway. "The best way to keep a secret—"

"Is to tell it to the police press office." Jackson nodded. "Not this time. I'm an eyewitness. And a reporter."

Hazel shut up.

If Sergeant Murchison wondered what it meant that these three people arrived at his desk together, nothing in his expression betrayed him. "Kidnapping," he echoed, straight-faced.

"Well, attempted kidnapping," said Ash, to whom accuracy was important. "Then they changed their minds and threw me out on the street."

"Why?"

"Because they saw me take a picture of them doing it," said Jackson with some relish. "If anything had happened to him after that, you'd have had a witness and photographic evidence in a murder hunt. They had to let him go. Doesn't mean they won't pick him up again another time."

"Let's have a look at this picture, then."

"Flat battery," admitted Jackson regretfully. "Damn shame, that. It would have gone down a blinder on my front page."

Ash was still rocking from the last thing he'd said. "*Another* time?"

Jackson was surprised at his naïveté. "You thought that was the end of it? Mickey Argyle wanted to talk to you enough to send his gorillas rather than a deckle-edged invitation, but he was put to rout by a middle-aged reporter with a camera phone? It's a nice thought, but I wouldn't stake *my* life on it."

Sergeant Murchison's ears pricked up. "It was Mickey Argyle? Did you see him?"

Jackson's gaze was caustic. "Don't be silly. If he was that stupid, you'd have nailed him long ago. I think it was his crew. I think Andy Fletcher was one of them. I can't be positive, let alone prove it, but you'd have to ask yourself who else in Norbold was going to pull a stunt like that. Mickey Argyle is about the only godfather we've got left." He said it as if he rather regretted the passing of the old days.

"What does Mickey want with Mr. Ash?"

"That's kind of the point," said Jackson, who'd somehow taken over the interview. "Ash isn't a client, and he isn't a rival. You'd have thought he was pretty much below Argyle's radar. So the next thing you have to ask yourself is, was it anything to do with what happened in the cells here the other night?"

Murchison stared. "How could it be?"

Jackson gave a cheerful grin. "Beats me. But Ash here, who's hardly been farther than his corner shop for years, was picked up after leaving the Cardys' house. So either they went there looking for him or they followed him. There was nothing random about it."

Now Murchison was staring at Ash. "What were you doing at the Cardy house?"

Ash gave an awkward shrug. "I wanted to express my condolences."

"Did anyone know you were going?"

Just barely he managed *not* to say, "My dog." He shook his head.

"Followed, then," said Jackson with unseemly satisfaction.

Murchison put his pen down. "This is CID stuff. I'm going to have to get hold of DI Gorman. I'll put you in one of the interview rooms while I track him down. Hazel, can you organize some coffee?"

It was like police station coffee everywhere: virtually indistinguishable from the tea, the hot chocolate, and the oxtail soup. The best that can be said was that drinking it gave them something to do while they waited. Hazel showed Ash to the washrooms and he attempted to clean himself up. Jackson ignored the SWITCH OFF MOBILE PHONES sign and called his editor.

Sergeant Murchison returned. "DI Gorman's going to be tied up in court for another hour, maybe more. Do you want to go on home? He'll call you when he gets in."

Outside the police station Jackson headed for his office and Ash turned the other way to walk home. But Hazel plucked his sleeve and said, "Come with me. I'll give you a lift."

"There's no need," he said, surprised. "I'm all right, you know."

"I know." She nodded. "I don't think you should go home alone."

"Why not?"

"They could be waiting for you."

He'd spent so long as the invisible man, shut up in his big house behind drawn curtains or wandering the blind streets with his dog, that being the focus of attention came as a shock. He genuinely hadn't thought of that. He looked askance at Hazel. "Are you armed?"

She laughed out loud, though it wasn't that funny. "No!"

"There were three of them. They were quite big."

Hazel thought that the correct response to that was, "I am a trained police officer. Armed with nothing but quick wits and a smattering of jujitsu I am more than a match for three large men armed with anything less than machine guns." What she actually said was, "I have Meadowvale on speed dial."

There was no one waiting for them. "They mustn't know about this place," said Ash.

"Or else they've already been here."

Ash looked at his dog. "Apparently not."

Hazel frowned. "What do you mean?"

He glanced up quickly, guiltily. "Patience would be upset if someone had been prowling around."

The constable seemed to accept that. "I still think you'd be wiser staying somewhere else for a few days."

Ash gave a tiny, helpless smile. "You know a B and B that takes dogs?"

Hazel shrugged. "Put her in a kennel."

It was as if she'd proposed something indecent. Both of them, man and dog, regarded her with silent, unblinking disfavor.

Hazel found herself breathing heavily at them. Which was odd, because she'd always rather prided herself on her patience. Something about Gabriel Ash got under her skin. Something about Ash and his dog made her want to bang their heads together. "You haven't forgotten that this is your safety we're talking about?"

"Why would anyone want to hurt me?" He wasn't arguing with her; he just wondered if she knew the answer.

Hazel sighed and lowered herself onto his leather chair, which bore the unmistakable circular impression of a sleeping dog and was still warm. "You made the classic mistake—you were in the wrong place at the wrong time."

"In the cell with Jerome Cardy?"

"It has to be. Somebody's worried about what he said to you."

"What he said made no sense."

Hazel shrugged. "You must be remembering wrong. Just a little bit—just enough to obscure what he was trying to say. Mickey Argyle has a pretty good idea what it was. Now he wants to know if you've worked it out."

"Worked out *what*?"

"I don't know," said Hazel, exasperated. "Something to do with drugs? That's Argyle's line of work. Jerome fled the scene of a minor accident he hadn't even caused—why? Was he carrying drugs for Argyle? Is that why he thought he was in deep shit—because he'd got himself picked up by the police while driving around with a suitcase full of cocaine?"

Ash stared at her in surprise and mounting admiration. It made more sense than anything he'd thought of. "Maybe that's why he mentioned the sniffer dog. To flag up the drugs connection." He frowned. "Where does Othello fit in?"

Hazel thought some more, then shook her head. "Beats me. Othello. Strangled his wife because he thought she was having an affair."

"Jerome was black, like Othello. But his father said he didn't have a girlfriend."

Hazel gave him an old-fashioned look. "He was a twenty-year-old student. There must have been someone. Even if he didn't tell his dad. Maybe it was a boyfriend rather than a girlfriend."

Ash's train of thought had turned up a branch line. "They could have killed me with that car. Then anything Jerome told me would have been lost. If this Mickey Argyle's such a bad lot, that would have been the sensible thing to do."

Hazel had never heard anyone described as a "bad lot" before. "He could still do it. Perhaps he wants to talk to you first in case it isn't necessary."

"What do you mean?" His gaze was honest, uncomplicated by any sense of irony.

Hazel chewed her lip delicately. "How am I going to put this? There's a general perception around Norbold that you're as dotty as Dundee cake. Don't look at me like that—I'm not saying it's what I think.

"But if I'm wrong and everyone else is right, Mickey doesn't need to shut you up. It wouldn't matter what Jerome said to you, it wouldn't even matter if you'd understood it, because no one would listen to anything you had to say. Argyle would only attract attention by killing you. I think that's why he wanted to talk to you—to find out if you're worth worrying about." She risked meeting his eyes. "Maybe that's why they threw you out of the car. They decided you weren't."

It was hard to take that as a compliment. But Ash's frown was more puzzled than offended. "Why?"

"You wanted to go with them. You thought something good was happening."

A faint flush crept up Ash's sallow cheek. "I suppose that does seem pretty crazy."

"What was going through your mind?" asked Hazel. "Who did you think they were? What did you think they wanted?"

For a couple of minutes, which is a long time to sit in silence with someone you hardly know, he made no attempt to answer. But she knew he was going to, so she waited.

Finally he said, "Jackson—the reporter—knows who I am. You don't, do you?"

Hazel shook her head. "Sorry. I've only just come to Norbold."

"Most people who've lived here all their lives don't know me from Adam, either. It didn't happen here—we were living in London, had been for years. I only came back here afterward."

"After what?"

He'd been trying to make them a pot of tea. The attempt fell apart in slow motion as he grew increasingly distracted, getting out cups that didn't go with the saucers, putting them back, getting out mugs, forgetting—and being quite unable to remember, even though he stood there racking his brains—where he kept the teaspoons, his shaking hands struggling with the jar until he dropped it and scattered tea bags across the countertop.

Hazel got up quietly, turned off the kettle, and drew him to the leather sofa, where the white dog was waiting, watching him with concern. "Sit down. Talk to me."

If she'd known she was asking him to strip his soul, she might not have pressed him. Or perhaps she would have. She was no psychologist, but there are human instincts that we all share, and human instinct was telling her that Gabriel Ash needed someone to talk to. She wasn't sure what he was going to tell her. She wasn't sure that it mattered. She thought he needed to talk about what was consuming him before his brain melted.

And it wasn't that any of it was a secret. As Nye Jackson had pointed out, it had once been national news. But news is ephemeral, and four years later only those directly involved remembered. Ash had got in the way of internalizing his grief not because the events were secret but because he was that kind of man. He had never worn his emotions openly. It said a lot about him that he would rather be thought mentally ill than recognized as the victim of a tragedy.

But perhaps things were changing. Partly it was that working with Laura Fry had made it possible for him to think of opening up to others. Partly it was because Hazel was a police officer, and Ash had been brought up with that unthinking respect for the law that is a defining characteristic of the middle class. And perhaps the shock of finding himself involved in something else—someone else's tragedy—actually made it easier. He took a deep, steadying breath. His arm slid around the dog's shoulders as a child clutches a comfort blanket. And he began to talk.

CHAPTER 12

"I WAS A GOVERNMENT security adviser," said Ash. "Don't read too much into that. I wasn't sitting at the prime minister's right hand or anything like that. It was a big department, a whole bunch of us with different backgrounds, different strengths. I was in counterterrorism."

He flicked her a self-deprecating little grin. "Before you ask, no, I wasn't licensed to kill. I wasn't licensed to do anything except read reports and watch video and interpret what I was seeing. I worked in an office in Whitehall. There are field agents, but I wasn't one. I trained as an insurance investigator. It turned out the skills you use, the techniques you acquire, are pretty much the same.

"Mostly, getting a feel for when you're being lied to. Spotting tiny inconsistencies in what you're being told. And then working out whether they mean the subject is genuinely doing his best, he's got something wrong precisely because he hasn't rehearsed what to say, or if it's a sign that things didn't happen how he says they happened. It's pretty much the same job whether you're investigating a claim for flood damage or a plot to blow up an airport. Except that the stakes are higher."

It had been a good job. Interesting, challenging, and important. He'd liked feeling he was making a difference. That people were alive who might have died without his input. He was good at it, had the right kind of mind—meticulous, analytical, but also creative and intuitive. It's not a combination you encounter every day.

"Cathy loved living in London," Ash recalled. "My wife. Like me, she came from a small town nobody'd ever heard of, and she loved the whole cosmopolitan thing. The bars, the restaurants, the theaters, the concerts. The choice. The fact that, whatever you felt like doing, whenever you felt like doing it, you could probably find it within a couple of miles of where you were."

He glanced shyly at Hazel. "Cathy was a lot better at the whole social thing than I was. I enjoyed taking her places I'd never wanted to go, because she got so much pleasure out of it. People loved being with her. All our friends were her friends—at least friends that she'd made. I knew a few people from work. By the time we'd been there three months, people waved at her if we walked down Portobello Road. She was *good* at people. I'm good at reading people. She was good at being with them. People liked her even before they knew her."

It hadn't escaped Hazel's notice that he was talking about his wife in the past tense. Divorce, of course, throws up all sorts of grammatical problems, but so does death. Youth isn't much protection, as events had recently underlined. Even short of murder, young people die of illness, accidents, suicide. If Ash had lost his wife to one of these, it might explain both his mental collapse and the obvious fact that he still loved her.

"Everyone said she'd have to slow down when the children came, but she didn't. If anything, pregnancy put an extra bloom in her face, an extra spring in her step. It was no trouble to her, either time. As if having children was something she'd been born to do. The midwife said she delivered them like shelling peas."

Remembering put a glow in his sallow cheeks and the words dried up. Hazel thought he'd forgotten she was there. When a couple of minutes had passed and he was still soft-eyed and silent, she prompted him gently. "What did you have? Boys, girls, or one of each?"

He blinked and came back to the gloomy, loveless room. "Boys. Gilbert and Guy. Two years between them. They'd be eight and six now."

That hit Hazel like a fist in the belly. Her womb turned over. That wasn't a question of syntax; it could mean only one thing. Gabriel Ash hadn't just lost his wife; he'd lost his sons as well. She felt her heart thudding wildly, a constriction in her throat like a physical lesion, and had no idea what to say next. Changing the subject would be like dropping litter on their graves. But there seemed a real danger that if she pressed him to continue, he would fall apart in front of her, so tenuous was the thread that tethered him to what was left of the world.

She needed help here, she realized. She'd done it again, charged in blithely where wiser souls would have exercised caution, and once again someone else was paying the price of her indiscretion.

But guilt was a self-indulgence, and right now she was fully occupied keeping an unhappy man from self-destructing in his own kitchen. She made herself speak calmly. "Gabriel, is there someone I can call for you? Someone you'd rather talk to? I'm not sure how much help I'm being. . . ."

The deep, dark eyes were hollow with grief, and with entreaty. "Please. I need . . . it isn't easy, talking about this. And I'm sure you've got better things to do than listen, but I need . . . to explain. What happened. Why . . ." Now his gaze dropped and his pale cheeks flushed as if with shame. "Why I live like this. Why I am like this."

Hazel was a public servant and Ash a member of the public: if he needed a sympathetic ear, she would provide it. But it wasn't just a professional obligation. Compassion demanded no less of her. "I'll stay as long as you want me to. I'll listen to anything you want to tell me."

He flicked her a grateful smile. Then he took a deep breath and started again. "I don't know how much you know about the arms industry." He paused, with a lift of one eyebrow, and Hazel shook her head. "There are two central points. One is that it's a field where the UK punches well above its weight. We're world-class when it comes to arms manufacture and export.

"The other is that the whole area is massively regulated. We don't want to sell state-of-the-art weaponry to people who'll fire it back at us. There's a long list of criteria that the government considers before it will grant an export licence, everything from our national interest and those of our allies to the human rights record of the end user and its ability to control its own borders so our munitions aren't diverted to terrorists."

Hazel said nothing. But she was thinking how articulate he suddenly became when he was talking about his own area of expertise. No rambling now.

Ash checked that she was with him so far, then continued. "It all takes time and effort, and expense, but everyone accepts that it's necessary. The manufacturers know that the hoops we make them jump through are necessary to stop their goods from being used for terrorism, torture, oppression, or warmongering."

"What went wrong?" Hazel asked softly.

"Pirates."

Whatever she'd been expecting, it wasn't that. She blinked. "What—skull and crossbones, pieces of eight, one-legged men with parrots on their shoulders?"

Ash knuckled his eyes. "I dare say some of them have parrots. I dare say some of them have wooden legs. What all of them have these days is RPGs and assault rifles, fast patrol boats, helicopters and half-tracks. And intelligence. Access to the information superhighway. Forget Johnny Depp. These are private armies. There are still large areas of the world where there is no law to speak of except that imposed by private armies. And it doesn't matter how careful we are about vetting end users if consignments of our arms are intercepted before they ever reach the customer."

"That was your job? Stopping pirates from taking our arms exports?" Just in time Hazel stopped herself from adding: "From a desk?"

Ash shook his head. "My department reported to the government on the status of end users. So when antiaircraft batteries approved for export to a conscientious African democracy were used to take out the ruling family of an Arab principality, we got a rocket, too, from Downing Street."

The first time it happened Ash was instructed to investigate where the blame for the disaster lay, with particular emphasis on how little of it could be laid at the feet of the British government. The report was accepted, passed on to the Arab principality, and forgotten about.

Until four months later, when it happened again. Again, all the criteria had been met by the manufacturer, all the appropriate licences had been obtained, the shipment was attended by all proper security—and this time it actually reached its destination airport before being hijacked on the tarmac and flown elsewhere.

"Was anyone hurt?" asked Hazel.

"Yes. None of the aircrew were seen again. We assume that when they'd flown their cargo to wherever the hijackers wanted it, they were killed and the plane destroyed."

"What was the cargo?"

"Mixed munitions. Assault rifles, shaped charges, and white phosphorus grenades."

Hazel's eyes flew wide. "There *are* people with a legitimate use for that kind of thing?"

"Yes. We have them in our arsenal, and other responsible states have them in theirs."

Hazel shook her head despairingly. "And now one of the irresponsible ones had them as well."

"The third time," said Ash, "it was ammonium picrate armor-piercing shells."

"For blowing up tanks? You could start a *war* with those!"

"Which is why we try so hard to keep munitions out of the hands of people who'll use them. Or at least, use them aggressively and without extreme provocation."

"And you were getting the blame for this."

"Not really. There was nothing wrong with our recommendations. The government couldn't blame the manufacturer, either, or the purchaser. Both of them lost out when the goods went walkabout. No, the reason we stayed involved was that report I'd been asked to write. I ended up with an overview of the situation that no one else had, so every time there were developments the Foreign Office came to me for an assessment of what it might mean."

It wasn't that Hazel was uninterested. It was a field she knew nothing about, but usually that made things more interesting, not less so. Right now, though, it wasn't what she wanted to hear about. "So what happened?"

"I talked to the manufacturers. I talked to the military

attachés of the end-user countries. The issue wasn't how the pirates got hold of the shipments but how they got hold of the information about where the shipments would be. That had to be happening within a fairly narrow band of informed personnel. I talked—"

"No. Gabriel." She caught his eye and held it. "What *happened*?"

In the urgent desire to protect innocent lives he'd made the oldest mistake in the book: he let it get personal. In his determination to move the inquiry forward he raised his head above the parapet. All the time he was gathering information about them, that well-armed, well-informed, entirely ruthless private army was gathering information about Ash. And they made a positive ID before he did.

"I never thought"—his voice cracked—"not for a moment, that I was putting myself in danger. I wasn't on the front line: I worked in an office, for God's sake—I drove a computer! And you see, there was no warning. At least nothing I recognized as a warning—nothing I associated with the case. There was an e-mail. . . ." The words petered out.

"An e-mail?" Hazel prompted gently. This seemed to be her role for the moment, to inject a little impetus when Ash ground to a halt. "What did it say?"

"*Stop*," he said, and the memory turned his deep eyes bottomless. "*Stop now*."

"Just that?"

"Just that."

"I wouldn't have known what it meant, either."

He gave a broken sigh. "But maybe you should have done. If you'd thought about nothing else for nine months, and you knew you were getting close, and you knew the men you were getting close to had already killed people, then maybe you *should* have recognized it as a warning. As the only warning you were going to get. And not dismissed it"—guilt colored his pale cheeks—"as an office joke."

That was understandable, too. The coming of the IT age, which had delivered such wonders of mass communication, had also put a powerful toy in the hands of many people who, intelligent and highly educated as they were, routinely behaved like ten-year-olds. The joke e-mail was the twenty-first-century heir to the photocopied posterior as the height of office wit.

Hazel Best could see how it happened as clearly as if she'd been there. He'd got the e-mail. He'd opened it and read it. He'd read it again, trying to see the joke. But this was Gabriel Ash, and he probably didn't have much of a sense of humor even before he lost his family. He'd be used to not getting the joke. He probably glanced around the office in case anyone was visibly giggling, then, failing to identify the author, deleted it without another thought. And only thought of it again after it was too late.

She whispered, a third time, "What happened?"

Ash shrugged, the awkward movement of a bird with a broken wing. "I don't know. I got home one evening and no one was there. There were no messages. There was no sign of a forced entry or a struggle. The car was in the drive. Cathy had taken her handbag but nothing else, for herself or the boys. None of their toys was missing. It was as if she'd popped out for milk and never come back.

"At first I thought that was what had happened." Hazel could tell from the odd flatness of his voice that he wasn't just reporting these events; he was reliving them. The need to bridle the surging panic still held his emotions in an iron fist. "She'd run out of something, walked to the shops, maybe got talking to someone. After an hour I was getting a bit uneasy, so I walked down to meet her. But they hadn't seen her in any of the shops. So maybe she'd met someone and they'd gone for coffee and lost track of time. After another hour I started phoning her friends, but still no one had seen her. At ten o'clock that night I called the police.

"Their first thought was she'd gone off with someone. A man—someone she was having an affair with. I didn't believe it, not for a moment. But it was only after I called my boss and he talked to an assistant commissioner or something that they started taking it seriously. I mean, really seriously. Put who I was, what I'd been doing, together with what had happened, and realized this was payback time."

CHAPTER 13

AMONG THE EXPERTS suddenly surrounding him was a trained negotiator. He'd taken Ash to a quiet room and explained that, sooner rather than later, he'd receive a ransom demand. Not for money, of course. What they wanted from Ash would be quite different.

"The negotiator warned me they'd do anything to protect their business. Anything. They could demand my life in return for Cathy and the boys. I said, if it came to that . . . But he said it wouldn't, that it was a negotiating ploy. All they needed was to get me off their backs and throw the investigation into disarray. But Alan—the negotiator—wanted me to be ready for something like that. I think he was afraid they might get past him—that I might get the demand without him knowing and act on it before he could offer an alternative."

So they sat by the phones. Hour after hour, day after day. But neither the pirates nor anyone representing their interests ever rang. Ash kept the laptop close, too, in case the approach came by e-mail again, but there was nothing.

"Alan said it was deliberate. Leave me to stew, so when they finally got in touch, I'd jump at whatever they suggested. In the meantime there were things we could do to show I wanted to cooperate. We replied to the e-mail, of course, but it bounced back—the account had been closed. He put out a press release—nothing dramatic, just enough that the papers would carry it and someone looking out for it would see it. An unnamed government security adviser had been sent on compassionate leave following an incident in Covent Garden. That was where we lived—Covent Garden. It was worded so most people reading it would assume I'd got drunk and shared state secrets with the flower traders. But whoever had my family would know what it meant. That I wouldn't be going into the office anymore."

Hazel heard a quiver run through Ash's voice, as if even the iron fist might not be enough to hold his emotions in check much longer. The dog heard it, too, lifted her head to gaze inquiringly at him. His arm tightened around her slim, strong shoulders. He sucked in a deep, steadying breath and continued.

"We thought it would be enough. That they'd wait until they were sure I wasn't still running the case at arm's length, then come up with the reward—send my family home. At least . . ." He swallowed. "Alan thought they might keep one of the boys to ensure my continued cooperation. He said if that happened I should take what I was given and get out of London, go somewhere far away, and not even send a postcard to the office. He thought if I did that, eventually they'd return the last hostage as well. After a month, maybe three. Six months after that I could probably go back to work, as long as I worked on something else. My boss said he'd get people with no dependents to take over my files."

But they didn't come home. None of them. Not after a week, not after a month. They didn't come home and there was no contact from the kidnappers. No demands, no threats—nothing.

"Alan said I should leave London anyway. Sever all ties—

break contact with everyone I'd worked with, everyone I knew. I took a cottage in the Orkneys. It was November by now, so taking a cottage in the Orkneys was a bit like stepping off the globe. There was no phone line. I changed my mobile and gave the number only to Alan. We thought if I was unreachable, they'd know I wasn't still working on the sly. I stayed there all winter, going slowly crazy. It achieved nothing. I never heard from them again. I never heard from Cathy again. To this day, I don't know if my sons are alive or dead."

He looked at Hazel then, his face twisting in a torment of uncertainty. "I'm not stupid. I know the chances are they're dead. I know the chances are they'd been killed before I realized they were missing. But you see, I don't *know.* Maybe the pirates kept them alive for leverage. At least the boys. They were only little. They could have been farmed out to someone, and after six months they wouldn't have remembered who they were. If they were dead—if they were all dead—there was nothing left to threaten me with. Nothing to stop me coming after them.

"Or maybe they are dead. All of them." He was able to say it without breaking up only because he'd lived with the possibility day and night for four years; and if he'd never become reconciled to the idea, he had at least become familiar with it, with the shape it made inside him. "Maybe that's why the bodies never turned up. Because as long as there's that doubt in my mind, I can't fight back. If I'd seen their bodies, there'd be nothing to stop me. The tiny chance that they're alive, that one of them is still alive somewhere, is enough to neutralize me. It's worked for four years; it'll go on working. I can't take the risk that my wife or one of my sons is still alive and could be hurt if I anger these people again."

Hazel had, quite literally, no idea what to say to him. What words could she possibly say that wouldn't sound banal to a man who'd lost everything? And yet, there's comfort in the most inadequate of human voices that is not there in silence. "Oh Gabriel," she whispered.

"I thought about killing myself," he told her honestly. "Not out of despair. I was desperate, but not that kind of desperate. I thought if they knew I was dead, there'd be no point holding on to my family. If they were still alive, they might be set free. If I'd known they were alive, I'd have done it. If I'd thought I could buy their safety that way, I'd have done it."

"I believe you," said Hazel softly.

"I could have done it anyway, on the off chance. But it seemed . . . like throwing away my last card, the last thing I could bargain with. And then, you see, I'd never have known." He looked to see if she understood. "What became of them. If they were dead. If the men who took them hurt them first. I'd never have *known*. I chose to go on living for the tiny possibility that one day I'll find out what happened. Who was responsible.

"Because, if I knew Cathy and the boys were safe—one way or the other—I'd finish the job. I could do it, I know I could. I was getting close—given another chance, I'd nail them. If I'd no one else to worry about, I'd find the men who did this to us and kill as many as I could before they got me."

He said it without any drama, without even much passion, a simple statement of fact. Another idea he'd spent four years getting used to. Hazel let a few moments pass, as much for herself as for Ash, so that when she spoke again she'd have some mastery over what she said and how she said it. She didn't want to break up in front of him—not because it was unprofessional, although it was, but because his own courage was strung together by gossamer. A breeze could break it now.

She took a slow breath. "Nye Jackson obviously knows at least some of this. How?"

Ash let his head rock back, staring blindly at the ceiling. "I said I went crazy on Orkney. That wasn't a figure of speech. Finally I headed back to London—hitching: I'd no car and no money—and showed up at my office in wellies with the soles worn-out and clothes I hadn't changed for a month, demanding access to the files."

Of course everyone who knew him was shocked at the state he was in. They'd pictured him sitting by a turf fire, smoking a pipe and reading Rabbie Burns. They tried to be kind. They explained that reappearing like this really wasn't a good idea, and tried to get him off the premises before anybody noticed.

"I wouldn't go quietly. I'd convinced myself that they'd given up. That no one was looking for my family anymore, that they could be found if only someone would try hard enough. It was desperately unfair to the people I'd worked with, but I told you, I was pretty crazy. When my boss tried to take me back to his place in a taxi, I decked him in the street."

If a Whitehall mandarin gets punched in broad daylight in Parliament Street, it's going to be noticed. It's going to be photographed, and the photograph is going to go global. Ash's department had about an hour to decide what to do next, and whether the priority was the man or his family.

"My boss, mumbling through broken teeth, and Alan, the Home Office negotiator, decided the most important thing was to make it clear that I wasn't back at work—that I wasn't fit to be working. They had me sectioned—carted off under sedation. And Alan drew up another press release explaining some of the background." He caught her look and shook his head. "Hazel, they were right. It was the only way of putting right the damage I'd done. If my family were still alive, we had to show that there was nothing to be gained by hurting them. I was no longer relevant. I only thought I was.

"I was in hospital for nine weeks while they sorted my head out. After that I was discharged on the basis that I'd stay out of London and see a therapist. I came back here. I still owned my mother's house. Luckily enough it was between tenants, and it was easier than going somewhere new. I see Laura Fry once a week. Life goes on."

Hazel swallowed. "And you've still no idea . . ."

"None," he agreed distantly. "No word from Cathy. No word about her or the boys. No sign of them, alive or dead. I never heard if my performance in Parliament Street did any harm. They must have seen the pictures. But either they accepted Alan's explanation, that I'd left the reservation but wouldn't be allowed out alone again, or it was too late to do anything more to them. Or maybe I'm wrong. Maybe I got them killed. I don't know. I don't think I'm ever going to know."

"So what . . ." She had to moisten her lips and try again. "What will you do?"

"Nothing," he said simply. "This. Wait."

After a moment she gave a little breath of understanding. "Ah."

Ash blinked. "What?"

"You thought it was them. The pirates." She felt silly saying it, but it was what they were. "When the car lifted you off the street, you thought it was the men who had your family. That's why you wanted to go with them."

He looked at her sideways. "Stupid or what?"

"Not stupid," said Hazel firmly. "Just desperate."

He couldn't argue with that. "If I'd had longer to think about it, I'd have known it wouldn't happen like that. I just couldn't think who else might want to see me enough to force me into a car." He frowned. "Actually, I still can't. Tell me again—who's Mickey Argyle?"

Hazel tried to remember what she'd been told. "He's a drug dealer. I mean, a *big* drug dealer—he employs the ones who work the street corners and nightclubs. He's about the last survivor of organized crime in this town, the one trophy Mr. Fountain hasn't been able to bag. Yet," she added loyally.

"Why would Norbold's last drug baron want to see me?"

"It has to be about what happened to Jerome Cardy. I mean"—there was no tactful way of putting this—"you haven't *done* anything else since you came back to Norbold."

"I didn't *do* anything much that night, either." Ash was still full of self-recrimination.

"You were the last person to be alone with that boy, except for the man who killed him. If Jerome was in a position to compromise Argyle, you were the only one he could have told."

"He didn't, though, did he?" growled Ash, bitter at his want of understanding. "He just wittered on about some dog he never owned."

"He told you he was in danger. He told you to remember that he knew he was in danger."

"He didn't say who he was in danger *from*."

"No. I wonder why not."

"Perhaps he did. Othello. I don't suppose it's Mickey Argyle's nickname or anything?"

Hazel gave a despairing little chuckle. "I wouldn't have

thought so. I could ask, but . . ." She tried to think her way back to basics. "Maybe we're going about this the wrong way. We should ask Robert Barclay why he killed Jerome."

Ash knew the answer to that one. "Because Barclay's a rabid racist. Because, after he was arrested for attacking the war memorial, he'd have dearly loved to knock seven bells out of you and your colleagues, but he wasn't able to; but he *was* able to knock seven bells out of the black kid he found hiding under his blanket."

"Yes," agreed Hazel. "Why did he attack the war memorial in the first place?"

Ash shrugged. "I've no idea."

"Me, neither. Can you think of any reason why anybody *would* attack a war memorial?"

"As a political statement? Against military action in Afghanistan, perhaps?"

Hazel raised a sceptical eyebrow. "This is Barking Mad Barclay we're talking about. I don't see him as a political activist. And if he was, he'd be with the National Front, not defending the rights of Islamic extremists to cut bits off one another."

Perhaps she had a point. But . . . "You don't think the clue's in the name?"

"Barking Mad?" She grinned. "You're a fine one to talk!"

He didn't understand. "Me? Why?"

"You know." The grin was becoming a little fixed. "Rambles?"

Still nothing. "Rambles?"

He *doesn't* know, Hazel realized, far too late. He doesn't know what all Meadowvale and half of Norbold calls him. What do I do now? Tell him? He might think it's funny. He might think it's deeply offensive. He just might retreat into his post-traumatic stress disorder, pull the psychosis up over his head, and never come out again.

She had to do something. He was waiting expectantly. She took a deep breath. "Most men," she said carefully, "would be flattered to remind people of a film star."

"What film star?"

"Kevin Costner."

He didn't look flattered, just puzzled. "I remind people of Kevin Costner?"

Hazel understood his confusion. If she'd looked in his mirror every morning and seen the pale skin and unkempt hair and battered clothes, she'd have struggled to see the likeness, too. "Sort of." She nodded. "You remember *Dances with Wolves*?"

"Ye-es." Suspicion made two syllables of it.

"People—not everybody but a few people—well, probably quite a lot of people, actually—I don't think they mean it unkindly . . . Gabriel, they call you Rambles With Dogs."

She looked at him. He looked at her. He said nothing. She said nothing more. They changed the subject.

Ash said, "So what would make a rabid racist head-butt a war memorial? He's just found out that Hitler lost?"

Hazel gave a helpless shrug. "Something must have brought it on. He's lived in this town for years and never attacked it before."

Ash was thinking. The fear he'd seen in the young man's eyes haunted him. The fear, and the certainty. "A man like that—a man so well known for his beliefs and his violence, a man whose random outbursts are in fact entirely predictable—could almost be used as a weapon. By someone who wanted to keep his own hands clean. And probably neither Barclay nor anyone else would ever suspect."

Hazel's brow furrowed with the effort to follow. "A weapon?"

"It's not easy to kill someone and make it look like an

accident," explained Ash. "There's almost always forensic evidence to say it's a lie—bruising on the body that's more typical of someone fighting for his life, fluid in the lungs that isn't the right *kind* of fluid, blood settling in the tissues that shows the body was moved after death. These are the kinds of things any pathologist would notice. It's a lot easier to get away with murder if you can shift the blame onto someone else—particularly if that person is helpful enough as to do the actual deed for you. So everyone thinks they know what happened and why, and nobody even wonders if something was happening *behind* what everybody knows. If someone else was pulling the strings."

He noticed the silence and looked up, to find Hazel staring at him. "What?"

"Er—nothing," she said hurriedly, and a more socially astute man might have seen the blush on her cheek. "Yes, I suppose it's possible, if someone was clever enough." For how could she say what she was thinking, which was, They're wrong, aren't they? They're all wrong. You're no more mad than I am, and when you get that traumatized brain in gear, it cuts like a laser.

And now everything you've said to me I have to reassess. Because I dismissed half of it, the half that didn't fit with what I thought I knew, in the belief that you probably imagined it. I don't think you imagined any of it. You may have got some of it wrong. You *were* concussed. But what you think happened is pretty much what happened, and what you think Jerome Cardy said to you is pretty much what he said. And if you think someone took him out of your cell and put him in another where, half an hour later, Robert Barclay was going to be slung, already foaming at the mouth and looking for someone to batter, there's a damn good chance that happened, too.

Ash had no idea what was going through her mind, but he

could see that something had pulled her up short. “Hazel? What is it?”

For a moment she didn’t answer. She was organizing her thoughts and trying to calm her jumping nerves. She had no illusions about what this might mean. Then she said quietly, “Gabriel, I need you to tell me again what happened. All of it. Everything you can remember.”

One thick eyebrow climbed. “Remember? Or just think I remember?”

“*Everything*,” insisted Hazel. “I think I’ve been doing you an injustice. I think we all have. I know I said you probably dreamed some of it. I think I was wrong.”

CHAPTER 14

When detective Inspector Gorman called, Hazel offered to drive Ash back to Meadowvale.

"I can walk."

"I have to go anyway. I have to talk to Mr. Fountain."

Ash regarded her with concern. "Is that wise?"

She managed a nervous smile. "I think it's necessary. I have information about a murder that probably no one else has. I have a theory that could explain what happened. I can't keep it to myself."

"If you're wrong, it could make things difficult for you."

"If I'm *right*, it'll make things difficult for me. I don't think it has to matter. If I *am* right and do nothing for fear of a backlash, what kind of a police officer does that make me?"

"I could tell DI Gorman."

That would keep her safely out of the loop. But it wouldn't have the same effect. "No offense, Gabriel, but he doesn't have to take anything you tell him seriously."

"Rambles With Dogs."

She nodded apologetically. "Mr. Fountain *does* have to listen if I make an allegation about another of his officers. He may not like it, he may not believe it, but he can't ignore it. And he will get to the bottom of it."

Hazel left Ash with DI Gorman and was heading for Fountain's office when she met Miss Patel in the corridor. The chief superintendent's secretary consulted a note on her clipboard. "Constable Best. IPCC want to see you. In the committee room."

"Now?" Hazel was taken aback. Not because she hadn't been expecting it, but because of the timing. "Can they wait half an hour?"

Miss Patel favored her with the sort of look Patience sometimes gave Ash. "I don't believe so, no."

There were two of them, both wearing suits. A man and a woman; at least one of the suits had a skirt. Intelligent, unforthcoming faces. They introduced themselves politely but without any warmth, any overlay of camaraderie. This was business from the moment Hazel stepped through the door to the moment they were finished with her, and they weren't going to forget it and they didn't want her to forget it, either. They weren't here to trick her or to trap her. They were here to get everything she knew, everything she thought she knew, and everything she only thought about the death of Jerome Cardy.

And that, in the end, is what they got. They didn't get it out of her by torture, by intimidation, even by particularly clever questioning, just by sheer thoroughness. Every word Hazel uttered was noted, analyzed, and explored for where it might take them. Thinking about it afterward she had no fault to find with either their manner or their technique. It was an object lesson in how to get everything possible from a verbal interview without crossing any of the lines. Hazel almost felt she should be grateful for the tutorial. And maybe she would be, when she'd finished feeling shell-shocked at how much she'd said, how unreservedly honest she'd been. Everything she'd meant to put before Chief Superintendent Fountain came out in the course of her interview with the IPCC.

As it was happening, it seemed the most natural thing in the world. Of course they needed to know about her suspicions—they were central to their investigation into the death in custody of a twenty-year-old law student. Only after they'd dismissed her, polite as ever, and she was splashing cold water on her face in the washroom did she begin to see how it would look. Now she really needed to talk to Johnny Fountain. And she really didn't want to.

Fountain heard her out in a silence that was worse than abuse. There were no interjections of "What?" and "Why?" and "In the name of God!" She didn't even hear him catch his breath. But the silence spoke volumes.

She'd known this was going to be a difficult interview. She was telling him something he'd never expected to hear about one of his longest-serving officers. And she had no proof, and her only witness was the village idiot. She'd known, driving Ash to his interview with DI Gorman, working out what she was going to say, that she'd have a thick high wall of shared history to break through. Fountain wouldn't want to believe her. He'd want to believe what his colleague of ten years, Donald Murchison, had told him, that he'd put Jerome Cardy somewhere safe and he'd be alive today if he'd stayed there.

But she thought that if she stayed calm and presented the evidence, including Ash's recollections, in an organized and coherent way, however reluctantly he would come to the same conclusion she had. That it might still be a combination of bad luck and coincidence, but the package as a whole was sufficiently worrying that it needed to be examined thoroughly. That she had no choice but to put it in front of him, and he'd have no choice but to open it.

That was before she was waylaid by IPCC. Now she was telling the chief superintendent that she'd given the parcel to someone else, whose priorities might be the same but whose modus operandi might be very different, so that whatever discretion the facts might have left him had been wrested away before they were even put before him. He'd been rendered impotent in his own police station.

So he was angry. Of course he was. Hazel understood that absolutely. She hoped *he* understood how it had happened—that she hadn't meant to put him in this situation, it had come about in such a way that she could only have avoided it by dishonesty. She couldn't tell from his face, and so far he had said almost nothing. She doubted this was a good sign.

When she'd finished, she stood in front of his desk—he'd asked her to sit when she went in, but she'd thought it better not to—with her hands behind her back, waiting to see which way the wind was blowing and how strongly. Still he said nothing.

He was thinking. Wondering how much damage had been done, and whether any of it could be repaired, and whether it would be better to try or to stand back and see what happened. A silly chit of a newbie constable, still wet behind the ears, had had an attack of the Nancy Drews and been stupid enough to tell IPCC. The fact that the investigators had heard her out didn't mean they believed a word of it. They'd seen a lot of overenthusiastic young constables in their careers, were well aware how badly they could misread a situation. How their judgment improved as experience grew and enthusiasm waned a little. How that first year they all wanted to catch Al Capone.

Finally he blew out a long sigh. "Okay, Hazel. I don't need to tell you that you should have come to me with this, not IPCC. I know that wasn't deliberate, but honest to God, girl, if you don't know just by instinct when to say what's on your mind and when to keep it there, I'm left wondering if this is the job for you. Have you any idea the harm you may have done? Not just to Donald Murchison—to yourself as well. Who else have you talked to?"

Hazel's eyes and voice were low. "No one."

"Keep it that way. The guys from IPCC know better than to spread it around, although these things have a way of leaking out under the door. If it does—if it gets out that you've accused Donald Murchison of covering up something this serious—I don't know if I'll be able to protect you from the consequences. I'll try, but it won't be easy."

"C—c—?" She swallowed and tried again. "Consequences?"

Fountain shook his leonine head as if surprised that the doings of young constables still had the power to wrong-foot him. "You don't know what you've done, do you? You really don't. Look. You know how many rules govern the way we do our job. Two hundred years of good policing distilled into paragraphs and clauses on thousands of printed pages. And some of them are laws, and some of them are regulations, and some of them are just guidance, but all of them are important. You know this—you studied hard, you got good marks in your exams."

The words might have been a compliment. The way his voice hardened suggested that no compliment was intended. "And you fell into the trap waiting for those who get good marks in written exams: You thought you knew it all. You thought a fresh eye and a good brain were worth more than thirty years of experience. You thought you'd spotted things, made sense of things, put things together that had escaped the notice and/or understanding of those of us who'd grown old and gray and dull-witted in the job.

"And then, Hazel," he bored on relentlessly, "you forgot the most important rule of all. Well, both of them, actually. The first is that you've got two ears and one mouth because you need to listen twice as much as you talk. And the other is that there are people in this police station who may one day have to die to protect you. They don't want to, they'll do everything they can to avoid it coming to that, but if it does, they will put their lives on the line to save yours. And they're willing to do it, accept it as part of the job, because they think if the need arose, you'd do it for them.

"When we talk about backing one another up, that's what we mean. Not covering for someone's iffy expenses claim. Not reconciling your statements in advance because you can't expect a magistrate to understand that there isn't always time to do things by the book. But standing shoulder-to-shoulder against the worst that the bastards out there can throw at us, and if we've nothing better to cover a colleague's back, we use our own. I've done that, and I've had it done for me. Everyone here has—well, everyone who's had time to wear out their first pair of boots. Donald Murchison has, several times."

His voice, that powerful, authoritative voice that made people a street away stand up straighter, had been rising until he knew he was in danger of shouting. He took a moment to calm his temper. But he had by no means finished with her.

"And you've accused him of—what? At best, falling asleep on the job and lying about it. At worst, conspiracy to murder a man in custody. Hazel, there are people here who've worked with Donald Murchison longer than you've been alive. I've worked with him for ten years. Don't you think if he was capable of something like that, I'd know? Or do you think it just didn't occur to me that it could be anything other than simple bad luck? *Of course it occurred to me.* I had all the information in front of me that you had, and rather more. I even had a statement from Gabriel Ash. What I didn't have was your touching belief that you can trust anything he says.

"As if that wasn't bad enough," he went on, the voice rising again despite his best intentions, "having come to this absurd conclusion, instead of discussing it with me, you took it to IPCC. The Independent Police Complaints Commission now knows that one of my officers, admittedly a very junior one, suspects a rather more senior one of being an accessory to murder." Finally he abandoned all efforts to hang on to his patience. "What the hell kind of a position do you think that puts me in? I can't back both of you to the hilt! The best I can do is point out to the IPCC that, in policing terms, you're still in nappies and the occasional mess on the carpet is only to be expected."

Hazel, white-faced, wondered if another apology might help. She wasn't sure it was called for, but if it would defuse the situation, she was willing to try. But a peremptory hand waved her to silence.

"They may accept that. They're going to give me some very funny looks, I dare say I'll be the butt of a few good jokes at the Division Christmas party, but with luck—with a lot of luck—it may go no further. If you believe in the power of prayer, that's worth praying for.

"I have to tell you, regaining your colleagues' trust will be harder. It may not be possible. If this gets out, they're going to feel you didn't just stab Sergeant Murchison in the back, you stabbed them, too. I don't know what you can do to persuade them that you won't do it again, the next time you want to make an impression on the top brass."

There are worse things for a police officer to do than bursting into tears, but not many. A bit like knocking over an elderly nun on a zebra crossing when you're taking your driving test, it's pretty much the end of the line. Another of those unwritten rules that you can't afford to break. You hold on. You wait till you're alone. Family, and very close friends, are the only ones who ever see you cry.

Hazel knew that if she cried in front of Chief Superintendent Fountain, he'd probably stop glaring at her in furious disbelief and put his arm around her instead, but that would be worse. The end of all her hopes. If none of her colleagues trusted her, and her chief superintendent thought she was pathetic, she could kiss good-bye to her police career. She'd worked hard to get here. People had expected her to go far. Now, it seemed, she had a great future behind her; and maybe she'd been wrong, and maybe she'd been naïve, but she'd acted from honorable motives and she still thought her concerns hadn't been given the consideration they deserved. But she was damned if she was going to cry.

"Sir, I really don't think you're being fair. I've given this a lot of thought. I believed—I still believe—that it could be coincidence, but the chances of it being something else were too high to ignore. I was on my way to see you when I was redirected to IPCC, and once there I answered their questions as honestly as I could. I thought, and I still think, that was my duty.

"I understand that this is the last thing you expected to have to deal with. I'm sorry it was me who came up with this instead of a more senior officer who'd worked for you for years and whose judgment you'd learned to trust. But that's not what happened. Maybe I'm wrong. I *hope* I'm wrong. But I think someone with a lot more experience on the job than me needs to look at it properly before you write it off as a rookie mistake."

He said nothing, just kept looking at her. But from the way his eyes widened slightly, she thought she'd managed to surprise him. Again. She wasn't sorry. She was already in such deep water that splashing probably couldn't do her any more harm.

Unless it attracted sharks.

Finally Johnny Fountain sucked in a deep breath, let it out in a sigh, and shook his head bemusedly. "All right." He almost sounded defeated. "If you want me to look into it, I'll look into it. I'll have to speak to Sergeant Murchison, and the other officers who were on duty that night. I'll even—God help me!—have to talk to Rambles. But you understand, any chance we might have had of playing this down goes out the window the moment I get involved. That's what you want, is it? You're sure?"

Hazel drew herself up to her full height and squared her shoulders: what had been described to her in training as "filling the uniform." She'd liked that, and remembered it, and she did it now not to impress and reassure a member of the public but so that Fountain would never know how devastated his assessment had left her, how uncertain she now was of what had seemed so obvious. But it was too late to back down. She'd rather be proved wrong, with all that would follow, than be thought weak and mean-spirited. Her career would be over either way, and she'd rather be shot down in flames than slowly choked. Like Desdemona.

"Yes, sir," she said, and wondered at the firmness in her own voice. "I think it's necessary."

"All right." He sat back, broad shoulders slumping. "On your own head be it."

CHAPTER 15

IT STARTED almost immediately.

No one spoke an unkind word to her. No one spoke to her at all, unless it was strictly necessary, when they said what they had to in as few words as possible and then moved away. Their faces remained expressionless. None of them could have been accused of intimidating her by word, deed, or manner. But oh, the power of silence.

Hazel was determined to see it through. It wasn't as if these people were her friends. Not really, not yet. They were colleagues, and they could go on working together whether or not they liked one another. She had done nothing wrong. She kept reminding herself of that. Others would decide if her suspicions were warranted, but even if they weren't, she'd had no choice but take them to someone with more experience, more seniority than she. Maybe those who'd known Sergeant Murchison since he was directing traffic onto the Ark would be proved right. That still wouldn't make what Hazel did wrong.

So if her colleagues at Meadowvale Police Station wanted to keep her at arm's length until the truth could be established, fine. Unnecessary, Hazel thought, and unkind, and maybe even cowardly, but fine. Sooner or later, whatever transpired, they would have to deal with her, and she'd still be here. She wasn't about to plead stress and go on gardening leave.

But for the first time since joining the police she couldn't wait for the end of her shift. When she went into the women's locker room to change that Saturday morning, everyone who was already there left. One left in her bra, pulling her shirt on as she stalked down the corridor.

Okay, thought Hazel Best, and just for badness she paused at the drinks machine in the foyer, bought a strong coffee, and took her time drinking it. Only then did she leave the building.

At first she drove around aimlessly, torn between thinking and trying not to think. Then she noticed the looks she was getting from people on the street, whom she'd passed three times, and realized they thought she was curb crawling. She left the car by the park gates and walked as far as the war memorial.

The urns had been restored to their proper positions, the uprooted shrubs replanted, the granite steps swept clean. Robert Barclay's blood on the obelisk had been washed away.

Why? she found herself wondering. *Why* had he wanted to head-butt it? Barking Mad or not, he must have known he'd hurt himself much more than the monument. Whatever was there about a granite war memorial to make him so angry? Hazel bent closer to read the inscriptions. But they were just names. The names of young men, and a few young women, who'd lived in Norbold and died on foreign fields in conflicts from World War I to present-day Iraq and Afghanistan.

There were even a couple of Bests. No relation. As far as she knew she had no family in Norbold, but that didn't stop the discovery from giving her a little jolt. In a way it didn't matter if they were close kin or not. They were all one. They'd come from roots like hers, and grown up in this place, expecting to be teachers and plumbers and, yes, policemen, and they hadn't had the chance. Some of them had died bravely, and some of them had died with their arms over their heads, crying for their mothers, but all of them had been trying to do a good thing and it had cost them their lives. Their loss had been felt in hearts and homes in every street in the town.

And Robert Barclay had found their monument so offensive that he tried to rip it down with his bare hands and indeed his bare head. *Why?*

Or maybe it didn't matter why. Maybe she was looking for some sort of logic where none existed. It wasn't what Barclay did here that was important; it was what he did in cell five at Meadowvale.

Unless Gabriel Ash was right when he suggested—it had been little more than an off-the-cuff idea, and they hadn't pursued it because they'd started talking about something else—that someone else had used Barclay to do his dirty work. Used him as a weapon, Ash had said—primed him and pointed him and stood well back to wait for the explosion. Mickey Argyle, perhaps, whose interest in Ash suggested he was in some way involved in Jerome Cardy's life, if not his death. A man like that, a serious player on the organized-crime scene—one of the last serious players in Norbold, thanks to Johnny Fountain—might have the nous to manipulate smaller thugs like Barclay if he also had the need. Hazel couldn't imagine why he would go to so much trouble to launch a stealth attack on a law student, but it wasn't necessary for her to know in order to find out if there was any mileage in the idea. To go back through Barclay's night, and possibly the previous day, to see if she could discover what made him do what he did that got him arrested.

The war memorial. He could have attacked any of the bus shelters on the way here, any of the shop fronts, or the art installation in front of the Town Hall, which had made Hazel reach for her truncheon more than once. He hadn't. He'd come into the park in order to attack the war memorial. She leaned forward, scanning the names. Not far up the long list from where she'd found the Bests, she found a Barclay. Lance Corporal E. M. Barclay of Second Battalion, the Parachute Regiment, died 1979 in Northern Ireland. Barking Mad's dad? She could check the custody records, but the man she'd tried to arrest looked to be around forty, making it perfectly feasible. Perhaps as a small child this big, violent man had stood on a railway station and waved goodbye to a soldier father he was never going to see again.

Was that enough? To make him put a brick through the window of the recruiting office maybe, but to attack the monument? Hazel couldn't see it.

As she backed away, nodding a tiny salute, someone was watching her. A dog walker, she supposed, waiting on the edge of the spinney while his charge investigated the fascinating aroma of something dead in the leaf mold. But there was no dog. As she moved, his shoulders moved to follow her.

Hazel turned toward him.

She thought he was going to hurry off—something about the way his body gathered itself in balance over his feet. But he resisted the urge and let her approach.

He was about sixteen, thin and pinched in the face, none too clean even for a teenager and wearing clothes too light for the April weather and trainers with holes over the toes. She thought he was sleeping rough, or the next best thing.

"Were you looking for me?" she asked, keeping her tone friendly.

He answered with a question, and a note of challenge. "Are you a cop?"

That surprised her. She was out of uniform, and hadn't lived around here long enough for everyone to know who she was and what she did. "That's right." She nodded. "Do you need some help?"

He disdained to answer that. "You were here three nights ago. After the nut with the dog got beat."

Hazel ignored his choice of words. "What do you know about that?"

The boy shrugged inside his thin clothes. "Nothing."

"You knew it was me dealing with it. You must have seen me."

"Nothing to do with me." Another moment and he really was going to run.

"He was all right, you know," said Hazel. "A bit bruised, nothing more. Which is a minor miracle, when you think about it."

"Yeah," muttered the boy.

"Yes." Hazel pretended not to notice the shiftiness of his demeanor. She thought she knew what this was about. "He said somebody helped him. That he'd have been hurt much worse if somebody hadn't taken the risk of helping him."

"Yeah?"

"By letting the dog go."

Saturday shot her a sideways glance from under overlong hair, half wary, half pleased. "They were going to kill him."

"Yes," agreed Hazel, "I think they were."

"It was the dog run them off. Cracking good dog, that."

"She couldn't have done it if you'd held on to her."

"He never done them any harm. Why'd they want to kill him?"

Hazel shook her head. "I don't know. They're not my friends."

"They're not mine, neither! They're . . ." He didn't finish the sentence. It was as if he was accustomed to being cut short. As if never being listened to had freed him from the mental discipline of having to think things through to a conclusion.

But Hazel was listening to him now, politely, her head tipped a little to one side like a curious bird's. "What, then?"

Like forcing a rusty hinge, like hand-cranking an unused engine, the boy made the feelings in his head shape molds for the underused words to flow into. At first they flowed like treacle. "Just, people I know. People like me. Wasters. No jobs, no money. Time to kill. You end up doing stupid things just to fill the day. Beating up on harmless idiots. Hanging out with people who beat up on harmless idiots."

"Why don't you do something else?"

His eyebrows rocketed. "Like what? Airline pilot? Bit of brain surgery? There's no jobs going for people much better qualified than me."

"That's not actually true," she chided him gently. "I know these are difficult times. But however tough the conditions, there are always some people who do better than others starting from the same place. The trick is to try to be one of them."

Saturday stared at her as if he really, genuinely thought she might have come from another planet. And, at least metaphorically, she had. A world where effort was by and large rewarded, and where people were motivated by the general expectation that it would be. Trucker's crew would have laughed the very idea to bitter scorn. Saturday suddenly felt jealous. He had no middle-class aspirations. He didn't even have any working-class aspirations. He knew, at a bone-deep level—the way he knew that if you aren't with the pack, you're the quarry—that he had no future beyond this daily drift toward the void.

He was never going to starve. They made sure you didn't starve, made a point of saving you from that. They never explained what it was they were saving you *for.* So far as Saturday could see, it was a kind of cosmic joke—to give you nothing to do, nothing to hope for, and make sure you'd all the time in the world to do it in. These days he didn't look very far ahead, not if he could help it, but when it sneaked up on him in the middle of a cold, unsleeping night, he knew with a cruel certainty that there was nothing ahead of him that was any better than what he had right now. Or any different. He was sixteen. Excepting violence, he might expect to live into his sixties. That meant there was three times as much living still to be done as he'd done already, and it was all going to be just like this. Just as pointless as this.

He felt his eyes grow hot on her smooth, nicely brought-up, and, above all, *clean* face—just a touch of makeup, long fair hair tied back neatly, wouldn't Mummy be proud, bet she's got a photo on the fireplace of Plodette in her lovely blue uniform and kick-ass hat—and somehow it mattered to him, more than making a fool of himself, more than making himself memorable to a police officer, which was not generally recommended for people in Saturday's position, that he jolt that smug self-confidence, that inbred knowledge of her own worth that informed her view of how the world worked. Maybe it worked like that for people like her, girls with nice accents and ponies and foreign holidays, but most of the world was more like him than it was like her and the least she could do was *bloody well recognize the fact*!

"Lady," he said roughly, "who the hell do you think you are? Who the hell do you think *I* am—Little Orphan Annie? Do you think that's all I need—a bit of motivation? That a Christmas cracker motto's all it'll take to turn me into a model citizen?" He gave a bleak laugh that made him sound far older than his sixteen years.

"I am not like you. Trucker and his crew, they're not like you. We don't do things because there's a good reason for it. We do things because we can—because you can't stop us. We take things, and scare people, and hurt people, because you can't stop us. Most of the time you can't even catch us, and when you do, the worst that happens is we get a warm bed and an extra meal every day for six months.

"I'm trash," he spat. "We're all trash. You know what makes us strong? Knowing it. Knowing we were born trash, and we'll die trash, and everything between is trash as well. Knowing that nothing you can do to us will make it any worse."

"And that nothing you do will make it any better," said Hazel softly. "That's what you think, isn't it? Not that you're strong, but that you're too weak to make things any better for yourself. And you don't try because the only thing that would be worse than staying where you are would be trying to leave and failing. As long as you don't try, you can tell yourself there's no alternative. But if you tried—if you pulled yourself far enough out of the gutter to see where the road leads—and then slipped back, you'd never again have the comfort of thinking that way. You'd know that I'm right. That if you tried hard enough, you might succeed."

The boy blinked at her. He was used to the blame-free approach of well-meaning social workers who'd been taught that poverty is a misfortune, which it certainly is, and largely beyond the ability of the victim to change, which Hazel had been taught it was not. Now that she had his full attention, she pressed home her point.

"*Hard* is the operative word. You want something in this world, you have to work for it, and I don't think that's a concept you're entirely familiar with. Taking, yes; being given, maybe; earning, not so much. But you're worth more than this, and that's how you get it. I'm not here to motivate you. Self-respect should be motivation enough."

Saturday stared at her in astonishment. It was like being savaged by a kitten. He'd thought she was soft and fluffy. He'd thought to bring a blush of shame to her middle-class cheek, and instead he felt himself growing hot and awkward. "You know nothing about it," he mumbled resentfully.

"Of course I do," Hazel retorted briskly. "I see it every day. I see more than you do—I also see the people who start off with nothing and end up with something. I'll tell you something you don't know. You're one of the people who could do it. I don't think Trucker is, I don't think any of his crew are, but you are. You're smarter and you're tougher."

A part of him didn't want to believe her. "I'm the same as them. . . ."

"No, you're not. While they were kicking nine bells out of a man on the ground, you were looking for a way to stop it. You didn't have to do that. You stuck your neck out doing it. You did it because you didn't like what was happening and you were willing to take a risk to stop it. Take another risk. Stop"—she looked him up and down, critically—"this."

The others weren't like this. They brought you soup at Christmas, and new socks and little homilies, but they didn't tell you that, essentially, it was your own fault you were living like this. That you could change it if you tried. Of course, new socks only lasted so long.

"Where do you live?"

"Up the Flying Horse." He indicated the direction of the estate with a wary jerk of his head.

"With family?"

"In a squat."

"With friends, then."

"I told you, I don't—"

"Have any friends," she said, finishing his sentence impatiently. "Except that you have. You've got at least two. Like it or not, I'm one. And the other"—Hazel's eyes narrowed as a train of thought that should probably have been shunted into a siding for inspection first went barreling through the points—"would probably like to meet you again, would like to thank you, and might be persuaded to make lunch for the three of us."

"I don't need feeding up, either," growled Saturday, as if there was something patronizing in the suggestion.

"Maybe you don't need to eat," said Hazel, ignoring the testimony of his gaunt young body, "so much as he needs to cook. And I need the company of people who aren't police officers. Come on, the car's this way."

He'd been right about one thing: she'd been nicely brought up. She resisted the urge to spread newspapers before letting him onto the front seat. "If we're going to be friends, we should probably know each other's names. I'm Hazel."

"Saturday," he responded in a low voice.

She looked surprised. "Really?"

He scowled. "No, not really. It's a street name."

She pursed her lips thoughtfully. "Like Acacia Avenue?"

The boy grinned and leaned back in his seat with his hands laced behind his head. Unaccountably he was starting to feel comfortable in this woman's presence. "My name's Saul Desmond. My family's Jewish, so the kids at school called me 'Excused Saturdays.' All right? Now, are we going to eat or what?"

CHAPTER 16

THEY ARRIVED AT the house in Highfield Road as Ash was letting himself in. Hazel lowered her window. "Everything all right?"

He hardly looked surprised anymore to see her. "Fine. Though Detective Inspector Gorman had no idea what Mickey Argyle might want with me, either."

"Nye Jackson was right, then—they were Argyle's goons?"

Ash nodded. "DI Gorman called them 'known associates.' I picked them out of some photographs he showed me." Belatedly, he noticed that she was not alone. "Er . . ."

"Yes," said Hazel, getting out of the car and beckoning her passenger. "This is Saul. Also known, apparently, as Saturday. You have actually met."

There was a silence that stretched to perhaps a minute. Long enough for Hazel to wonder if she'd done the right thing bringing the boy here. Long enough for Saturday to wonder if he should run. Even long enough for him to remember that on the other side of that door was a dog with the speed of a greyhound and the jaws of a mantrap, so that a head start of anything less than about a quarter of an hour wasn't worth taking. He stood his ground. But his eyes were wary and his body tense.

Finally Ash said quietly, "Yes, I remember."

Saturday still didn't know if he was in for a meal or a thrashing. "I done my best, mister. I'm sorry you got hurt, but it wasn't my fault."

"They were your friends."

"No. They weren't. I haven't got . . ."

Hazel was making *Don't let's go there* gestures behind his head. "Gabriel, can we go inside? I don't like you hanging around out here. Just in case someone's watching."

He hesitated a moment longer, then opened the door. "Come in." And, after the briefest pause: "Both of you."

The dog was waiting in the hall. Hazel—and probably also Saturday, though he was too proud to show it—experienced a moment of concern, because dogs aren't sophisticated thinkers and if she associated the boy with the violence in the park, things could quickly get unpleasant.

She gave no warning signals. No growling, the curtains of her lips drawn back from the scimitar teeth, no lifting of the hackles along her smooth back. She stood four square at the end of the hall, regarding the visitor steadily, both with her gold-rimmed eyes and with the constant twitching of her nose. Then she waved her tail, just once, and everyone relaxed.

"Come into the kitchen," said Ash. "I'll put the kettle on."

"Actually," said Hazel, following him, "I could murder something to eat. If you've nothing in, I'll fetch fish and chips."

Ash looked at her, then at the boy, then at Patience. "There's stuff in the freezer."

What was in the freezer was mostly fish and chips, too. Ash cooked with immense concentration, as if even at this modest level entertaining was a forgotten skill. He'd eaten off trays for so long, he couldn't find a tablecloth.

Hazel found one buried in the airing cupboard, shook out the creases, and threw it cheerfully across the kitchen table. "That's better. Plates, glasses, cutlery—have you enough for four?"

Ash stared at her blankly, and when she realized what she'd done, she colored to the roots of her hair. It was his fault—he'd got her talking like something out of The Famous Five! The dog *was only a dog and didn't warrant a table setting.*

"Anything to drink?" Saturday asked hopefully.

"You're too young to drink," said Ash disapprovingly, and unrealistically, and Hazel jerked a thumb at the kitchen tap.

"Adam's ale."

Despite the awkwardness it was—nice. Eating together. For all of them, for different reasons. For Ash, because he didn't get much company. For Saturday, because he didn't get much food. And for Hazel, because today she desperately needed a success of some sort, and this was better than nothing. It had been a good idea and it reassured her that her instincts had not entirely gone AWOL.

Afterward she made Saturday help her load the dishwasher. It hadn't been used in a while. A dog and a man with no appetite don't produce much washing-up. As she worked she said over her shoulder, "Had Dave Gorman anything useful to suggest?"

Ash shook his head. "He didn't offer any suggestions. He just asked questions."

Hazel thought he seemed low. Whether it was the shock sinking in, or disappointment because for a moment he'd thought something good was happening to him, or even resentment that she'd brought to his house one of the gang responsible for his involvement with Jerome Cardy, she had no way of knowing. Or maybe it was none of the above. Maybe this was normal for him—not so much peaks and troughs of emotion, more troughs and deeper troughs.

She tried to reassure him. "That's his job. He will get to the bottom of this, you know. He'll find out what Mickey Argyle is up to, and whether it's anything to do with . . . what happened at Meadowvale. You're in good hands."

Ash shrugged. "At least he listened to me. Of course, having a reporter as an eye witness couldn't hurt."

"Mickey Argyle?" Saturday had abandoned the washing-up and was looking at Hazel with an air of casual curiosity totally betrayed by the sharpness of his gaze. "What's he got to do with anything?"

Hazel frowned. "You know Mickey Argyle?" But of course he did. Trucker's gang and all the wasted youth hanging around the street corners of the Flying Horse were the bottomless reservoir from which he tapped the help he needed. They ran errands for him, kept watch for him; the more promising among them ended up on the staff. If Mickey Argyle was interested in Gabriel Ash, Saturday probably knew. Or, if he didn't know, could probably find out.

Hazel gave a somewhat disingenuous shrug. "We don't really know. Some men wanted to talk to Mr. Ash. They were interrupted and drove off before they said very much, but someone thought they worked for Mickey."

"If Mickey wants to talk to him, they'll be back," said Saturday darkly.

"I expect so," said Hazel casually. "I don't suppose you've heard anything?"

The boy shook his head quickly. She thought it was the truth. He'd been surprised to hear Argyle's name mentioned.

"What about Trucker?"

"What *about* Trucker?"

"Would it be worth asking him?"

"No, it wouldn't," said Saturday forcibly. "It wouldn't be worth you asking him because he wouldn't tell you anything. And it wouldn't be worth me asking him because he'd rip my frigging head off!"

"Fair enough," said Hazel mildly. "I just thought you and Trucker must hear a lot of stuff. And you probably know these people better than I do. Mickey Argyle. Robert Barclay."

Somewhat mollified, Saturday sniffed. "Barking Mad Barclay. That's what everyone calls him."

"That I knew. But not till after I tried to stop him head-butting the war memorial."

"That was you?" The boy's eyes widened, though possibly more in astonishment than admiration. He barked a little chuckle. Hazel could hear nights on a cold street in his chest. "Jesus, you really are new in town, aren't you?"

"That's me," she agreed wryly. "Everything to learn, and only till yesterday to learn it in. Like, why would anyone want to nut ten tons of granite?"

Across the room Ash sat still. He didn't know much about angling, but he knew you need to keep very still when there's a fish nosing at your bait. He'd only just realized Hazel had a line out. With luck the fish hadn't realized it yet.

Saturday gave the glassy grin of a child who's coming to realize that what seemed like really good fun to him isn't striking the adults in the same way. He turned back to the dishwasher. "Trucker's idea of a joke," he mumbled.

And you don't yank until you're sure the hook has taken. "That was Trucker, too?" Hazel gave a light laugh. "Seems to me, if we knew where Trucker was holding his birthday party and locked the doors, we could put a stop to most of the mischief in Norbold."

Saturday grinned at her again, back over his shoulder, happier now.

"Still—*how*?" Hazel wondered aloud. "I couldn't make Barclay let me clean the cuts on his head. How did Trucker make him beat himself up?"

"He told him half the names on the war memorial weren't even English."

Robert Barclay, the well-known racist. Who probably thought of himself as a patriot. Who probably thought that the town's war memorial honored men just like him, and only men who were just like him. He may have left a poppy there every year, but he'd probably never bothered to read the inscriptions until a troublemaker pointed out that there weren't just Barclays on the list of the glorious dead; there were also Badawis, Bajramis, Balasundarams, Barzaqs, and a Bassakaropoulos as well. "So that's what blew his tiny mind." Hazel whistled.

Ash said nothing, but shock deepened the hollows of his eyes. Someone's idea of a joke had resulted in a young man's death.

Hazel kept her tone light, inconsequential. "Who put him up to it?"

Saturday didn't look around, but his shoulders stiffened. "I don't know. Nobody."

Hazel shrugged. "He must have had a reason. Not even Trucker's going to wind up Barking Mad Barclay on a whim. It must have been for a bet."

The boy relaxed a fraction. "Maybe."

"Or else somebody paid him."

Hard to know if he saw the trap or if he was just naturally

cautious because—living as he did—it was the safest way to get by. But Saturday clammed up tight. He echoed her shrug but refused to say any more, and soon afterward said he had to leave. He declined Hazel's offer of a lift back into town, leaving her and Ash to consider what they'd learned.

"You were right," said Hazel. "Somebody found a way to use Barclay as a weapon."

"But why?"

"Barclay killed Jerome," Hazel said carefully, "because he was black and Barclay's a racist. On Wednesday night he was primed to explode because he'd just found out his father shared the war memorial with a bunch of guys who were neither English nor white. But that's not why Jerome was killed. He was killed because someone, possibly Mickey Argyle, arranged to have Barclay spitting tacks when he was put in the same cell."

Ash was struggling with the details. "I can see how he could get Barclay locked up. He paid this Trucker to wind him up so much he was bound to get arrested. But how could he make sure Jerome would be in the cells that night? Anyone could have lit Barclay's blue touch paper, but how do you get a well-behaved law student behind bars?"

"That would be the hard part," agreed Hazel. "That's why he had to be arrested first. Only once Jerome was in custody was it worth picking Barclay up."

Ash nodded slowly. "Jerome was arrested after a traffic accident. No"—he corrected himself—"after fleeing the scene of a traffic accident. An accident that wasn't his fault. Why would he do that?"

"He had something to hide?" hazarded Hazel.

"Maybe." Ash nodded. "Or some other reason to be afraid of policemen. Once he decided to run, everything else fell into place. The police were bound to give chase, to arrest him when they caught him, to put him in a cell. So the question is, why was he scared of a routine encounter with the police?"

"He was a law student," said Hazel. "He knew what was expected of him. And how very ordinary a piece of business it would have been. He *must* have been up to no good if he preferred to look like a criminal than do what was required of him. Maybe there was something in his car that shouldn't have been there."

"Do you usually search the cars of people who've been involved in minor traffic accidents? The innocent parties in minor traffic accidents?"

He was right: if Jerome had had something to hide, his best defense would have been to play the innocent party. Wait for the police, make a statement, express the hope that the other driver would get home safely, and go about his business.

"That boy wasn't afraid of what the police might find," said Ash. "He was afraid of the police. We all have encounters with police officers from time to time. We think nothing of it. We know it isn't personal—you're just doing your job. But what if Jerome thought it *was* personal? That the police were looking for him, and he was going to be in danger if they found him? Wouldn't that be enough to make him flee the scene of a traffic accident?"

Hazel was trying to remember what she'd heard in Meadowvale. "Mrs. Wiltshire said he became agitated when she insisted on calling the police. That he tried to talk her out of it."

"He was scared. He knew something bad was going to happen to him. He knew the moment the other driver said she wanted to call the police."

Hazel was constitutionally inimical to the notion of a respectable citizen being afraid of the police. "It makes no sense. If he'd done nothing wrong, he'd nothing to be afraid of. This isn't a police state. We aren't allowed to intimidate people even if we want to."

"Two possibilities," said Ash, brows knit in a pensive frown. "Either Jerome wasn't the thoroughly decent young man he seemed and was up to his neck in something he knew would come out if the police ever had a reason to pull him in, or he *was* a thoroughly decent young man, in which case he believed—it may not have been true, but he believed it—that the police were gunning for him. That it was worth taking any risk to stay out of their grasp."

Hazel's eyes were round with astonishment. He wasn't talking about a world she recognized. She made a determined effort to follow his train of thought, expecting it to hit the buffers at any moment. "But still, why? If he'd done nothing wrong, *why* would he think the police were gunning for him? Even if he did, why wouldn't he suppose there'd been a misunderstanding and go into Meadowvale to sort it out?"

"He must have considered doing just that," said Ash, "and obviously he dismissed it. He must have thought it would make matters worse."

"Worse than trying to outrun a police car?" Her tone was brittle with skepticism.

"He believed so," said Ash. "Hazel, I was with him. He was genuinely afraid. He didn't tell me why, but *he* understood what was happening to him. And what was going to happen to him. He knew his life was in danger. So even if we don't know why, we can assume that something had already happened to make him feel that way. Someone had threatened him. Or he'd seen or heard or done something that made him a target."

"And what's the first thing you'd do in those circumstances?"

demanded Hazel. "You'd go to the police and demand to be protected! Unless you'd been up to no good."

For a moment Ash tried to avoid her gaze. But he knew it would only make him look shifty, and no one can afford to be thought both mad *and* shifty. Certainly no one who has to say what Ash was about to say.

He made himself look her in the eye. "There's another way to explain his behavior. It may not have been Jerome who was up to no good. It may have been the police."

One of the first lessons Hazel had learned at police training college was that there's a time to exercise authority, when there's a good chance it'll nip trouble in the bud, and there's a time to keep things calm and casual, when the exercise of authority will act as a red rag to a bull. But there's never a time when matters will be improved by losing your temper.

So she counted to ten, and thought about her pension, and didn't do what she wanted to do, which was slap his face; and when she was sure she had her voice under control, she said quietly, "That's a pretty poor joke, Gabriel."

He was watching closely for her reaction. A part of him seemed to expect the slap. But he didn't take the easy option and back down. "It isn't a joke."

Two things had knocked the wind out of Hazel's sails. One was what he'd said. The other was—even after the week she'd had: the suspicions, the worry, the way she'd been treated—how much she resented the insult to her profession. How much it hurt that he thought the police were not to be trusted. Beneath the shabby clothes, behind the shambling and muttering, Gabriel Ash was an intelligent man with some experience in the field of law enforcement; and even he thought that a credible explanation for what had happened was that Meadowvale Police Station had gone rogue. If Ash thought that, what chance was there of convincing the ordinary man and woman in the street, the people whose rates and taxes paid her salary, that it might make good television *but things like that didn't actually happen*?

Pain affects people in different ways. Some internalize—curl up around it, seek a quiet corner, in the room or in the mind, where they can deal with it in privacy. Some run—fleeing in blind panic, conscious of nothing but the distance they may put between themselves and the cause of their pain, forgetting that an injured soul is like a broken bone and comes with you wherever you go until you get it seen to. And some fight back. The strong, the desperate, and those who think that they have something worth fighting for. Anger eclipses pain. Hazel Best felt herself growing angry.

She didn't shout when she got angry. She grew cold, and precise, and picked her words very carefully. "And that's your explanation, is it? Jerome Cardy was running from the police not because of something he'd done but because of something they'd done? Sorry—something *we'd* done. I presume that this accusation includes me, too."

"I'm not accusing anyone," Ash said in a low voice.

"Of course you are. You're saying there was a conspiracy at Meadowvale to round up Jerome Cardy on some pretext and put him in the same cell as Barclay. No one officer could have done what needed doing. First of all he'd have had to arrange for Jerome to be arrested for something. Perhaps he bribed Mrs. Wiltshire. Then he had to get Jerome past the custody officer, whose job it is to ensure that people aren't banged up without a damn good reason. Then he had to tell Trucker to find Barclay and make sure he, too, got arrested. Oh, and he had to tinker with the CCTV so he could transfer Jerome to a vacant cell without anyone noticing. Apart," she added sarcastically, "from you and Patience, of course.

"Finally, when Barclay was brought in, he had to ensure that he'd end up in Jerome's cell. And that once again no one would notice. No one would notice that a cell the size of the average bathroom was already occupied. Jerome himself, polite to the end, wouldn't yell, 'Hey, man, you're not leaving me here with *that*! I'm going back to the nutter with the dog.'"

They were regarding each other intently over the coffee table. Hazel's jaw was rigid with anger. Ash's face was pale, his breathing unsteady. He hated confrontation. The last few years he'd avoided all social intercourse, had lost any skill he'd once had for managing his own emotions or those of anyone else. Instinct told him to run from this, too, even if it was his house. He could leave and come back later.

But human beings are not creatures only of instinct. He knew that fleeing the argument would be the wrong thing to do. It would fatally undermine any hope he might have of being taken seriously. It would be the end of the embryonic friendship between him and this earnest, graceful young woman.

Neither of which really mattered, except a little in his head. He'd lost the right to be taken seriously when he'd struck his head of department in a London street. And he was realistic enough to know that what he thought of as friendship might be nothing more than a nicely brought-up young woman treating the local idiot with kindness.

What kept him from leaving the battlefield to nurse his wounds in privacy was the possibility that he might be right. That was all it was—a possibility. A cogent argument could have persuaded him he was wrong. But thinking about the matter this way finally enabled him to explain things that had seemed inexplicable, and until someone came up with another viable theory, he wasn't going to let this one go by default. Not because he was prideful or stubborn, although on occasions he could be both, but because if he *was* right, it was vitally important to find how far the rot at Meadowvale had spread and cut it out before it cost the life of another decent young man.

"Please," he begged her, "hear me out. I know one man couldn't have done all that. But maybe two men could. Three could do it without much difficulty. I'm not suggesting that everyone at Meadowvale is corrupt. I'm suggesting that a small group may be. You know the place, Hazel, you know the people. Is that so utterly beyond the bounds of possibility? Might there not be two or three people, out of all those who work there, who've got themselves involved in something they shouldn't have?"

"Something they shouldn't have?" Incredulity sent Hazel's eyebrows soaring. "Like murdering witnesses, you mean? Yes, I can see how that would happen. Anyone can make a mistake—fill in the wrong form, enter the wrong charge, throw a twenty-year-old boy to a homicidal maniac. There but for the grace of God, as they say . . ."

She was willfully misunderstanding him and Ash knew it. He just couldn't seem to find the words to stop her, to make her think about it, not as a fellow police officer but as an intelligent and concerned individual. To grapple with the idea in her head, not her heart. To remain open to possibilities however distasteful they might be.

He shook his head helplessly. "That's not . . . Hazel, you *know* that's not what I'm saying. I've known a lot of police officers. A lot of them I'd trust with my life—*have* trusted with my life, and things that meant more to me. But I also know, and so do you if you're honest, there are a percentage who are not trustworthy. Who went into the job for the wrong reasons, or got frustrated or disillusioned somewhere along the way and started wondering what would make them feel better.

"And once you take that turning, there's no coming back. You take the first bad decision out of greed, and the second to protect yourself from the consequences of the first. Men who never wanted anything more than an extra week in Marbella with the wife each year end up trashing serious inquiries because they're in too deep to say no to whoever's pulling their strings."

In the honest heart of her—and her heart was nothing if not honest—Hazel could not have argued with a word that he'd said. But she was no longer capable of an entirely rational response. She was angry, and hurt, and beleaguered by what felt like a personal attack; and somehow the fact that she had already entertained doubts about one of her colleagues made it worse, not better, by adding guilt to the mix. On top of that, it rankled that these accusations came from someone she'd gone out of her way to be kind to. Someone she'd tried to help and protect, and listen to, when everyone else was dismissive. She felt Ash owed her better than a sneak attack.

"There's no one pulling my strings," she shot back, hammering the words out like bullets. "I make my own mistakes. Like this one. People warned me about you. Told me not to get involved. Told me you weren't reliable. I thought they'd got it wrong. Hadn't looked deeply enough, hadn't given you a chance. I thought if I treated you like a normal, intelligent, responsible individual, you'd behave like one.

"And that was naïve. You can't, can you? It's asking too much. If you could behave normally, you would, and that dog"

—she flicked a bitter glance at Patience—"would be just a dog, not a kind of alter ego. You live in a dream world, Gabriel. Nothing you say or think has any basis in reality. Which means the stupidest thing of all is that I would even *care* what you think of me!"

And with that parting shot she spun on her heel sharply enough to bring tears to a drill sergeant's eyes, and stalked out of Gabriel Ash's house—and, she believed, out of his life—and back to her car.

Ash stood staring in amazement and distress as the door quivered on its hinges.

Goodness, said Patience mildly. Little Miss Grumpy.

CHAPTER 17

NYE JACKSON HAD always known he wanted to be a reporter. He knew when the other boys in his class still thought they were going to be astronauts and firemen. He was the only eight-year-old boy his English teacher had ever known who not only owned a dictionary but wrote his name inside it so it wouldn't get lost.

But somewhere along the line the dream had bumped into real life and come off worst. He'd never been a front-line war correspondent. He'd never worked for Reuters. He wasn't a hard-bitten investigative journalist on one of the national tabloids. He was senior reporter (out of three) on a small-town biweekly newspaper that filled its centerfold with wedding photographs and its back pages with under-fifteens soccer and racing pigeon results.

Even that wasn't the worst of it. He wasn't much past forty; he could still have made his name as a crime reporter, if only he hadn't ended up working in the town with the lowest crime rate in the Midlands. The sort of town where a reign of terror amounted to two little boys letting off bangers. Where he'd once written the headline BEAST OF NORBOLD: FEAR EMPTIES STREETS over a story about Queenie Porter's potbellied pig, Nigel, who'd taken to breaking out of her backyard on a Friday night and going looking for sex and/or curry-house leftovers.

Jackson was a disappointed man. Somehow he'd expected his life to be better than this—more exciting, more important. He wasn't sure where he'd gone wrong. Lying wakeful in his lonely bed in his rented flat above a grocer's shop, listening to Nigel rooting around in the bins below, more than once he'd tried to identify the point at which he'd had the chance to live the dream and not taken it. He'd gone for jobs with the big news-gathering organizations, but there'd always been somebody better qualified, more experienced, perhaps more photogenic after the same job. For a long time he thought the broadcast media had something against a Welsh accent. When Huw Edwards did so well for himself, Jackson had to accept that it wasn't his accent putting off the news moguls; it was him. The *Norbold News* was going to be the high-water mark of his career.

What happened yesterday had made him think again. Made him wonder if there wasn't a little bit of life left in the dream. If the right story might not even now propel him to the fame he still secretly craved. Not a Pulitzer Prize, of course, but perhaps a British Press Award?

The right story. Well, maybe. At least some of the elements were there. The holy fool with his tragic background. The murdered boy. The O.K. Corral standoff between the last godfather and the lawman who'd made all the others history. If he could tell it right—if, first of all, he could work it out—this could be it. The breakthrough story. The one that the nationals, and the radio and TV, all picked up and ran with. And kept coming back to Nye Jackson for updates and analysis. He just had to get his byline repeated enough times and people at the sharp end would start thinking of him as one of them. This could be how—if he handled it right.

Gabriel Ash was the key. Jackson didn't know how—he didn't think Ash knew how—but journalistic instinct insisted that it was so. Of course, like any other storyteller, a journalist wants a tidy outcome, all the loose ends neatly tied. It makes the story more satisfying both to write and to read. It's easy for novelists. In this as in so many ways, life is messier than art.

If only he'd got the photograph. However fuzzy and pixilated, however stubbornly the story refused to come together, a real-time picture of a murder witness being bundled into a big dark car and a caption explaining how, and by whom, he was rescued would have made front pages across the country.

Except possibly, and Jackson still had to get his head around this, in Norbold. When he left Meadowvale to return to his office, to his surprise his editor had not so much congratulated him, or even suggested that it might have made still better news if the kidnapping had been allowed to continue, as warned him off.

Discreetly, of course. Journalists are an obstinate and contrary bunch; almost the only way of making them throw everything they've got into their work is to tell them there are stories they can't write. If Desmond Burnham had told his senior reporter to hold back on the Jerome Cardy murder, that he didn't want to publish any more than a bare statement of facts until someone was charged and convicted, the editor would have known that a rival paper would have the unexpurgated version before the end of the week, with everything but a *Look you* in the intro to identify the author.

So he hadn't done that. He'd talked about the relationship between the *Norbold News* and the town's police, and how it benefitted both parties. He reminded Jackson how fragile a relationship was when it relied entirely on trust, and how vital it was to do nothing to jeopardize that trust. Finally he let Jackson know—

Jackson wasn't sure now that he'd actually said the words—that Chief Superintendent Fountain would deem it a personal favor if the *News* could refrain from speculating about the Cardy murder until the IPCC had worked out whether there was more to it than met the eye, and if there was, found out what and charged somebody.

Jackson had stared at his editor with shock giving way quickly to outrage. "He wants to muzzle us?"

"Of course he doesn't want to muzzle us," retorted Burnham sharply. "And if he did, do you suppose I'd let him? He's trying to keep the bung in the powder keg. This isn't just a murder. It's the murder of a black youth by a white racist while they were both in a police cell. Are you old enough to remember Brixton and Broadwater Farm? There's nothing nastier than race riots, nothing harder to put back in the box.

"Right now there's one thing standing between Norbold and the sort of scenes that'll flash around the world before bedtime: that by the merest stroke of luck, Jerome Cardy was not a street kid from the Flying Horse but a law student and the son of a respectable, hardworking family. Not the obvious poster boy for a gang uprising. But the longer this goes on, the more likely it is that people will start to focus on the color of his skin. That's where it goes ballistic."

He gave a world-weary sigh. "That's what Fountain is desperate to avoid, and if he thinks we can help, I'm not going to tell him we're not prepared to. You'll get to write your story, when you can write the whole story and not leave gaps to be exploited by people who'd like nothing more than a good black-and-blue barney culminating in running battles through the center of town. This newspaper is not on the side of people who want to manufacture race riots."

And the words, even to Jackson's recalcitrant ears, made sense. Journalism is not now and never was a matter of dumping raw facts in front of the public. It is always necessary for someone to choose which facts to report and which to discard. It's what the word *editing* means. The most that can be hoped for is that the person doing the choosing is governed by good and honorable motives.

And yet . . .

Jackson had known his editor for six years. Des Burnham had been appointed over him, which caused a certain amount of irritation. He hadn't wanted the job, but he'd have liked the opportunity to turn it down. It wasn't even that Burnham was a world-class editor. He was overcautious, worried too much about what the owners wanted, what the advertisers wanted, and, yes, what the police might want. But he was straight. He had no hidden agenda. He did the job to the best of his ability.

This was different. Sitting on a story like this, for whatever reason, *couldn't* be the right decision. It had to be told. Carefully, yes, depriving anyone with an interest in rabble-rousing of ammunition, but told and told fully. A boy had died. A man had probably escaped the same fate by the narrowest of margins. Mickey Argyle was probably in it up to his neck. And Des Burnham, and Johnny Fountain, wanted to play it down?

"Bugger that for a game of soldiers," muttered Jackson, heading for his car.

The *Norbold News* was founded in 1898 and had published once or, later, twice every week since, including through the General Strike, two world wars, and the Winter of Discontent. That's a lot of back copies to file in a small and generally chaotic office. Like many newspapers, the *News* kept its archive on microfiche in the local library. That was where Nye Jackson went that Saturday afternoon.

He wasn't interested in copies going back a hundred years. He was interested in copies going back perhaps five years. Five years ago Jerome Cardy was fifteen—Jackson couldn't imagine he'd done anything much before that to annoy Mickey Argyle.

It was, he was ready to admit, quite a leap of faith, from the Cardy boy's being beaten to death by a local head-case to ultimate responsibility lying with Norbold's last surviving godfather. But reporter's instinct was putting it to him something like this: If something really bad happens in a town from which nearly all the really bad people have been removed, it makes sense to run a suspicious eye over those remaining. That was what he was doing: running a suspicious eye over Mickey Argyle and any connection he might have had with Jerome Cardy. He was doing it in the Norbold General Library because it was safer than chatting to the bouncer outside Argyle's snooker rooms.

Five years' worth of a biweekly newspaper is still over five hundred copies; at an average of twenty-eight per issue, that was fourteen thousand pages to scan. Jackson didn't propose to read every word on each of them. But, not knowing exactly what it was he was looking for, he knew he'd have to skim pretty well every item to be sure he wasn't missing anything. Then there were the photographs. There might be a hundred of them to an issue. Any one of them might hold a clue. He'd have to look at every one to be sure it didn't.

Although Argyle had run the drug trade in this town for longer than Jackson had lived here, the reporter was not so naïve as to expect to find a reference to that. When someone was picked up peddling his drugs, it wasn't Argyle's name that went on the charge sheet. When someone was dumped at Norbold Royal Infirmary A&E with his head broken by a snooker cue, Argyle may have been the prime suspect, but without evidence no one risked saying it aloud, let alone putting it in print. Mickey Argyle made the *Norbold News* when his club sponsored an under-fourteens snooker tournament, when he gave away his elder daughter in marriage to a Brazilian polo player, and when he bought himself a 1950s Rolls-Royce in a millionaires' charity auction. Those were the only references Jackson was able to find in five hours of hunting.

Funnily enough, in view of their respective significance to the town, there was more on Jerome Cardy. Jerome, age fifteen, winning the debating competition at Norbold Quays High School. Jerome, age sixteen, receiving the English Literature Award from his mother. Jerome, age seventeen, running a marathon for charity. Those were just the highlights. It had been a short career but an illustrious one. The boy full of promise grinning out of the photographs would have grown into the man he was born to be if he'd only had time. You'd like to think that anyone's death will be mourned by someone. But even the notoriously unsentimental Jackson recognized Jerome Cardy's death as a loss to all Norbold.

In the end he nearly missed it. It was just another photograph, pretty much like all the others he'd spent the last several hours looking at. This time it was Jerome Cardy presenting the mayoress with a bouquet of flowers after the school production of *The Tempest.* He'd played Prospero; she, if the photograph was anything to go by, had been bored.

It wasn't either of their faces that drew Nye Jackson's gaze. For half a minute he wasn't sure what it was. His brain was telling him there was something in that three-year-old group photograph that was significant, but for half a minute he couldn't see what it was.

Then he did. He'd seen one of the other faces in the picture before—not long before, while he was scrolling through this bloody microfiche. It took him another ten minutes to find it again, and to confirm that his eyes weren't playing tricks on him. The strange sparkly makeup might have confused him, but when Jackson made copies of both pictures and held them side by side, he no longer had any doubt.

It might mean nothing, or it might mean everything. Jackson needed to find out what it meant.

CHAPTER 18

HAZEL HAD EXHAUSTED all the other possibilities. She'd sought counsel inside her own head and done what she believed was right. She'd looked to her colleagues for support and met only silent recrimination. She'd even tried to find some sort of common ground with Gabriel Ash, only to have her offer of friendship thrown (so it felt) in her face. What do you do when the world turns against you? You go home.

It was a long drive—three hours, even using the motorways as far as she could, even on a Saturday afternoon. She didn't begrudge the time. It gave her the space to work out what she wanted to say—how to broach the subject without sounding pathetic. It mattered to her that her father didn't think she was pathetic. Not because he'd task her with it, but precisely because he wouldn't. He was—now, at fifty-nine, and had always been—a strong man who didn't need to trade on others' weaknesses to prove it. But she'd spent all her life admiring him and trying to live up to his example. It was going to be bad enough admitting to him that she'd failed. Letting him see how miserable she was would break her.

It was easy to find his cottage, even for strangers. You followed the signs for the big house, and Alfred Best lived in the gate lodge. He'd turned joiner when he left the army at forty, took a job maintaining the woodwork at Byrfield House. Peregrine, Lord Byrfield was often to be seen holding his ladder steady and peering anxiously up at his beetle-challenged rafters.

Hazel had grown up in the gatehouse. It had been an idyllic childhood, all the freedom of the Byrfield estate without the appalling prospect of inheriting it. When she'd left home, she'd thought it would always be here, always the same. But within twelve months her mother had died. Alfred had shouldered the loss as he shouldered every tribulation he met: manfully, with dignity, keeping his tears for when no one was around. Hazel had never seen him cry, but she knew it would be stupid, insulting even, to think that he didn't. That his grief had been any less than hers.

Now there were just the two of them. She saw him every six weeks or so. As soon as he heard her car on the gravel he knew there was a problem. He wasn't expecting her for another fortnight.

He was wearing the big canvas apron with all the pockets, rulers, pencils, and chisels distributed around them apparently at random, when he came out of the side gate. He'd been in the workshop. "Hazel? Is everything all right?"

She cast him a wan smile as she climbed out of the car. "Not exactly, Dad." Then all her good intentions went by the board, and she flung herself into his strong arms and wept down the front of his apron.

He said nothing more until he'd got her settled in the big armchair in the parlor, her hands wrapped around a mug of tea. Fred Best made possibly the worst tea in the civilized world—spoons didn't just stand up in it, they went toe-to-toe and fought. Hazel had never enjoyed a cup of bad tea more.

"All right," he said finally, the words rumbling up from the depths of his chest like lava, "what's happened?"

So she told him. All of it. All the things she thought she'd done right. All the things she was pretty sure she'd done wrong. All the likely consequences, and how quickly they'd kicked in.

Best listened in silence. It's something soldiers are good at. But he took it all in—every detail, every inflection of his daughter's voice, every expression that flickered across her face. By the time she'd finished he knew everything she did, and possibly understood more.

"So then you got in the car and drove a hundred and forty miles, and I'm supposed to make it all better?" His eyes were a clear bright blue, filled with compassion, sparkling with anger, and laced with just a little bit of humor because this was how they had always faced the world—together, and without self-pity.

"Making me *feel* better will do," said Hazel, smiling at him through the steam off her tea.

"You don't need me to tell you that what you did was right."

"No?" It was more than half a question. "I thought it was right when I did it. I think, when I'm looking back in two years' time, I'll think it was right again. Today, I just don't know."

"Yes, you do," said Fred Best.

"Yes, I do," admitted Hazel. "I just . . . I didn't expect it to be so *hard*. I thought people would at least *try* to be professional. I know they've known Murchison a lot longer than they've known me. And maybe, in spite of everything, I'm wrong. But I thought they'd see that I had no choice. I *couldn't* think what I did and say nothing. Not when someone had died. If I've got it wrong, the IPCC will say so. I'm willing to wait for the result of the inquiry—why can't everyone else?"

"*Because* they've known this sergeant a lot longer than they've known you. They don't want to believe he's capable of letting them down like that. It's much easier to believe that someone they've known for just a couple of months is being stupid, or even malicious." He refilled the mugs from an enormous dark brown teapot. All his movements were slow and deliberate, and that was the way he thought, too. Slow, deliberate, and to fine tolerances. "What about this man Ash? Do you believe what he told you?"

"That the whole of Meadowvale has gone rogue? Of course I don't."

Best regarded her steadily. He wasn't a big man. But even wearing an old apron and holding a mug bearing the legend *Carpenters have a vice—they do it on the bench,* he had a presence. All her life he'd been the rocky core at the center of Hazel's existence. "Is that what he said?"

She made herself revisit the conversation, or that part of it before she lost her temper. "Not exactly. He thought there *was* a conspiracy—anything from two or three people up."

"He thinks two or three people out of the whole Meadowvale staff are up to no good. And you're pretty sure at least one is. Tell me again why you're so angry with this new friend of yours."

"He's not really . . ." she began, then the logic of what Fred was saying caught up with her. She sighed. "You're right, aren't you? And so's Ash. If Sergeant Murchison couldn't have done everything that was done alone, then he had help. Whether he was acting alone, or there were a few of them involved, really isn't the central point. I don't know why I flew off the handle when he suggested it."

"Because you're feeling vulnerable," said her father, "with every reason. You've found yourself in a position no one in their right mind would want to be in—you're the new girl in school and you've caught the head prefect cheating. That's bad enough, without thinking half the upper sixth is involved as well!"

Almost against her inclination, the image made her smile. "I expected a bit more support from the headmaster, too."

"I suppose he has a vested interest in believing you're mistaken. If there's something rotten in his police station, what does it say about his leadership? One of two things: either he knew or he should have done."

Despite everything that had gone before, Hazel was moved to defend him. "That's a bit harsh! Johnny Fountain has worked wonders in Norbold. It's not his fault if a couple of bad apples have got into the barrel."

"No," agreed Fred. "But it's part of his job to lift the lid from time to time and have a good sniff."

As always, talking with her father, coming up against his yeoman blend of insight and pragmatism, put things into perspective for Hazel. He grounded her. When he died, she'd be cut adrift from the greatest source of her strength. Like a sail flapping free: all noise and activity, no power or direction.

If she'd had no choice about the course she'd taken, there was nothing to agonize over. Whether she was proved right or wrong, and wherever the fault was deemed to lie, she'd done what was required of her, as a police officer and as a decent human being. If her colleagues couldn't cope with that, it was their problem. Maybe they'd come around. Maybe they'd hold a grudge, like children. Hazel had been a teacher; she'd dealt with sulky children before. The main thing, she'd found, was not to buy into their illusion of being mistreated. All children, even sulky ones, respect fairness. Continuing to treat them fairly, and keeping a sense of humor, won over most of them in the end. Probably what worked for sulky children would also work for policemen.

Hazel felt a new sense of purpose, of weight lifting off her shoulders, of blood coursing through her veins. It had been worth the drive. It always was.

"Get cleaned up. I'm taking you out for dinner. And then," she added reflectively, "I owe Gabriel Ash an apology."

As soon as he thought Monday-morning assembly would be over, Nye Jackson paid a visit to Norbold Quays High School. The head of the English department was Mrs. Cardy; as she was on compassionate leave, Jackson asked for her deputy. He was directed to the staff room and told Mr. Burtonshaw would be along in ten minutes.

Before Mr. Burtonshaw arrived, though, someone had told the head teacher that a reporter was hanging around, and Miss Lim descended on the staff room like a small, exquisitely groomed typhoon.

All her life Elizabeth Lim had been mistaken for something soft and delicate. It's true that she was small and had the composed and modest manner of many Asian women. But concealed among the cherry blossoms was a mind like a blade and a steely determination. It's not easy for anyone to become the head teacher of a sizable English comprehensive school. For a girl from a family of Chinese immigrants it was a major achievement; but most people found their surprise diminishing as they got to know her. In repose she had the stillness of a fine porcelain figurine. But the Chinese didn't just invent porcelain. They also invented fireworks.

Nye Jackson had been thrown out of more places than he could remember, sometimes verbally, sometimes bodily. He always went back, and he usually got what he'd gone for, and he looked on it as an occupational hazard, like parking tickets—an inconvenience rather than a humiliation. All the same, being thrown out of a school by someone who was smaller than he was *and* wearing a twinset and pearls wouldn't be quickly forgotten.

"Mr. Jackson," she began—she spoke perfect English, with not so much an accent as a slightly distinctive rhythm of speech—"I believe that if you have questions to ask in my school, the person to see is me." On paper it looks a fairly mild opening gambit. But it wasn't. There were ninja stars in every word.

"Sorry, Miss Lim, I thought the head of English should be my first call." It wasn't entirely sincere—he'd hoped to avoid the head teacher precisely because she'd give him the third degree—but it was close enough to the frontier of reasonable to draw some of her venom.

"Mrs. Cardy is on leave," she replied stiffly. "I thought you'd be aware of that."

"Yes, of course. But Mr. Burtonshaw produces the school play, doesn't he?" He was in the photograph along with Jerome and the mayoress.

"Usually," Miss Lim acknowledged warily. "Mr. Jackson, what is this all about?"

He produced the photocopy he'd made at the library. "I was putting together an obituary on Jerome," he lied fluently. "I thought I might use this photograph. I hoped Mr. Burtonshaw could tell me who the other people in it are."

Largely mollified by now, Miss Lim was saved from having to admit that Ernest Burtonshaw was indeed the man Jackson needed to speak to by the timely arrival of the deputy head of English. He was older than either of the women he worked under, bald to the point of having nothing to comb over, and wearing the English teacher's uniform of a corduroy jacket with leather elbow patches.

He took the photocopy and angled it to the light. "*The Tempest*. That's—what, three years ago? Jerome as Prospero, Mary Miller as Miranda, the Woods boy with the broken nose as Caliban. He was a shoo-in. And just about the best Ariel I ever saw. Do you remember?" he asked Miss Lim. "Everyone told me it was crazy casting, but I knew it would work. Ariel's a sprite, for God's sake—whoever you cast, there's got to be some suspension of disbelief!"

"I remember," said Miss Lim with a slow smile. "It was a very fine play." She looked over his shoulder at the photocopy, at the tall black youth in the center, and gave a whisper of a sigh. "So much promise. Such a loss."

Some instinct for tact Jackson hadn't known he had urged him to allow a moment for their memories. Then, pen poised, he said, "And who was it playing Ariel?"

CHAPTER 19

HER HEART FORTIFIED by her father's words, her mind calmed by a weekend in his company, and her intestines armor-plated by his tea, Hazel drove back to Norbold on Monday morning. She headed first to Meadowvale, parking her car in the most prominent spot she could find. The fact that it bore a small plate with the words SENIOR STAFF ONLY caused her no concern, only a grim satisfaction. She wanted it to be seen. She was ready for an argument. She might move the car, because she had no right to the spot, but that was about as far as she was going to compromise.

She was heading for Chief Superintendent Fountain's office when he met her on the stairs, gripped her arm in one large hand, and had her heading down again before she knew it. "What do you think you're doing?" he demanded softly.

"Reporting for duty, sir." Hazel made no effort to keep her voice low. "I thought I'd just let you know . . ."

He stopped dead, and again she had no choice but to match him. He looked at her with a glowering mixture of annoyance, incomprehension, and grudging respect. She looked at his hand. After a moment he let go, and she looked him full in the face.

She'd changed. He didn't know what had happened, but

something had. And now it didn't matter what was best for Meadowvale, or what was best for him, because nothing he or any of them could do would intimidate her. She was calm, polite, and utterly determined. The Maid of Orleans at the head of her army. Except that Hazel Best had no army behind her, only a basket-case neurotic and his mangy dog. And everyone knows what happened to Joan of Arc.

"I thought I'd let you know," she repeated, clipping the words out like thumbing rounds into a magazine, "I'll be working my shifts from now on unless I'm told different."

Fountain found himself blinking. "Is that a good idea, do you think?"

"It's what I'm paid for," said Hazel levelly.

"You could take some of your annual leave."

"Right now, there's nowhere I need to be as much as I need to be here."

Fountain sighed. It was hard not to admire her. Even if she had no idea what she was letting herself in for. "Not everyone's going to be happy working with you."

"Then perhaps they should take *their* annual leave. Sir," she said, "let me make this clear. To the best of my knowledge and belief, I have done nothing wrong. I had suspicions, and I reported them. As I am required to do. Maybe the inquiry will prove me wrong. I hope it does. But that won't alter the fact that what I did was right. This is awkward for all of us—Sergeant Murchison, me, you, everyone who works with us. But we're all adults, so I suggest we try to behave that way. Put this to one side and do our own jobs until the people whose job it is to investigate have done theirs.

"Donald Murchison isn't going off on leave, is he? And I don't imagine you are. Well, neither am I. I'm not going to act as if I created this situation. If you can't cope with having me here, you'd better suspend me."

Their eyes met with a clang like hammer on anvil. Hazel was utterly astonished at herself. She *never* spoke to people like that. And this was her chief superintendent, the man who held her professional life in the palm of his hand. All she could think was that she'd burned so many boats already, the hot resin smell and the merry crackle had gone to her head.

And yet she wasn't sorry. It had needed saying; she had needed to say it. Maybe it would be easier to live with the consequences of taking on the police establishment and losing than being afraid to take it on at all.

"Don't make me do that." The regret in his voice was genuine. He'd hardly noticed her before all this came up; now there was no ignoring her. It was a damned nuisance, and she was leaving him with few options, but he still couldn't help feeling that the service needed more officers like her, not fewer. Only, somewhere else and some other time.

"I don't think I've any choice," said Hazel doggedly. "If I'm not on shift today, and people ask why not, I want it clear that it was your call, not mine. If it turns out to be a bad one, it won't affect your career. But if people here think I'm afraid to face them, it'll destroy mine."

"It matters that much to you?" he asked softly.

"Yes." She sounded surprised. "It seems it does."

He thought a little longer, but not much. "Suspension it is, then. In the interests of the efficient operation of this police station. On full pay, of course, pending the outcome of the IPCC inquiry." He managed a tight-lipped little smile. "Who'd have thought a Hazel would turn out to be such a tough little nut? You want it official, it's official. And when this is all over . . ."

Hazel grew tired of waiting and prompted him. "What, sir?"

"I hope neither of us has any regrets."

An idea was starting to form in Nye Jackson's ginger head. He had no evidence for it, not in the photograph, not in anything Ash had said. Perhaps it had its genesis in his own fund of knowledge—of human nature in general and Mickey Argyle in particular.

If there was any truth in it, the evidence would exist somewhere. The question was where to look. So he started from where he was and worked toward where he wanted to be. He started with the photograph of *The Tempest* and the Woods boy who was a shoo-in for Caliban.

Tom Woods had graduated from schoolboy rugby—which was how he'd broken his nose originally—to the proper grown-up game, where he'd broken it twice more. His profile was now like the contour map of a banana republic. When he wasn't playing rugby, he was studying for a structural engineering degree at Coventry University.

Jackson arranged to meet him at the college library. He got the impression that he was more familiar with libraries than the student was.

He produced the photograph as a memory aid, but Woods remembered well enough. A big grin spread across his striking and still oddly handsome face. "Old Burtonshaw was an absolute gag! He should never be trusted among the young and impressionable. The man's an total anarchist."

"*Were* you that impressionable?" asked Jackson doubtfully.

"Oh no, not a bit," said Woods cheerfully. "None of us were. We were all pretty well grounded. And, it should be admitted, fairly anarchistic in our own right."

"Including Jerome Cardy?"

"Jerome? Well, less than the rest of us. He suffered the terrible handicap of having been nicely brought up. One day he'll make someone a wonderful mother."

Jackson felt the jolt somewhere under his heart. "You haven't heard."

Tom Woods read the sports pages and, if pressed, papers on engineering. "Heard what?"

The reporter told him what had happened. He watched the blood drain from the young man's face. "That's . . . crazy! He was the *last* one to get involved in anything. . . ." The sentence petered out.

"I'm sorry," said Jackson. "I didn't realize this would be news to you."

"When?"

"Last week. Wednesday night."

"And it was as . . . as mindless as that? He was just in the wrong place at the wrong time?"

The reporter shrugged, a shade disingenuously. "Seems like it. There'll be a police inquiry, of course, but that's the theory."

"And . . . what do you want from me? I haven't seen that much of him lately." Woods might have been shocked, and he might not have been the most intellectual student at Coventry, but he wasn't stupid. He wasn't going to elbow in on the story because he was flattered to be asked.

"The school play," said Jackson, showing the photocopy. "That was one of his triumphs at Norbold. I thought it would be nice to ask fellow actors for their memories of him."

"Oh—yes, okay."

"I've talked to Ernest Burtonshaw. And you. What about Ariel?"

Despite the shock, Woods smiled, remembering. "That was a brave bit of casting. I don't think anyone's ever thought of Ariel as a girl's part. But Alice was superb. She dusted talcum powder through her hair and put something sparkly in her slap, and she looked absolutely like some kind of elemental."

"I imagine she'll remember him."

"Oh yes . . ."

There was something about the way he said it, and then didn't say anything more, that set bells ringing in Jackson's synapses. As if Woods had stumbled over a trip wire attached to the journalist's toe. "Tom?"

"Nothing," said the student quickly. "I was just . . . thinking . . ."

Jackson regarded him levelly. What it was Tom Woods was thinking he clearly didn't want to share. That didn't mean he couldn't be persuaded to. "Did they keep in touch after they left Norbold Quays? Jerome and Alice. Were they, in fact, a bit of a number?"

It was a complete shot in the dark. Nothing anyone had said suggested as much. But if true, it opened up a shedload of possibilities. And if it wasn't, Woods would probably know and say so, and save Jackson a lot of time and effort.

Tom Woods remained circumspect. "No harm to you, Mr. Jackson, but it's not my place to comment on something like that to the *Norbold News*. Especially if—now—Jerome's dead. Certainly they were friends. We were all friends."

"That's not the sort of friendship I'm talking about," said Jackson quietly, "and you know it."

The rugby player flushed. "You should ask . . ." Again he ended the sentence without finishing it.

"I should ask Alice?"

"Yes. No! Look, it's difficult. You know who her father is, don't you?" Jackson nodded. "And Jerome was . . ."

"Jerome was black."

If he'd been that forthright with someone of his own generation, they'd have hemmed and hawed and said there were lots of reasons, because racism was something they abhorred in principle but suspected they might still harbor in practice. Tom Woods's generation had come out the far side of political correctness. They were much more confident of their antiracist credentials.

"Well spotted," said Woods tartly. "Which wouldn't have mattered if she'd been just about *anybody* else. If her father had been anybody else."

"He didn't like the idea?"

Woods looked at the reporter sharply. "No, he didn't like the idea. That wasn't the problem. The problem was, he's the kind of man who doesn't just settle for disapproval. We're not talking Spencer Tracy and Sidney Poitier here—if he'd found out about them, he'd have . . . done . . . something . . ." His expression changed as the words distilled the thoughts. His voice came hollow. "And now Jerome's dead. Don't tell me that's a coincidence."

Jackson gave a little shrug. "There's no question about who killed him. There were only the two of them in there."

"What does that prove?" demanded Jerome's friend. "People get killed in prison because someone on the outside wants them dead. People on the *outside* get killed because someone inside wants them dead. Mickey Argyle is not just bad, he's powerful. He has a long reach. You want a story, Mr. Jackson, you find out how Alice's father could have set a maniac on her black boyfriend."

CHAPTER 20

NOT FOR THE FIRST time, Hazel Best thanked whatever gods watched over her that she'd found lodgings in town rather than taken the easy route of bunking in the station house. At least in the back bedroom of Mrs. Poliakov's Villa Biala she could avoid policemen without it looking as if she was avoiding policemen.

She lay on her bed for ten minutes, listening to Mrs. Poliakov cleaning—the redoubtable Polish woman devoted great time and energy to household duties, although she had no talent for them—and looking over the rooftops to the uppermost branches of the trees in the park. It wasn't the kind of view that tourists would flock for, but Hazel had always found it both pleasant and calming. It was the main reason she put up with Mrs. Poliakov's cooking.

Then she got up and went out again. She had fences to mend with Gabriel Ash, if he'd let her in.

For a surreal moment she thought the dog had answered the door. The explanation was much more prosaic. It wasn't closed properly, so it opened when she reached for the knocker; the dog just happened to be in the hall at the time.

The unsettling thing about Gabriel Ash's world, she thought, was that it existed just on the cusp of sanity, where in an unguarded moment a normal person might cross the line without noticing. It was important not to allow herself to be drawn into the fantasy, to keep one eye firmly fixed on what she knew to be real. He was a man with a dog; that was all. He talked to it because he'd no one else to talk to. But it was just a dog—an intelligent dog, a dog that benefitted from its owner's undivided attention, but still just a dog. It didn't answer doors. It didn't smile a welcome, or glance an invitation to the kitchen, and when it barked, just once, it wasn't calling anyone; it was just reacting to the appearance of an intruder.

Despite knowing all this, Hazel didn't feel remotely threatened by the barking dog in the hall, and she did go into the kitchen and sit down.

A moment later Ash appeared with a book in his hand. He glanced at her as if she'd popped across the road for a paper, not stormed out forty-eight hours earlier with a volley of parting shots that were, if memory served her right—and she was horribly afraid it did—both insulting and offensive. "I'm reading *Othello*," he said by way of a greeting.

"Er—good," she said. "Gabriel, I owe you an apology."

He looked up blankly. "Yes?"

"I was very rude to you. And I jumped down your throat when you didn't deserve it. All I can say in my own defense is, I was suffering from divided loyalties. But I am sorry."

He had a way of focusing on what most people considered unimportant details. "Was?"

Hazel drew a deep breath and nodded. "I still consider myself part of the police family, but it seems no one else feels the same way. I went into Meadowvale this morning and found my bag metaphorically packed and waiting on the stairs."

Ash's eyes widened. "They've *sacked* you?"

"Suspended me." It wasn't much of an amendment, but Hazel felt it necessary to make it. She flicked him a smile that came and went in a moment. "On full pay."

"Oh, that's all right, then." But the words were ironic—his eyes were appalled. He knew what it meant to her. He also knew what had provoked it. She'd supported him. She'd listened to him and supported him. "Hazel, I'm so sorry. . . ."

"Don't be." The smile lasted longer this time, bright and brittle. "In a way it simplifies things. I thought we could all be sufficiently professional about what happened to get on with our work until there's some kind of a resolution. But that was naïve. This is just too huge."

"So . . . what will you do?"

She put out her hand for the book. "I'll read *Othello,* too."

Ash didn't surrender the volume. His expression was somber, concerned. "Hazel—don't give the impression you're working against them. Fountain and the rest of Meadowvale. If it turns out we're right about the rotten apples, they just might, in time, forgive you for raising the suspicion. They'll never forgive you for trying to prove it."

"Then sod them," she snarled. "I didn't join the police in order to make other police officers happy. I joined—sorry to sound so pious—to help the vast majority of the population who *aren't* police officers. And no one's going to convince me that the public interest is served by protecting officers who are lazy, stupid, or corrupt."

Hazel heard herself, heard the anger in her own voice, and

made a conscious effort to lower her tone. "Sorry. It's just that, for a while there, I wondered if it might be worth backing off for the sake of a quiet life. I suppose I'm rather ashamed of that."

"You have nothing to be ashamed of," Ash retorted firmly. "You've shown real courage. But now it's time to keep your head down. You don't need to rub their faces in the fact that you were not only bright enough to see that something was amiss at Meadowvale when no one else was but also brave enough to do something about it. IPCC will work out what Sergeant Murchison did, whether it was an honest mistake or something worse, and whether anyone else was involved. They don't need any more help from you."

"IPCC won't have . . ." Realizing she couldn't finish the sentence without giving offense, Hazel let it hang. Immediately, though, she knew it was too late. She hadn't known Ash very long, but already she knew he had a talent for hearing not only what had been said but also what had nearly been said.

"Won't have all the information?" he said, finishing the sentence for her. "Why not? You've told them everything you know."

"Yes. But . . ." This time she took a deep breath and said it. "I believe that you heard and saw pretty much what you say you heard and saw. They won't."

"They won't?" He thought about it, got a picture of himself as others saw him, and nodded ruefully. "Ah. Rambles With Dogs."

"And that'll be the end of it"—she nodded fiercely—"if I leave it to the IPCC. Donald Murchison will get a slap on the wrist. They may think he made an honest mistake. They may think something else but be unable to prove it. He'll get a slap on the wrist, you'll be written off as an unreliable witness, and I'll get a note in my file saying I'm a troublemaker. And that's three injustices. Maybe you don't mind what people say about you, but

I do. I'm not going to wait patiently to hear whether I'll be trusted with a responsible job ever again."

Ash looked worried. "What are you going to do?"

"Try to put it together." Until she said the words, Hazel hadn't realized the idea was anywhere in her head. But as soon as they were out she knew it was the right thing to do. "We've got a lot of the pieces already. What Jerome said to you. What you heard and saw later that night. What Saturday said about Trucker and Barclay. If Argyle wanted Jerome dead, he could have sent Trucker to get Barclay riled up and got Donald Murchison to do the rest. Murchison knew how to kill the CCTV so there'd be no record of it. All we're short of is a motive. If we had that, IPCC would know it wasn't just bad luck."

A terrible thought struck Ash. "You're not going to ask him? Go to Mickey Argyle and ask him?"

Hazel had to think for a moment but then dismissed the idea. "No, of course not." It would have been a mistake. Not because she was afraid of him, although she was, but because he wouldn't tell her anything—and he *would* then know she was on his trail. That would be both dangerous and counterproductive. She could prove nothing if he locked her in a room with one of his thugs. "Our tutors always used to say, 'Try not to ask questions until you've at least some idea what the answers should be.'"

"Who else could you ask? Someone at Meadowvale?" The look she gave him was answer enough. "What about the local paper?"

"That reporter—Jackson." Her voice sharpened with sudden possibility. "He seemed to know a fair bit about Argyle, didn't he? And he knows that he's involved—he saw his heavies snatch you off the street. Okay. I'll call the *News*."

"Wait." For the first time in their acquaintance Ash reached out and touched her—laid his hand on top of hers as she pulled out her phone. The strength in his long, bony fingers surprised her. "Think about this."

"*Think* about it?" she echoed, startled. "I've thought about nothing else for nearly a week! I haven't slept for thinking about it. If I think any more about it, I'll go mad. It's time to *do* something."

"Thinking about it might cost you sleep, but it won't make you mad." He spoke as one who'd done the experiment. "Doing something may very well get you hurt. It could get you killed. If there *was* a conspiracy to murder Jerome Cardy, and if you draw attention to yourself, those responsible may decide it would be safer to silence you than to let you rattle on."

"'Draw attention to myself'? Gabriel, that boat's sailed! They're sticking pins in little Hazel dolls all over Meadowvale! Everybody knows what I've done, everybody has an opinion. Pandora's box is wide open, it's too late to start stuffing things back in. And do you know, I'm not sure I would if I could? Covering up awkward facts is not what I joined the police to do. Let them out—let them all out where the air can get at them! Do you know what was left at the bottom of Pandora's box when all the evils of the world had escaped?"

"Hope," murmured Gabriel Ash.

"Exactly."

"You think, if you can prove you're right, you can wipe the slate clean."

"I don't know. But I know this. When you're in too far to turn back, through is the only way out."

Nye Jackson drove back to Norbold, his lips shaping silently Othello's closing speech. The boy hadn't been raving, and neither had Gabriel Ash. Jerome Cardy had made the same mistake as Othello, and he'd found a way of telling his cell mate without the policeman at the door noticing. He'd been a smart boy—at least in most respects. He'd also taken a gamble—that Ash would remember what he said and pass it on to someone who might make sense of it. Most people who knew Ash wouldn't have thought it a gamble worth taking. But Jerome hadn't had many options, so he worked with what he had.

Jackson parked in his accustomed spot behind the boot factory, on a bit of waste ground handy for the newspaper's back door. As he locked the car the words were dancing in his head. *Then must you speak of one . . .* He hadn't remembered the lines exactly. He'd used his phone to look them up on the Internet. And there it was: the reason Jerome had to die. What he'd done that was so terrible another man wanted to kill him for it. . . . *Of one that loved not wisely, but too well.* Jerome Cardy, talented actor, promising law student, and black, had fallen in love with Mickey Argyle's younger daughter.

Jackson had been a reporter for too long to think that all he had to do was write the story and justice would be served. The toughest libel laws in the world made it possible for a dishonest man to sue an honest newspaper for reporting the truth and walk away with millions. But Jackson knew what had happened now, and he knew what to do about it. First talk to his editor. Then talk to Dave Gorman and Johnny Fountain. And while they were investigating there was nothing to stop him putting some of what he'd learned on record. He could write about Jerome Cardy without risk of prejudice. Remind people of his outstanding school career, and that memorable production of *The Tempest* where he shared the acting honors with the girl who played Ariel.

He was thinking along these lines, and resisting the urge to skip, as he crossed the rough tarmac of the back alley.

He almost got there. Another three strides and he'd have been safe in the *News* building, at least for now. Of course, the car that hit him didn't come out of nowhere—they never do. But he didn't see it coming, certainly not in time to avoid it, not even in time to recognize it. It swept him up like a sudden tornado, threw him into the air, and flung him down on the back steps of the *Norbold News*.

CHAPTER 21

ASH SAW HAZEL'S face change as she talked on—or rather, listened to—her phone. Age crept up on her. So he knew it wasn't good news.

When she'd finished, she quietly put the phone away and turned to meet his troubled gaze. "Nye Jackson's dead."

At first, for more than a few seconds, Ash thought he'd misheard. "Sorry—he's . . . what?"

"He's dead, Gabriel." Her voice was flat, the calm of the professional at delivering bad news, but her eyes were shocked and appalled and filling with tears. "He was run down by a car in Tanner's Alley about an hour ago. He was dead before they got him to A&E."

There were probably forty thousand cars in and around Norbold. Most of them would not be large and black. In spite of which, Ash felt he'd seen it happen. "Not an accident." It wasn't even really a question.

Hazel shrugged helplessly. "No one saw. There's a security camera over the back door at the *News* offices, but it missed what happened. Just caught a corner of the roof as it sped off. A big estate, they thought. Black. No registration."

No, thought Ash. Entry-level blagging for men who worked for Mickey Argyle would include the field of view of every CCTV in town. Finally he said, "It was Mickey Argyle. You know that, don't you?"

Hazel nodded. Her head felt like someone else's. "I imagine so. Why?"

"Because he interfered when Argyle sent for me." Guilt thickened Ash's voice.

It may also have clouded his judgment. Hazel wasn't convinced. "His people didn't hurt you—why should they hurt Nye? You might, if you were that sort of man, kill the eyewitness to a murder. You don't kill someone who saw you drop litter."

He saw her point. It wasn't a proportionate response. Whatever it was that Jackson prevented, all he actually saw was a man being helped into a car and then helped out of it. Nothing Argyle could do to Nye Jackson was as smart as nothing at all. Any attack on him would have elevated a minor incident into a major one; killing him told the world that the reporter was on to something big. Norbold's last surviving godfather had no reason to draw attention to himself like that. "Then why?"

Hazel was trying to think. "Where did he go when he left us?"

"Back to his office to talk to his editor."

"That was on Friday. What's he been doing since?"

But Ash had no idea. "I haven't seen him."

"I bet Mickey Argyle has," Hazel said curtly. "I bet Mickey Argyle had him watched from the moment he took that pretend photograph outside the Cardys' house. But that's not why he killed him. He killed him because of something Jackson discovered in the last twenty-four hours."

Ash could go very still when his attention was engaged. "Like what?"

"Like what's had us all puzzled—the link between Argyle and Jerome Cardy. We know there has to be one. I think Nye Jackson found it."

"And Argyle killed him because of it." Ash reached a decision. He put his book down and tried to steer Hazel toward the front door. "You have to leave. Now. Leave here; leave Norbold. Go and stay with your father. It's not safe for you here."

Hazel blinked. "Me? What have I done?" Then she saw it from Argyle's viewpoint. "Apart, of course, from telling IPCC that his tame policeman facilitated the murder of a twenty-year-old boy who'd somehow displeased him. Yes, I see what you mean."

"There's no one to protect you now," warned Ash. "The people at Meadowvale have shut you out. Argyle would have hesitated at taking on the local police, but now he's wondering if he needs to think of you as police anymore. You're alone and you're vulnerable. Getting rid of you would serve both Argyle's needs and Sergeant Murchison's."

"This isn't Chicago! Things like that don't happen here." But even as she said it Hazel knew that she was wrong. The evidence was there. Jerome Cardy was murdered in a police cell at the behest of Norbold's last gangster; and a man'd who made it his business to find out why was lying in the morgue at Norbold Royal Infirmary. Of course she was a target. She'd dared to suspect the unthinkable. If Argyle's handy little setup was under threat—if he was in danger of losing his insiders at Meadowvale, and the freedom and power they bought him—it was her doing.

If she were to disappear now, the possibility that she'd been neutralized by Argyle might not be the first thing IPCC thought of. They knew how difficult things at Meadowvale had become for her. They knew Fountain had put her on suspension. They'd wonder if she'd run away with her tail between her legs because the whole thing had suddenly got heavier than she ever expected. If she'd let her imagination run away with her, and was only now realizing how slight her evidence was and how unlikely she was to be vindicated.

Ash saw in her eyes when the understanding fell into place. He nodded. "If you disappear, they'll all think you had second thoughts and couldn't face admitting it. They'll finish the investigation, they'll have to, but it won't be much more than a paper exercise if they think the whistle blower has cut and run. They'll rap some knuckles, tell Mr. Fountain to tighten up his procedures, and in all probability that'll be that."

"That's what'll happen if I bugger off to my dad's place, too!"

"Maybe. But you can come back from . . ." He raised an expectant eyebrow.

"Byrfield," Hazel told him "It's near Peterborough."

"From Byrfield. You can't come back from the foundations of Mickey Argyle's kitchen extension."

For someone who, for four years, had rationed his words like a smoker finishing his last packet before quitting, Gabriel Ash had an unexpected facility with them. The picture they painted hung before Hazel's unblinking eyes. This wasn't an exercise she was involved in, a challenge to her deductive powers, or even a moral dilemma, but something that could get her killed. Something that had already claimed two innocent victims would have no difficulty claiming another. She was twenty-six. This had the potential to stop her from reaching twenty-seven. Unless she got out, and got far, far away right now.

Her voice stumbled. "I can't go to my father. Anyone could find me there."

"All right. Go somewhere you've never been before. Go

pony trekking in Snowdonia. Take a Mediterranean cruise. Anything. Go, go now, and don't leave a trail. You can phone me to see if there are any developments. I won't phone you. I don't want your number."

Their eyes met and neither was prepared to look away. She knew exactly what Ash was saying. That he didn't want to be able to betray her if Argyle hurt him.

Finally Hazel understood that the damaged man in front of her knew more about these things than she did. That he'd operated at a level that made the apprehension of disorderly drunks and the confiscation of the occasional machete seem trivial. His experience, his expertise, made her look like a school monitor. But for the atrocity visited upon him, Constable Best would never have heard Gabriel Ash's name until it appeared on an Honors List for undefined services to the nation.

He had a clearer idea what to expect than she had. It didn't matter if he talked to his dog: if he talked to *her*, she had to listen. And not just to what he said but to what he didn't want to say. Hazel let out a slow, careful breath. "If it's not safe for me to stay here, it's not safe for you."

Ash tried to make light of it. "I'll be fine. Nobody cares what I think because nobody believes what I say."

"Argyle's already tried to grab you once. He knows who you are. He knows you were there when Jerome was murdered."

"I don't think he'll try to kidnap me again."

"*I* don't think he'll try to kidnap you again, either," retorted Hazel sharply. "Things have moved on from there. He's not taking any more chances. That's why Nye Jackson's dead. If Argyle deals with both of us, he has nothing left to fear."

Ash tried for a confident grin. He looked like a schoolboy telling fibs to his teacher. "Patience will look after me."

Hazel looked at the dog. Then she looked back at Ash. "Bulletproof, is she?"

Ash swallowed. "Probably not. What do you suggest?"

"That we both leave. All right"—she anticipated his objection—"that all three of us leave. Now—as soon as you can pack a bag. We'll find a motel and book in under a false name, and we'll stay there until it's safe to come home."

"Er . . ." Hazel thought for a moment that it was the idea of booking into a motel under an assumed name with a young woman that was making him hesitate. Because he still thought of himself as a married man. But it wasn't that. "I don't think a motel . . ."

She realized where he was going before he'd finished the sentence, and rolled her eyes to the ceiling in a *God give me strength!* kind of way. "No, you're right. A motel might not take the dog. So we'll look for a farm cottage, maybe, or a caravan park. We'll find something. Look at it this way. The harder we have to hunt, the harder it'll be for Argyle to find us. We'll leave no trail for him to follow. I'll let IPCC know what we're doing, but nobody else—and after I've talked to them I'll dump the phone and buy a new one. We have to be very, very careful. We have to think of everything. If we do that, we'll be safe."

"For how long?"

"As long as it takes."

He persevered. "As long as *what* takes? Hazel—how do you think this is going to end?"

She hadn't actually got that far. "I suppose, one of two ways. If we're not careful enough, it ends with both of us dead, Barking Mad Barclay in Broadmoor, and the file on Jerome's murder closed. If Argyle can't get to us, it ends when someone gets to him."

"Who? Fountain? IPCC?" The problem with that was that

Mickey Argyle wasn't IPCC's problem, and Johnny Fountain had been trying to get him for ten years, without success.

"He killed Jerome Cardy! He killed Nye Jackson. They'll pull out all the stops—they'll have to." Hazel was trying very hard to believe it.

"Only if they see the connection. There's no more evidence that Argyle is responsible for Jackson's death than there was tying him to Jerome's. I *know* they didn't believe what I told them. If they dismiss what you told them as well, there isn't much of a case left. We could be in that farm cottage a long time."

"We'll convince them," said Hazel doggedly. "We have to. No offense, but I'm not spending the rest of my life in a rented cottage in Leicestershire with you and Patience."

Ash nodded as if he understood. "Fair enough. Only, why Leicestershire?" He was already pulling a battered suitcase out from under the stairs.

"There's a lot of nothing in Leicestershire. Easy to get lost."

CHAPTER 22

"WELL—THIS is nice."

It wasn't. It was a dump. It smelled of rodents and damp bedding, and they were to find that the nose had it in both cases.

But the cottage offered something that none of the others they'd passed could: total anonymity. If they'd tried to rent a property from an estate agent, they'd have been asked to prove who they were and a record of that would have existed on a computer. What exists on one computer can be accessed by another, if the operator is clever enough, and a man who could hire both killers and policemen could certainly hire a computer geek.

This run-down little hovel, hardly better than animal housing, had been home more likely than not to some elderly farmer's unmarried sisters until the last of them died, leaving the overflowing gutters to meet the rising damp halfway up the stairs and the farmer's eldest son with a barely habitable property to let out until probate could be finalized. He'd made the To Let sign with some paint he had left over from doing his cow shed, and seemed astonished beyond measure when someone came to his door to express an interest. He didn't ask them to prove who they were. It was enough that they offered him cash.

"I'll get a fire started."

Hazel was still looking around in horror and incredulity at where she was proposing to spend the next weeks or months, or possibly the last days, of her life. Mrs. Poliakov's, or even the station house, seemed like gracious living by comparison. There were three bedrooms upstairs, each with a single bed that hadn't been changed since its last occupant left feetfirst. Dust bunnies played in the corners of the rooms when she opened the doors. "Sorry . . . what?"

"It'll seem better once we've got a fire going."

"No, it won't!" she cried, despairing. "It's a dump!"

"I've stayed in worse. I'll see to the fire. Why don't you drive into town and get some sleeping bags, food, and a kettle. There are pans in the kitchen."

"Call me fussy," said Hazel grimly, "but I think I might buy some new pans, too."

"While you're away Patience can make a start on the livestock."

Hazel shuddered and left.

Oh I can, can I? said the white dog, looking down her nose at Ash.

"Of course you can. It's in your blood. Generations of your ancestors were bred for ratting."

Your ancestors used to hunt woolly mammoth, Patience observed pointedly. It doesn't make you Mr. Self-Sufficiency. *You* don't like seeing a fish with the head on.

"Please," said Ash. "Try. For Hazel's sake. You might enjoy it."

Oh, all right. She got up with dignity and began sniffing

along the skirting boards. And though she was in many ways a remarkable animal—probably—she was also a lurcher, and her pulse quickened at the ripe, musky smell that gathered in her nose, and the imminent prospect of a chase that would end in a sharp, damp squeak.

Hazel also wanted to buy a new phone. She drove through the first village she came to and on to the market town ten miles beyond. In between was almost nothing. A few farmhouses across the fields with no obvious way of reaching them; a tractor at work on the horizon; a woman on a horse, who turned and stared as if an unfamiliar car was a remarkable event in these parts. Hazel hoped she'd be able to find her way back to the cottage. If she didn't, she thought Ash—miles from anywhere and without transport—would quietly starve to death.

Once she had the new phone she used the old one to call Meadowvale. It took a minute to connect her to IPCC investigator Daniel Rossi; if it had taken a minute and a half, she'd have rung off. She didn't want to make it easy for anyone to trace her call, even him. Perhaps she was taking caution to ridiculous lengths, but she didn't want her famous last words to be, "I never thought of that!" When this was all over, they could laugh about the things they'd done that there had been no need to do. But only if they were still alive.

She couldn't tell from Rossi's tone whether he believed what she was saying or not. She told him everything: everything she knew, everything she believed, everything she and Ash had worked out. "Nye Jackson was working on it, too. I think he'd got more than we had. I think that's why he's dead."

"Mickey Argyle." Rossi's voice was flat, expressionless.

"Yes."

"Why?"

"Because Jackson found out why Argyle had Jerome Cardy killed."

"Why?"

"I don't know," Hazel was forced to admit. Then a little of the old spirit stirred within her. "But if a small-town reporter could nail it in a couple of days, a squad of professional detectives ought to be able to work it out as well, sooner or later."

The silence lasted long enough for her to wonder again if he was trying to triangulate her location. Actually he was trying to classify her. He was familiar with police officers making mistakes, even stupid ones; he was familiar with idle officers trying to protect their pensions and dishonest ones trying to cover their backs; he was familiar with those who joined the police to Make a Difference (the capitals were integral), to Make the World a Better Place, to offer care and support to the unloved and the unlovable, who saw it as their duty to guide old ladies across roads whether they wanted to go or not. Hazel Best didn't seem to fit any of these templates exactly, and it bothered him. He considered the possibility that she was simply a more straightforward person than he was accustomed to dealing with: good-hearted rather than a do-gooder, someone who was both pragmatic *and* principled. His head sunk low into his shoulders. That was all he needed. He was much more at home with people who lied to him.

Finally he said, "Assuming there's something to all of this, Constable Best, what exactly is it that you expect me to do?"

Her response jolted him with its immediacy, its simplicity, and its magnitude. If she wasn't a silly girl getting a kick from playing detectives, then she was laying a huge burden on his shoulders. A burden he'd carried before, to be sure, but one he'd half-hoped to shed when he took on a job that was half pencil pusher, half Gruppenführer.

She said, "I expect you to keep me alive, sir. Me, and my friend Gabriel Ash. I want us to walk away from this. And I don't think we will unless you can find out why Jerome Cardy died and put Mickey Argyle behind bars."

Daniel Rossi had been on the point of packing up for the evening. After Hazel rang off, he went on staring at the phone in his hand for a full minute. Then he spread the file once more across his borrowed desk.

Hazel finished her shopping, dropped her old phone regretfully into a Dumpster, and drove back to the cottage. She had no idea if what she'd said to Rossi would do any good, but saying it had made her feel better. She'd put responsibility for their safety into better-paid hands than her own. There was no point worrying about whether she would come out of this with her job when she was by no means sure she'd come out of it with her life. The fact that she'd done the best she could was some consolation. As she drove she found herself humming the Monty Python classic "Always Look on the Bright Side of Life."

She'd wondered if she should arrange a password with Ash, decided there was no point. If Argyle found them, a cottage door wasn't going to keep him out, whether or not he knew the password. All the same, she was taken aback to find the front door not only unlocked but standing open. The white dog emerged from the tangled shrubbery, looking faintly embarrassed at having been surprised at her toilette.

Hazel couldn't see why the door couldn't be both shut and locked, and Patience could wait to be let in like normal dogs. She went inside alone, loaded with carrier bags and sleeping bags, ready to tell Ash as much. What greeted her dried the words in her mouth.

You can't make a silk purse of a sow's ear. But if you try this hard, what you get is arguably more valuable. Ash had spent every moment of her absence sweeping, scrubbing, dusting, ejecting the irredeemable, and tidying what was left into some semblance of a habitation. He turned at the sound of her tread, his gaunt face flushed with effort, shy and hopeful, as if unsure what her reaction might be. "Er—better?"

Hazel put her shopping down where it wouldn't spoil the effect. "Much, much better." There was a lump in her throat. She steered Ash by the shoulders to the newly excavated sofa. "Sit down. I'll put the kettle on."

She'd closed the front door as she came in. So she was surprised, as she carried the mugs through to the sitting room, to meet the white lurcher trotting down the hall toward her. Ash appeared not to have moved.

"Did you let her in?"

He shook his head. "She opens doors. She can close them, too, but you have to insist."

Hazel put the mugs down and went to close the door, again. She found herself studying the lever handle. Yes, it was possible for a tall dog to rear up, put a paw on it, and let its weight do the rest. It was possible that a dog could be trained to close the same door by rearing up on the other side. Perhaps the world was full of smart dogs who'd worked out that they need not stay in the rooms where they were left if they didn't want to. And having opened a door, of course they'd prefer it to stay open. A closed door was always going to restrict a dog's movement around the house, particularly if it was carrying something. The newspaper, perhaps, or its knitting . . . Hazel recognized just in time that her train of thought had been diverted down the siding named Surreal and she went back to Ash and the coffee.

He was looking at her politely, as if he was waiting for a reply. Seeing the blankness of her expression, he repeated the last thing he'd said. "Did you get through to IPCC?"

"Oh—yes. I talked to the guy who interviewed me."

"Useful?"

"I don't know," she said honestly. "He wasn't giving anything away. Of course, they don't. I told him how things looked from this end and told him to sort it out." She gave a self-satisfied little chuckle at the recollection.

"Had they connected what happened to Jackson with the Cardy case?"

"I don't think so. Rossi asked for evidence and I said we hadn't got any. I told him Mickey Argyle was behind it, he asked how I knew, and I told him it was the only thing that made sense. I don't know if he believed me. I don't know if he'll do anything about it."

"He'll do something," said Ash. "At least enough to cover himself if we turn up dead."

"Terrific," growled Hazel. She changed the subject. "How are you getting on with *Othello*?"

"I don't think English literature is my forte," confessed Ash. "Somebody keeps being referred to as ancient, when he's clearly nothing of the kind. Somebody borrows a handkerchief, and because of that someone else strangles his wife. I thought *I* was irrational till I met these people."

Hazel laughed. "If everyone behaved sensibly, there would *be* no art. No one would go to the theater to watch Othello take his wife aside and say, 'Iago says you've got the hots for Cassio,' and her tell him, 'Iago's cross because you didn't promote him.' Othello sacks Iago, Cassio marries Bianca, Othello and Desdemona live happily ever after. End of play, curtain, back to the bar, where they haven't even washed up the first lot of glasses."

"Not a lot of scope for the kind of speeches people will be quoting four hundred years later," agreed Ash ruefully.

"'Then must you speak of one who was no mug,'" essayed Hazel. "No, it isn't as catchy as the original."

Something odd was happening in Ash's face. His lips were still smiling, but his eyes were clouding over and a frown was gathering between them. He got up without a word and went into the next room, and came back with the book, leafing through it not at all casually.

"What is it?" asked Hazel. "What are you thinking?"

"I'm not sure," he said without looking up. "That's Othello, isn't it—after he's killed Desdemona and Iago's treachery has been revealed. And he says—I want the exact words—he says . . ."

It was the only quotation from the play that Hazel knew by heart. Probably, that most people know. "Then must you speak of one that loved not wisely, but too well."

Now Ash looked up, looked directly at her. "Is that it?"

"Pretty much."

"No. I mean, is that it? Is that what Jerome Cardy wanted me to know? That the mistake he made, that was going to cost him his life, was to fall in love?"

Hazel was forgetting to breathe. "Who with?"

"Does Argyle have daughters? It had to be someone close to home—he didn't go to this much trouble because he disapproved of Jerome's love life in a general sort of way."

"Let's find out."

Some things are a matter of public record. For more than ten years Mickey Argyle had kept officialdom from knowing, or at least proving, that he was a criminal, the overlord of numerous other criminals, and the main conduit for drugs in the Norbold area, but when his census form turned up, he filled it in like every other householder. Except for the fact that he gave his occupation as club proprietor, he told the truth. That his household consisted of himself, his wife, Phyllis, his son, McAuley . . . and his younger daughter, Alice.

It took Hazel longer to get an Internet connection than to flesh out the information on Facebook. Alice Argyle was a year younger than Jerome Cardy. She was into athletics, modern art, and the theater. She was studying English literature at Durham University. She had an unfeasibly large following of friends, and a habit of reporting even the most trivial aspects of her life. And one of the pictures on her Facebook page was of her triumph as Ariel, playing opposite a handsome black youth in a turban.

"Durham?" asked Ash. "She's at Durham University?"

"Yes. Why?"

"So was Jerome."

"Different courses."

"Yes. Same campus."

Hazel returned to the Facebook entry. It hadn't been updated for nearly a week. For a girl who thought people wanted to know what shoes she was going to wear to a party, this struck Hazel as significant.

"Who would know if Jerome and Alice were an item?" Hazel was talking to herself, but Ash thought that was something only he did, so he answered.

"His parents?"

Hazel turned from her laptop and looked at him as his mother might have done. "So, you were never actually a teenage boy? You went straight from infancy to middle age? Of course he didn't tell his parents. If he told anyone, it was friends—male friends. Or maybe just one friend—the one he was closest to. Someone at university, probably."

Chastened, Ash nodded. "Maybe his parents would know who."

"Yes, maybe. Give them a call."

"I don't know their number."

A couple more keystrokes and Hazel had it.

"What should I tell them?"

"Anything you like. The truth. Or a lie. Just tell them you want to talk to his best friend and do they have a number for him."

He did as she said, using the new mobile. Hazel noted how he was all fingers and thumbs with it. Phones had got a lot smaller in the time he'd been out of touch with the world.

Ash was relieved when Mrs. Cardy answered the phone. He knew her husband doubted his motives, would have wanted to know why before parting with the information. Jerome's mother seemed to accept that he was trying to help.

"Actually, Mr. Ash, his best friend was a boy he was at school with. A moment while I find his number."

Moments later she was back. She reeled off a string of digits. "Tom Woods. They knew each other since junior school. Tell him you've been talking to me, if you like."

Hazel made the call. Without a flicker of guilt she introduced herself as a constable at Meadowvale Police Station. And that was the first they knew that they were following a trail blazed twelve hours earlier by Nye Jackson of the *Norbold News*.

"I didn't want to talk to the press," said Woods, "but he seemed to know most of it already. Jerome and Alice *were* serious about each other. They knew how many obstacles would be put in their way. Her family of course, but also members of *his* family thinking his own kind weren't good enough for him anymore. It didn't have to matter.

"That's not true," he said then, editing as he went along. "It *did* matter to them—this wasn't a joke, something they'd come up with to outrage people's sensibilities. But being together mattered more. When Jerome proposed and Alice said yes, they were never more serious about anything in their lives."

"They were going to get married?" Hazel heard her voice soar, coughed it back to a professional level. "When did they decide this?"

"About five weeks ago," said Tom Woods. His voice didn't break; that didn't mean his heart hadn't. "I was going to be best man."

CHAPTER 23

"SO THEY'VE BEEN friends for years, all through high school and now at the same university," said Hazel. They were eating breakfast in the cottage, balancing on rickety kitchen chairs while Patience watched from the sofa. "They have the same interests—literature, theater, sport. They have everything in common except for two things: the color of their skins, and the fact that *his* family is respectable. Getting married isn't something they've rushed into. But with graduation looming they decide it's now or never and they can't face the idea of never.

"What's the first thing you do when you get engaged? You tell the parents. But that was going to be the biggest hurdle they faced, so they put it off. For maybe a month they held back, knowing they were going to light a cigar in a gun powder factory. Then they did it. They thought they'd get the Argyles out of the way first. Maybe Alice told them on her own, or maybe they did it together—who knows? Whatever they thought would be safest." She looked up at Ash. "But it wasn't. Safe. Mickey Argyle said—and I'm paraphrasing here, but I'll bet you anything this is pretty much exactly what he said—'Before I see you marry my daughter, I'll kill you, you . . .' Supply the racist invective of your choice."

Ash was nodding slowly. Finally it was making sense. "He won't be the first father to feel that way about his daughter's intended. He won't even be the first to go crazy. Usually, though, given a bit of time people calm down. Or even if they don't, they lack the means to carry out their threats. There's nothing stopping Argyle. He's ruthless enough to do it, he has the kind of help to get it done, and he can afford to pay for it. If he told Jerome he was going to kill him, Jerome would know it wasn't empty rhetoric. And Alice would know exactly how much danger he was in."

Hazel took up the story again. "They decided he should get out of Norbold right away. He probably wanted to tell the police that he was being threatened, but Alice knew her father had people inside Meadowvale. She told Jerome, 'Don't stop for anything. This time the police are not on your side.'"

"But he did stop," said Ash. "When Mrs. Wiltshire ran into him."

"He was a decent, law-abiding citizen. He wanted to make sure she was all right. When he saw she wasn't injured, he made a run for it before the police arrived."

"But now there was good reason for them to give chase. Leaving the scene of an accident without observing the proprieties. This was what Argyle's man inside Meadowvale—"

"Sergeant Murchison," Hazel reminded him. Her voice was low, as if even now she didn't like admitting it out loud.

"—Sergeant Murchison was waiting for. What Argyle had told him to find, or to make—an excuse to get Jerome Cardy into the cells. When the patrol called in that they'd arrested Jerome, he thought the boy was doing his job for him. He put him in a cell and called Argyle to see what he wanted to do next."

"What Argyle wanted," Hazel continued grimly, "required

privacy. It couldn't be done in a cell he was sharing with someone else. So Murchison cleared a cell—sent home the only woman prisoner that night—then he nobbled the CCTV and took Jerome across the hall. He wasn't wandering around looking for somewhere quiet to sleep. The custody sergeant took him to another cell and locked him in there."

"And he tried to leave me a coded message," murmured Ash, "because he didn't dare speak plainly in front of a man he knew was in Argyle's pocket."

Hazel nodded slowly. "Meanwhile, Argyle—or more likely one of his crew—was talking to Saturday's friend Trucker, who found Barclay, plied him with drink, and told him about the names on the war memorial. Anyone could have guessed how that would end—with Jerome alone in a cell and Barclay flung in with him, already foaming at the mouth. He never had a chance."

"And he knew it." Ash's face was gray. "As soon as he was arrested he knew what was going to happen to him. He desperately needed help." He swallowed. "What he got was me."

Hazel regarded him with compassion. "Gabriel, he was *lucky* to get you. You listened. You cared. And you tried to find out what had happened. You think any of the usual drunk-and-disorderlies we have for bed and breakfast would have done that? The people whose job it was to protect him didn't do it either, and how much of that was down to carelessness and how much to corruption, I don't know. You couldn't save him. But if we do this right, we can get justice for him. It has to be worth something."

After a moment he nodded. "Yes, of course it is. I'm sorry, I'm not much good at this anymore. I used to be a dab hand at solving puzzles. That was when I was able to think of it as a puzzle, an intellectual exercise. When it became personal, the objectivity went out the window and I've never been able to get it back."

"You're not doing badly."

He smiled. When he smiled, it was as if all the grief, all the trauma, coalesced into a dark mask, and behind the mask, and looking through the mask, was the man he used to be. Around the edges of the mask he seemed almost to glow. "You're not doing so badly yourself."

"For a rookie," she qualified ruefully. Then she chuckled. "A rookie cop and a washed-up analyst. And a dog. Not exactly the Sweeney Todd, are we?"

Ash looked puzzled. "The demon barber?"

"The Flying Squad," Hazel explained patiently.

The dog whined. It seemed to remind him of something, because Ash blinked, and Hazel saw the little perplexed frown gather between his eyebrows again and his lips purse on the beginnings of a question.

"What?" she asked. "Gabriel, what is it?"

"So—where's Alice?"

"At Durham." She thought he'd forgotten.

"You reckon? You think after her father murdered her fiancé she had a little cry, and a consolation shopping trip, and tootled off back to read Chaucer at Durham? A girl strong enough to know that she wanted Jerome Cardy despite all the trouble she knew they'd face? And to want to do it properly—not to run off and marry in a registry office before her father could catch up with them, but to face him first and tell him that she knew he wouldn't be happy but this time he wasn't going to get his own way. You think a girl like that wouldn't be talking to policemen before Jerome's body had cooled?"

"Whatever else he is, he's her father," Hazel pointed out.

"And people make allowances for family," agreed Ash. "She must have known what he did for a living. She kept quiet about it because he's her father. You could understand that. This is something else. He killed the boy she loved. You think she'd keep quiet about that? This girl? Alice Argyle, who must have been scared to death of her father but faced him anyway? Because I don't."

"Then . . . what do you think?" Fear is contagious; she was catching it from him.

"I think," Ash said slowly, "that even if Argyle loves her as much as normal people love their children, he knows he can't trust her with this. That she'll betray him if she's ever free to do so. He'll never be safe while Alice is alive, and I think that somewhere in the bitter, twisted heart of him he knows it."

Hazel stared at him in horrid disbelief. "You're not suggesting he'd kill her? His own daughter?"

Ash took a deep breath. "Yes, I am. Not yet. He probably thinks he can talk her round—convince her that what he did was for the best, that he was only thinking of her, that one day she'll understand that and when she does, he'll let her go. I think he's taken her somewhere she can't get help or talk to anyone, and he thinks he's only got to keep her there until she starts seeing things his way. But she won't. And a time will come when Argyle will see that. See that he's all out of options."

Hazel stared at him dumbstruck for half a minute. Then she felt herself getting angry. "His daughter?" she repeated. "You think he'd kill his own child rather than go to prison?"

"Men kill their own children all the time," Ash said bleakly. "Not just men like Mickey Argyle—ordinary men, not psychopaths. They kill them because they don't love them, or they love them too much, or they get drunk, or angry, and lose control just long enough for one irreversible act. They shake the baby, they push the child, they hit the teenager. The inhibitor that's meant to cut in and prevent you from harming your own offspring fails momentarily and they do what every parent has thought about doing: they hit out. And men are strong, and children are weak. The wonder is not that it happens, but that it doesn't happen more often."

Hazel shook her head. "But we're not talking about a man losing his temper with a stroppy teenager, are we? We're talking about a man weighing the pros and cons and deciding that his liberty is worth killing his daughter for. I don't believe it. Not of Mickey Argyle; not of anyone."

Ash had seen more of the world than she had. It was a long time since he'd seen anything through rose-tinted glasses. "Look what he's done already. He didn't kill Jerome in a fit of fury. He planned it, meticulously, because he didn't just want to stop his daughter from marrying a black man. He wanted to make sure there was no trail back to him. Even the people he used didn't know what they were doing, or why, or who for. That wasn't a crime of passion. It was an act of cold, calculated vengeance."

"Jerome wasn't his child!" exclaimed Hazel, exasperated. "There's all the difference in the world between what a man like Argyle would do to anybody else's son or daughter and how he'd treat his own. I'd have thought—"

She almost managed to leave the thought in her head, the words unspoken. She did succeed in cutting it off at the knees, the bit that got past her completely innocuous. It could have been anything that she'd started to say and then thought better of.

But it wasn't just anyone she'd started to say it to. Gabriel Ash had made his living by reading signs that were hardly there and extrapolating from fragments of evidence to the facts they were evidence of. He heard what people hadn't said, what they had carefully avoided saying. Almost, he heard their thoughts. He heard Hazel's thought, and it went straight through his armor and exploded in his gut.

"You thought I'd have understood that?" His voice was low, his dark eyes burning. "What, as a father myself? As the father of dead children—is that what you meant?"

Regret for her clumsiness rose in a dull flush up Hazel's cheek. "Gabriel, I didn't mean—"

"Of course you meant it. You thought that the way I feel about my sons is the way Mickey Argyle feels about his daughter."

"I didn't mean to hurt you."

"Oh, that boat has sailed!"

They stared at each other for another moment, then Ash looked away. He gave a sigh of infinite weariness. "I'm sorry. I . . . overreact. I know you didn't mean anything by it. You may even be right. Being a career criminal doesn't prevent you from loving your children the same way law-abiding fathers do. Maybe I'm wrong, and Mickey Argyle would lay down not just his liberty but his life for any of his children, and do it willingly.

"But what if I'm right? What if all those years of preying on other people's children have left him incapable of holding normal feelings for his own? What if it's not that big a step from selling the drugs that kill other men's daughters to deciding he'd rather sacrifice his own than spend the rest of his life behind bars?

"Men—not career criminals, but what you'd call ordinary men—have killed their children for crying during *Match of the Day*. Can you be sure that Alice Argyle, who defied her father and fell in love with a black law student, who faced up to him and told him so, who knows her fiancé is dead and who's to blame, is going to do what's necessary for his safety? Can she keep her mouth shut? Can she convince her father she'll go on keeping it shut even when he's not there to muzzle her?"

And when he put it like that, Hazel felt the doubt creeping back. Alice could be in real danger. "We have to find her, check that she's all right. Give her some options about what happens next."

She made some phone calls. To Durham University, where Alice had missed a week's lectures. To some of her friends there, none of whom had heard from Alice since the previous Tuesday. Even, posing as one of those friends, to the Argyle house, where Phyllis Argyle said her daughter was unwell and couldn't come to the phone.

"But she's all right?" pressed Hazel. "She's going to be all right?"

"Of course she is, dear," said Mrs. Argyle; and it could have been imagination, but Hazel detected a hollow quality to her voice that was less than reassuring.

After she'd rung off Hazel sat for a moment looking at Ash. Then she passed a hand across her mouth. "You're right. At least, you *may* be right. Nobody can contact her. Her mother says she's at home in bed, but she sounded scared. I think she knows Mickey could hurt the girl and doesn't know what to do about it."

"What do *we* do about it?"

Hazel knew the answer to that one. "If someone's in danger, that's a job for the police. I'll call . . ." And there the reality of the situation ambushed her. "I can't call Meadowvale because Donald Murchison, and anyone else on Argyle's payroll, will be keeping him informed. I could force his hand—push him into killing her now in case he doesn't get the chance later."

"IPCC?" suggested Ash.

"Yes." Hazel nodded. "I could tell Rossi. What I can't do is make him believe me. All he knows of me is that I've told him a story that's radically different from everyone else's at Meadowvale.

If he has me marked down as a fantasist, telling him Argyle might murder his daughter won't make him revise that opinion."

"Then what?" Ash was on his feet, his arms clasped about his thin body, his voice rough with a kind of angry despair. "What do you suggest we do? There's a nineteen-year-old girl out there somewhere, she's already lost her fiancé, and if we know she's in danger from her father, you can bet your life she does. What are we going to do about Alice Argyle?"

"I could try Mr. Fountain," said Hazel reluctantly.

"Chief Superintendent Fountain? Who suspended you for telling the truth?"

"Maybe he hadn't much choice. You know, rock. . . . hard place . . . *him.* He always treated me with respect, even when he didn't want to believe what I was telling him. I don't think he thinks I'm lying. I think he hopes that I'm wrong, because it'll be easier to deal with an overenthusiastic constable than a corrupt sergeant. But I think he'll listen if I go to him with this. I think he'll do something about it."

"You can't go anywhere near Meadowvale. It isn't safe."

"No. I'll phone him."

"All right," said Ash. He had nothing better to offer. "Give it a try."

CHAPTER 24

HAZEL KEPT HER guard up. She didn't want all Meadowvale knowing she'd been in touch again. She told the switchboard she was calling from Division about a management seminar being organized for the deputy chief constable. It was a clever deceit: it sounded both official and uninteresting, and something that required her to talk to Chief Superintendent Fountain in person. If he wasn't there, she'd have to call back.

God was on the side of the small battalion. Miss Patel asked Hazel to wait a moment, and then the unmistakable gruff Yorkshire voice came on. "*What* management seminar?"

"Sorry, sir, I made it up." She thought, from the quality of the silence and the way it stretched, that he recognized her voice immediately. But she didn't want to give him an excuse for hanging up on her, so she said it anyway. "It's Constable Best, sir. I know—you were looking forward to some peace and quiet. But you need to hear this."

To his credit he heard her out, and neither snorted nor laughed when she said where her concerns about Alice Argyle had originated. When she'd finished, after another protracted pause Fountain said, "What exactly do you want me to do?"

"Make sure Alice is safe."

"Do you know where she is?"

"No, sir. But if she isn't updating her Facebook page, I'm guessing she's nowhere with wi-fi access. Not at Durham and not at home."

"You want me to find her."

"You have the resources. I don't."

"True enough." Fountain considered. "I still don't have any evidence—actual evidence, the sort of thing juries like—against her father."

"You don't need it. You don't need to accuse him of anything. Just say that you're concerned for her safety and need to see her. What responsible father can say no?"

"*Responsible* and *Mickey Argyle* are two things not normally found in the same sentence."

"I know that," said Hazel, "and you know that. But Argyle can't use it as a reason for not producing her! He may know that the only threat to his daughter is him, but he can't say that, either. If you ask, he has to cooperate. He's giving you grounds for suspicion if he doesn't."

More silence while the chief superintendent thought. "You're not afraid that an approach will bounce him into doing something rash?"

Hazel had already considered that. "Not yet. It's less than a week since Jerome was killed—he probably still believes he can talk Alice around, convince her either that it wasn't his doing or else it was for the best. In another week or two, if she's still not buying it, that's when he'll start wondering what he has to do to protect himself. He can't keep her under wraps forever. Even if he could bully his family into keeping quiet, she'd be missed at Durham."

"But in that case," rumbled Fountain, "he's not going to want her talking to me. He can't risk her telling me that her father killed her fiancé!"

"It *is* a risk," agreed Hazel, "and he won't like taking it. But what choice does he have? If you ask to see Alice, he has to decide which is the most dangerous—refusing, or producing her, with the caveat that she's in a terrible state emotionally, she hardly knows what she's saying, the poor girl even thinks *he* might have been involved. . . . He has to take the risk. He can put the fear of God into her first, he can no doubt produce a medical certificate from some tame quack saying she's in a state of grief-induced psychosis and nothing she says can be counted on, but I think he has to let you see her."

"All right, so I see her. What then?"

"Protective custody?"

"Constable Best," he said wearily, "were you absent from training college the day they covered *just cause*? I can't take someone into protective custody because someone with a good future in the police behind her and someone else who talks to his dog think it might be a good idea!"

The way he put it was unnecessarily brutal, but Hazel had to concede his point. "The mere fact that you've asked to see her should be enough to keep her safe. If Argyle knows you're watching him, he can't hurt her. He knows what you'd find if he gave you a reason to look."

"I've been looking at Mickey Argyle for ten years," growled Johnny Fountain. "Don't you think he'll assume that, if he's been smarter than me for that long, he can be smarter than me for a bit longer?"

Hazel had no answer to that. She'd thrown every bit of persuasion she could muster into her argument. If it wasn't enough, it wasn't enough. The problem was what it had been all along: the lack of forensic evidence. If Chief Superintendent Fountain thought her case too flimsy, he wouldn't want to pin his reputation to it.

But it was a girl's *life* they were talking about. The life of a nineteen-year-old girl. And whatever her father had or hadn't done, and whatever he might or might not do in the future, Alice was entitled to the protection of the law as much as anyone else. And Johnny Fountain was the embodiment of the law in Norbold. He *had* to find a way to help her.

After an agonizing minute and a half, it seemed that was the conclusion he'd reached. He vented a gusty sigh that reached all the way from Meadowvale. "Hazel, Hazel." She could hear him shaking his head. "What a dull place Norbold was before they posted you here! Yes, all right. I'll tell Argyle I need to see his daughter. After all, if she knew the Cardy boy, it's reasonable enough that we should want to speak to her. Then I suppose we play it by ear. If she says anything, I'll act on it. And if she doesn't, maybe Argyle will take the view that she never will. I'll let you know how I get on."

Even then, with relief washing around under her heart, and even at the risk of offending him, Hazel remained circumspect. "I'll call you, yes?"

Fountain seemed not to notice her lack of trust. "Give me twenty-four hours. And Hazel . . ."

"Sir?"

"Be careful. You did the right thing. But as you've discovered, righteousness isn't always a shield. Sometimes it's a target."

* * *

Ash took Patience for a walk. Hazel tidied the cottage. He made coffee; she made lunch. Three hours had passed. Ash washed the pots and Hazel took Patience for a walk. The road turned to a track beyond the cottage, so she went that way.

It wasn't picture-postcard countryside. It was too flat, and the stretching vistas of new green crops needed the punctuation of trees and houses and people. Right now, though, it was ideal for Hazel's purposes. She wanted space around her, and no people. She didn't want to be worrying what lay behind the blank canvas of strangers' faces, or whether a passing car was just that or a sign they'd been discovered. She saw a tractor perhaps a mile away, and one car trundling along a stretch of elevated laneway not much closer, and no people at all.

Town dwellers are afraid of what might befall them in remote, unpopulated areas. Hazel—essentially a country girl—knew that, ninety-nine times out of a hundred, the biggest danger to people is other people. If you want to feel safe, being alone is a good start.

She sat on a bank amid the primroses, her knees drawn up to her chin, watching the white dog root around under the hedge. After a while, feeling her gaze, the animal turned with an amiable grin and ambled over to sit beside her, scratching an ear with a back paw.

"So what do you make of all this?" asked Hazel. "I suppose *you* think we're on holiday, and it's a nice change from cars and crowds and pavements. Although what I suspect you *really* think," she went on, warming to the task of second-guessing a dog, "is that you don't care where the hell you are as long as you're with him." She glanced back the way they'd come. "Which is the best thing about dogs, and why people put themselves to trouble and expense to keep one. Dogs love you without qualification. It doesn't matter to you that folk think he's crazy. It wouldn't matter to you if he *was* crazy, as long as he looked after you. A very simple view of the world, dogs have. Which is not altogether a bad thing."

The white dog turned her head to look into Hazel's face, happy drool trailing from the corners of her mouth. Then she licked Hazel's nose.

"Er—thanks." She went for her handkerchief; then she paused, worrying that she might cause offense; *then* she reminded herself, impatiently, *It's just a dog!*—and wiped the cool wet spot off her face. So far as she could tell, Patience didn't take umbrage.

They strolled back to the cottage.

Or almost. A hundred yards from the garden gate the dog suddenly froze. The hackles on her shoulders rose and a low growl like machinery came from her chest.

All Hazel's instincts were honed for danger. Maybe it was just a wandering badger the lurcher had got wind of, or the local stud come to check out the new bitch on his patch, but Hazel wasn't taking any chances. She grabbed the dog's collar and crushed the pair of them into the hedge. "Shhh!"

For a long minute, concentrating with all her senses, she saw and heard nothing untoward. The cottage looked as it had when she left half an hour ago. The car was where she'd parked it under the lean-to. The door was closed; the curtains were open. No sound of voices reached her on the spring-scented breeze. Nothing was wrong.

Something was wrong. Patience knew it, and Hazel knew it, too. Finally she saw what it was that her senses had picked out automatically. A shadow where no shadow should have been. The afternoon sun was casting a shadow that was separate from the shadow of the house, and half an hour ago there'd been nothing in the backyard to explain it. Someone had driven to the cottage in the time she'd been away, and had parked discreetly around the back.

Visitors don't do that. If it had been a neighbor calling with milk and a welcome, or a particularly desperate candidate for the parish council canvassing for support, they would have parked at the gate. These visitors wanted to go unnoticed. Not by Ash, who'd have heard the car arrive wherever they parked it, but by her. She was meant to walk unknowing into an ambush.

So where were they? Watching for her, for sure. Had they spotted her before the dog growled? If not, would they wait? Or were they out looking for her already? If she ran, would they catch her?

She was young and fit. Mickey Argyle's men were probably also pretty fit, and stronger. She'd be outnumbered. They could use their car to cut her off. Oh yes, they'd catch her. Unless she got a good head start.

Before she committed herself, she took a moment to wonder if running was the best option. She'd be leaving Ash to his fate, at least until she could round up some help. On the other hand, if Argyle had them both, he could kill them both, dispose of the bodies, and defy anyone to tie him to the disappearance of a couple of misfits. If he only had Ash, he'd probably wait until he could be sure of tying up all the loose ends.

The decision made itself. It wasn't just in her best interests to stay free; it was in Ash's, too. The question now was, how.

By getting off anything you could call, however generously, a road. Their car would be no advantage if she took to the fields. Afraid Patience would head back to the cottage, she put the dog's lead on, found a weak spot in the hedge, and forced a way through. She needed to put some distance between herself and the interlopers before she started trying to explain all this on the phone.

* * *

Gabriel Ash knew he was going to die the moment he heard the car draw up outside. Hazel had gone for a walk, leaving hers in the lean-to. No one else was supposed to know they were here. Except—his heart lifted for a moment—the farmer they'd rented the cottage from. He might have come around to check that they weren't trashing the place. Then Ash remembered what they found when they first opened the door and his heart sank again. Lighting a bonfire in the sitting room would have counted as home improvements.

Also, the man who owned the cottage would probably have knocked before entering, he wouldn't have brought two friends, and they wouldn't have come in through the front door, the back door, and the sitting room window simultaneously.

Ash was sitting in the chair in the kitchen. It took an effort of will, but he stayed there. It was too late to do anything except try to hang on to some dignity.

"You're Ash," said the man who'd come through the back door. They had actually met before, in Windermere Close. He was the man Nye Jackson recognized as Andy Fletcher. "Don't try and deny it."

"I wasn't going to," said Ash.

"Where's the girl?"

"She's gone."

"Gone where?"

He tried to think fast, and look like he wasn't thinking at all. "To the village. For some food."

"The car's outside," said the big man, scornfully. "Walk, did she?"

"Yes," Ash said simply. "She took the dog."

One of Fletcher's companions came in from the hall. "She's not here."

"He says she's walking to the village shop."

"It's bloody miles!"

"She took the dog," Ash said again, helpfully.

"Unless she took a tent and a sleeping bag as well, she hasn't gone to the village," decided Fletcher. "We didn't pass her in the lane, so she's gone the other way. I'll wait here. You two go look for her. While we're waiting"—he pulled a bentwood chair out from the ancient table—"I'm going to sit here with Mr. Ash and we'll have a nice little chat."

When they were alone, he said conversationally, "You know, I don't really go for it."

"For what?"

"This dummy act of yours. I don't think you're stupid. I think it's like camouflage. I think you hide behind it." He was a man of about Ash's age but a hand taller and twice as far around. He wore a black leather jacket that strained to meet at the front.

"Yes?"

"I think *you* think that if everyone thinks you're crazy, nobody'll bother you."

"Not really working, is it?"

Fletcher grinned with a confidence born of knowing he could deal with anything Ash might try. Ash knew it, too, and wasted no time wondering if he could make a fight of it. If they fought, Ash would lose. He hoped he had an intellectual edge on a man who thought with his fists, but that was only an advantage over someone with decisions to make. This man had come here with orders, and probably nothing Ash could say would stop him carrying them out.

"See?" said Fletcher, pleased. "That's not what a dummy would say. I won't make the mistake of underestimating you."

"Okay."

The man gave a puzzled frown. "What, no arguments?"

Ash shrugged. "You're asking me if I think I'm sane? What possible faith could you put in the answer?"

Fletcher chuckled, but there was a slight uneasiness behind his eyes that hadn't been there when he came in here. "Lots of people talk to dogs."

"Yes, they do."

"It's what you do if you've got a dog. It's *why* you have a dog."

"Do you have a dog?"

"Yes. For the kids, mostly. But you get fond of them, don't you? I like a dog about the place."

"Do you talk to it?"

"Course I do. It's *normal.* I ask it if it wants its dinner. I tell it it's a good dog for *eating* its dinner. I ask it if it wants a walk, or should we just go down the shed for a smoke on account of it's starting to rain."

As an insight into the home life of a professional thug it was fascinating. "So there's nothing abnormal about talking to dogs is what you're saying."

"Exactly."

"How about when they talk back?"

CHAPTER 25

ON GOOD GOING, you can cover a couple of hundred meters in a minute without much exertion. Two hundred meters over plowed fields was going to take longer than that. Hazel plugged on until her chest began to crack and her muscles burned. Glancing back, she saw no sign of pursuit, so she labored a little farther until she could drop into the shadow of a hedge, where she pulled out her phone. Her nice new phone that hadn't protected them for a whole day.

How Argyle could have found them so quickly was something she'd have to think about, but not right now with her lungs trying to squeeze out through her ears. She'd thought she was fit. She *was* fitter than most of her colleagues. But running over broken land and burgeoning new crops was as much of a workout as Hazel could take.

Who to call? Fountain first, obviously—he needed to know they were in trouble. He'd mobilize help from somewhere closer than Meadowvale. But with her finger on the button, Hazel hesitated. Maybe she should take time to think this through. She'd taken every precaution to ensure Argyle couldn't find them. The only person she'd called was Chief Superintendent Fountain. But somehow Donald Murchison had got hold of . . .

Of what? She hadn't told Fountain where they were. If Murchison was listening at his door, or scanned his blotter with an ultraviolet lamp as soon as the chief went out, he still couldn't have sent Argyle's heavies after them.

Coincidence, then? They hadn't left a trail a bloodhound could follow. Only the farmer knew they were in his cottage, and he didn't know they were hiding, let alone who from. It didn't seem possible. She even wondered for a moment if she'd misread the situation, overreacted to the visit of a particularly determined Jehovah's Witness.

But in a way it didn't matter. She had to get help. If it turned out she didn't need it, she could apologize then. If she did nothing and *that* was the wrong call, it would be too late for apologies. So she called Fountain. She didn't bother with subterfuge this time—the secret she'd been trying to protect was already out.

But Fountain wasn't in his office. His secretary tried to raise him on his mobile, but it was switched off. "Shall I have him call you back?"

There wasn't time. "Put me through to Detective Inspector Gorman."

It was a gamble. She had no reason to suspect Dave Gorman of taking handouts from Mickey Argyle, but then, she'd had no reason to suspect Donald Murchison until someone died in his cells. If Gorman was involved as well, no help would come. If Gorman was involved and it really *was* a Jehovah's Witness parked behind the cottage, Mickey Argyle would come.

Either she told him what was going on or she didn't.

Reduced to a choice that simple, Hazel decided to take the chance. When Detective Inspector Gorman came on, she gave him a zip file of the essential facts in less than a minute and the whereabouts of the cottage to the nearest half mile, which was the best she could do.

Then she went back.

She told herself it was the last thing Argyle's men would expect. She told herself that she could creep up on the cottage from behind and work out what was happening while they were scanning the far distance with binoculars. But really, she was going back because she couldn't face leaving Ash to whatever Argyle had in mind.

The dog was a problem. If Hazel let it go, it would run to the cottage and warn those inside that she was returning. She could keep it on the leash, but it's hard to sneak up on someone with an excited dog bouncing up and down beside you. Or she could tie it to a fence somewhere, in which case it would almost certainly bark. In the end she did what Ash would have done: bent down, looked it in the eye, and whispered, "It is really, really important that you keep quiet."

Patience returned her gaze in that solemn, down-the-nose way that only something with a greyhound's face can, then fell into step at Hazel's left heel, silent as a ghost.

Hazel looked at her phone. Five minutes since she'd spoken to Gorman. How long before she could expect help? Another twenty at least, and only then if there was a patrol as close as the nearest village. How long before these people gave up on finding her, bundled Ash into their car, and drove him off into the sunset, never to be seen again? Again, impossible to know, but maybe not too long now. She walked more quickly over the rough land.

Delay was the name of the game. She had to keep them

from leaving while Gorman organized a relief squad. What would happen if she simply presented herself at the door? Would they grab her, grab Ash, and leave immediately? Or would they relax because their job was done and it was no longer a matter of urgency to be on their way? Would it be better to barricade the only exit? If this had been livestock country, she'd have opened every gate she could find and chased every animal into the lane. But it was arable, and you can't herd turnips. She found a couple of gates anyway, cut the baler twine securing them, and threw them across the lane. But they weren't long enough; all they did was turn a straight into a slalom. The car might have to slow down a little, but it wouldn't have to stop.

The only ace left in the pack was Hazel herself. She leaned against the blind side of a tree, steadying her nerve. She could just hide and wait for reinforcements. But there was no knowing what orders these men had. They'd run Nye Jackson down with a car—quite possibly *this* car. They wouldn't slap Ash's wrist and tell him to mind his own business in the future. If she was with him, perhaps she could protect him. . . .

Or she could die with him. She thought about that for a moment. To her surprise, the mere possibility was not enough to end the mental argument. There *are* things worth dying for, and Hazel Best wouldn't be the first police officer to decide that doing the job well was one of them. Johnny Fountain had the power to suspend her; he had no way to stop her from being a police officer, accepting the obligation to protect the public even at the risk of her own safety. Gabriel Ash was a member of the public, and he certainly needed protection, and unless DI Gorman had managed to whistle up a passing helicopter, she was the only member of the police service close enough to help. Looking at it that way, she really didn't have much choice.

She was stepping out from behind the tree when she heard the car start.

They'd given up on finding her. Plan B began with manhandling Ash out to their vehicle. Fletcher checked that the car in the lean-to wasn't going anywhere, not with knife slashes in two tires; then he got into his employer's 4x4 and they set off.

Fifty meters down the lane the young woman they'd wasted the last half hour looking for stepped out in front of them.

"What do you want me to do?" asked the driver tersely. He was a much smaller man than Fletcher, and had answered to the nickname "the Rat" for so long that Fletcher could no longer remember his proper name.

The big man thought, but not for long. "Flatten her."

Hazel, waiting in the middle of the lane, expected them to stop for her, thought that was what they were here for. Only when the driver floored the accelerator and the big black car leapt forward did she realize that death was coming for her, right here, right now, and she'd never get the chance to help Ash. That she'd thrown her life away for nothing.

She jumped then, as far to the side as she could from a standing start; but it wasn't far enough. The wing of the car, as high as her midriff, caught her in midair and tossed her like an angry bull, flinging her against the tree she'd been hiding behind. Not that she knew anything about it.

Gabriel Ash saw it from the backseat of the car, and something inside him snapped. It wasn't a very robust something to start with. He hadn't seen what happened to his wife and sons, he didn't even *know* what had happened to them, but this was close enough to drive a dagger into the same coil of his innards that had been hacked apart when he lost them.

He cried out in horror and grief; and neither was inappropriate, because though Hazel Best wasn't an old friend, he'd known her just long enough and well enough to feel a personal pain that went beyond the shock any decent man would have felt at witnessing a murder. In a way he could not have explained, the horror and the grief, and the rage, were compounded because he'd been here once before and the pathways of his brain were primed.

The men on either side of him took a wrist each and twisted them up behind him. But the elastic snapping in his head had catapulted him to a place where pain and fear and even the threat of death had very little meaning. He fought them with all his strength, a heart full of pain and a howling in his throat, and he succeeded in shaking off one of them and using the fist thus freed to cannon the other's skull into the reinforced glass of the window. Then he launched himself forward, fists pounding on the head and shoulders of the Rat, who let out a yelp of shock and then cowered over the wheel with scant regard for the way bits of landscape that were racing at him at forty miles an hour.

If it hadn't been for Fletcher, possibly all of them would have died, bent around a tree or somersaulting into a field. But Fletcher recovered quickly, and he had a gun. For half a second—and half a second was all he had—he considered shooting Ash there and then, and explaining to his boss how he'd had no choice. But in fact there was another option, and he took it. He palmed the gun and swung it as best he could in the confines of the rocking car.

Fireworks burst behind Ash's eyes. He left off what he was doing with an odd little pant, and blinked, and his free hand moved uncertainly toward his head. It was halfway there when the blackness took him.

Not long afterward, the blackness that had taken Hazel began to thin. Not all at once. First she was aware of sounds—the sound of a car, then a man's voice. Then she felt strong hands and thought of her father. But he didn't know where she was, let alone that she needed him, so probably it was Mickey Argyle's men come back to finish the job their big black car had started. There was nothing she could do to stop them. She waited, not resigned exactly, just too tired to help herself.

"Open your eyes." Though it certainly wasn't her father's, it was a voice that she recognized, even if for the moment she couldn't place it. "Hazel, open your eyes and look at me. I know you're in there."

She was also too tired to argue. She did as she was told.

Seeing the figure bent over her did nothing to dispel her confusion. She was still imagining things. If it couldn't be Alfred Best, it couldn't be Johnny Fountain, either. "Wha' . . . ?"

"That's better," growled Fountain, straightening up. He'd eased her into a more comfortable position under the tree, his folded jacket under her head. "You're concussed—you've had a crack on the head. And you're going to be pretty sore all over, but I don't think there's anything broken. Do you think there is?"

"What?"

He sighed and tried again. "Are you in pain? Can you move your arms and legs? How are your ribs?"

When she tried, she found he was right—she was sore all over. But there was no sharp, unignorable pain that said something wasn't going to be better after a hot bath and a good night's sleep. "I'm okay," she mumbled.

It wasn't true, and Fountain knew it wasn't true. He could see a glazed sickness in her eyes. "Don't try to move. I'll call an ambulance. They'll get you checked out at A&E. I'm sorry, I can't wait with you. I need to find Ash."

"Ash!" She'd all but forgotten. "Mickey Argyle has him."

"You saw him?" The lowering of his heavy brow concentrated his gaze on her like a searchlight. "Argyle was here?"

Hazel went to shake her head, then thought better of it. "His heavies. At least, I guess so. No one else had any reason. . . ." But the effort of putting the words together into sentences was helping to clear her head. She looked at Fountain oddly. "Nobody knew we were here. Even *you* didn't know we were here. Only Detective Inspector Gorman, and that was after they found us."

"I know. He called me. You got lucky—I wasn't fifteen minutes away. Heading home from a working lunch in Leicester. I thought I could get here before the local CID."

Against his advice, Hazel was struggling to sit up. Fountain let her, watching to see if she'd topple over again. She didn't. "You're going after them? Argyle's men, and Ash?"

The chief superintendent nodded.

"I'm coming, too."

"Don't be ridiculous! You're waiting here for the ambulance. You're in no fit state. . . ."

"I'm coming," she said again firmly—so firmly it ended the discussion. "I'll stay in the car. I'll work the radio. But I am coming."

CHAPTER 26

FOUNTAIN HELPED her into his car, and by the time she'd remembered how a seat belt works they were on their way. She'd no idea how far ahead the 4x4 was, nor where it was heading. Back to Norbold? To a rendezvous elsewhere? Her hands dropped helplessly in her lap. "I don't know where they'd take him."

"I have an idea," grunted Fountain. "Mickey has a workshop outside Liddam, this side of Norbold. I think it was a blacksmith's shop. He took it in settlement of a debt years ago. Most people don't know it's his."

"You think that's where they're going?"

"Nobody lives there and there are no passersby. If I wanted to talk to someone who didn't want to talk to me, that would be my choice."

Hazel tried not to focus on the implication that a meeting between Mickey Argyle and Gabriel Ash could get noisy. And messy. "Maybe Alice is there, too."

Fountain shot her a sideways look. "You still think she's in danger?"

Hazel made her protesting body swivel sideways on the car

seat. She knew she must look like death warmed up. "He killed Jerome. He killed Nye Jackson. He thinks he killed me, and he means to kill Ash. Why would he draw the line at Alice?"

Fountain made no reply.

As her wits found their way back, like swallows settling on a telegraph line, Hazel remembered Patience. "The dog, sir! Ash's dog. What happened to her?"

He shrugged. "I didn't see it. It wasn't there when I arrived. Did they take it with them?"

"I don't think so. She was with me, until . . . unless they came back for her, and why would they do that? It's not like she can be a witness against them."

"It must have run off."

Hazel shook her head slowly, the picture unfolding behind her eyes. "No. She's following them. She's following the car."

"Then she's got a long journey ahead of her," grunted Fountain. "We'll probably catch up with her on the road." But they didn't.

Ash, too, woke to a sensation of hands. One hand, anyway, slapping his face—not gently, but with an insistency that rocked his battered brain. A voice was calling him, though not by his name. "Hey, dummy! Wake up. I want to talk to you."

Brain damage, which is what concussion is, surprises even the professionals with its puckishness, the way it may affect one faculty profoundly and leave another untouched. Ash couldn't see for the constellation of stars exploding in the dark room, and couldn't move for vertigo even though he was lying down. But he could hear, and he could think, too. He knew what had happened. He knew what was happening now, and he knew what was going to happen. He knew his ability to influence what was going to happen was limited by the proximity of a number of men, all of whom were stronger, fitter, and tougher than him.

"Mr. Argyle," he slurred, mostly into gritty concrete. He concentrated all his efforts on getting his face off the floor. "About time, too. Now, where's your daughter? You'd better not have hurt her."

It was a long time since anyone had surprised Mickey Argyle. No, that wasn't true. His daughter Alice had surprised him—shocked him to his foundations—only a couple of weeks ago, but before that he couldn't remember the last time.

Men like Argyle can't afford to be surprised. They need to know what's going on around them all the time. They need to know how the people they're dealing with will react in any situation. If they get it wrong, they can pay with their lives, literally or at least in a penal sense. Mickey Argyle didn't like anyone saying or doing something unexpected. He spent serious money surrounding himself with the kind of help that could keep the unexpected at bay.

Sprawled on the floor of his blacksmith's shop, grime on his tramp's clothes and blood on his hands and face, was the Norbold village idiot, beaten helpless, his long, thin limbs as capable of doing his bidding as bits of well-chewed string. His eyes were sunk deep in a gaunt face masked by dirt, blood, and bruises; he was struggled to keep them open. And yet he knew things that nobody should have known. That his *wife* didn't know. Things that existed only in Mickey's head. For all that she'd done, he hadn't laid a finger on Alice. He'd only thought—briefly, guiltily, dismissing the idea almost if not quite entirely—that he might have to. *How could the village idiot know that?*

If he couldn't, he didn't. Argyle got a grip on himself,

clamped down hard on the stunned expression that had crept over his face, and replaced it with the usual one of rigid, ruthless control. "What are you talking about?"

"Alice," said Ash carefully. He'd levered himself pretty well upright against the timber block that held the anvil in the middle of the floor, and if it had cost him blood, at least it had restored to him a little dignity. "Your daughter Alice. Who knows what you did. Who nobody has seen for days. Where is she? What have you done with her?"

"You've been spying on me? On my family?" Argyle heard himself losing his cool again, which wasn't good. Not that he cared what Ash thought. He cared what his crew thought. They did what he told them because he paid them to, but also because they were scared shitless of him. They'd have admitted as much. It was part of the deal: they probably wouldn't have worked for someone they *weren't* scared of. So it mattered if it appeared that Argyle was not on top of things. That there was someone *he* was scared of.

Of Gabriel Ash? Rambles With Dogs? How could a man like Argyle be scared of something like that? He only had to say the word and Ash was history.

But Ash's ghost could still come back to haunt him. He needed to know what Ash knew, how he knew it, and who he'd shared the information with. Not the reporter, who'd been dealt with, or the girl, who'd lost to a tree in a head-butting contest, but who else? Who else had he talked to that Argyle knew nothing about? Who *does* a village idiot talk to when he's not talking to his dog?

He hadn't thought it mattered. He hadn't thought Ash was capable of rational thought, or that anyone who was would have paid him much heed. But somehow he'd managed to convince both the Whoopsie and the hack. The fact that they'd both been neutralized didn't blind Argyle to the danger that Ash had also spoken to, and been believed by, someone else. Someone he knew nothing about.

The only one who could tell him was Ash. He leaned slowly over the man on the floor. "Tell me everything you know, and everything you think you know, and I'll let you go."

Ash rocked his head back and regarded the man laconically. Physically he felt exhausted, drained, and sick. Oddly, his mind felt light. He smiled. "No, you won't."

Argyle blinked. He was an older man than Ash by maybe ten years, of a similar build but more muscular, with thinning black hair slicked back in a manner that was more fashionable once than now. He had brown eyes without a hint of warmth in them. He frowned, puzzled by the smile. "What do you mean? *I* don't want you, and the kids are too old for pets. But you've been telling porkies about me and I need to set the record straight. Talk to whoever you've been talking to and explain how you get things wrong sometimes."

It wasn't a bad pitch. If Ash had done all his thinking inside his own head, he might have wondered if he'd made a fundamental mistake. But he hadn't. He'd hammered it out with Nye Jackson and Hazel Best, two professional people with their feet firmly on the ground; and now—he didn't think there was much doubt about this—both of them were dead. By and large, people don't get murdered to keep them from telling fairy stories.

He nodded a rueful agreement. "I *do* get things wrong sometimes."

Argyle, too, nodded, and smiled. The smile was as warm as the eyes. "It's easy done. And you haven't been well. It's easy to start imagining things. Let's talk about it, sort out what's real and what isn't."

"Then what?"

"Then we'll take you home, and I'll put things right with anyone you've accidentally misled."

"Put things right."

"Yes."

"You mean run them down with your car."

Argyle feigned shock. "Of course not. Why would I do that?"

"Hell, I don't know," said Ash disingenuously. "The same reason you've done it before? To stay out of prison?"

"I thought we talked about this." Argyle was speaking through clenched teeth now. "About how you get things wrong sometimes. I'm not going to prison. I haven't done anything to go to prison *for*."

Ash's smile broadened. He rested his forehead on the back of his wrist and propped his elbow on his bent knee. "Of course not, Mr. Argyle. It was all a misunderstanding. You're an upright citizen, an honest businessman, and a loving father, and these people"—his gaze flicked toward the men from the car—"are your valet, your accountant, and your personal astrologer. I may be mad, but I'm not a fool. I know what you did. And I know what you'll end up doing."

"I'm not going to kill you!"

"I don't mean killing me," Ash said dismissively. "I know you're going to do that. You have to. I mean, killing Alice. Because eventually you'll have to do that, too. Eventually it's going to be her or you, and when you can't make her toe the line, you'll kill her."

Mickey Argyle slapped his face. That shocked his crew as much as what the dummy had just said. They'd seen Argyle deal with people who crossed him in a number of different ways, involving everything from lump hammers to concrete galoshes. If he'd kicked Ash to a bloody pulp, then cleaned up the mess with a welding torch, they wouldn't have turned a hair. But he slapped his face. That made it personal, and they struggled with the idea of their boss having personal feelings.

And, a little, with the possibility that the dummy might be right. Fletcher said, "Boss?" uncertainly, as if seeking reassurance.

Argyle didn't spare him a glance. All his attention was on Ash. He loomed over the man on the ground like a thunderstorm. "Who have you talked to?"

"The reporter—Nye Jackson."

"Yes. And?"

"Constable Best."

"Who else?"

Ash considered for a moment. He didn't expect to walk away from this. If he talked, it would be over fast; if he didn't, it would take longer. Faster would be easier, but slow held out the faint hope that something might happen. That someone might come to his aid. It was only a very faint hope, but it was the only one he had. He lifted his head to meet Mickey Argyle's stare. "I may have mentioned it to my dog."

CHAPTER 27

HAZEL FELT MORE human with every mile that passed under the big, comfortable car's wheels. Not enough to feel equal to whatever lay ahead, perhaps, but enough to try some joined-up thinking.

"I tried to get through to you, sir. I couldn't. But DI Gorman could?"

Fountain was concentrating on the road. It wasn't designed for speed, although speed was what they needed. "I switched my phone back on after I left the meeting."

"I don't want you to think I went behind your back."

"You did what you had to do."

"Yes. There wasn't much time."

"Hazel, it's all right. I'm just glad I was close enough to help."

"Me, too." She frowned. "*I'm* glad I wasn't waiting for the local guys to arrive. They don't seem to be treating it with much urgency, do they?"

"They'd a long way to come. When I get a minute, I'll let them know we've left."

Hazel nodded carefully. "I suppose, after ten years, you must know Mickey Argyle better than most people. Well enough to know about this blacksmith's shop, for instance."

Fountain shrugged like a bear, hunched over the wheel, reading the road. "A lot of info crosses your desk in ten years. Even if you can't always use it, you don't forget it."

"Do *you* think he'd kill his daughter?"

Fountain risked a brief sideways glance. "God, I hope not!"

"He killed her fiancé. And she must know he did. And *he* must know he'll never be safe while she's alive."

"She *may* be in danger," conceded Fountain. "But not while you and Rambles are still around."

"He has Ash and he thinks I'm dead." She didn't want to ask, but she had to. "He's going to kill Gabriel, isn't he?"

A slightly longer look. "That matters to you, doesn't it?"

Hazel was taken aback. "Of course it matters! It's my job to keep him safe." She refrained, just barely, from adding: "It's your job, too."

"I know that. I mean, it's personal now as well. You've become friends. You've got fond of him."

She was about to deny it, when she realized that would be lying. "I suppose I have." She sounded surprised. "He's a good man. He's a *clever* man. Yes, we've become friends, but that isn't really the point. We—the police—would have the same obligations to him if he didn't have a friend in the world."

This time he looked her full in the face, for so long that he had to snatch at the wheel as the road came around unnoticed. "All right. Listen to me, Hazel Best, and listen good. When we get to this forge, I will do everything in my power to save Gabriel Ash. But you will stay in the car. There's nothing you can do to help, and you'll only put yourself at risk if you try."

Hazel found herself gaping. "You can't go in on your own! I'll call for backup. . . ."

"I already did," said Fountain calmly. "While you were out cold. They'll arrive soon after we do. I'll be fine. I can look after myself. I can probably look after Ash. I'm not sure I can look after all three of us."

She bit her lip. "Are you armed?"

"Don't be silly," snorted Fountain. "Mickey Argyle isn't stupid. He can't murder a chief superintendent and hope to get away with it. He'll compromise."

Hazel couldn't see any room for a compromise. "He's killed already. We *know* he's killed already. If we walk away, he doesn't, and vice versa."

Fountain sighed. "You have the makings of a good police officer, Hazel, if you'll just stop seeing everything in black and white. There's *always* somewhere to compromise. If it's only giving him five minutes of a head start before I call it in. To a man facing life in prison, a five-minute head start can look pretty attractive."

"I thought . . ." She didn't finish the sentence. "You know, when I got this posting, I was thrilled. I don't want to embarrass you, sir, but the reason was you—what you've achieved in Norbold. It's remarkable. Ten years ago the town was mired in crime of every variety. Now it's not. You must be very proud of that. I know Division is."

Fountain kept looking ahead, concentrating on the road. "You do what you can."

"If you *could* get Mickey Argyle, it would be a perfect score. The drugs scene would collapse overnight. We'd round up the little-league players who'd try to move into the vacuum, and Norbold would be as close to a crime-free town as anyone's ever likely to see."

"If," grunted Johnny Fountain.

"Of course," Hazel said quickly. "I'm not underestimating the scale of the task. I mean, you've been trying for ten years. You must have tried every trick in the book. You'd almost think the bloody man was fireproof."

"He's good at his job." Fountain shrugged. "As good at his job as I am at mine. He's been doing it nearly as long. It matters to him as much."

"Stalemate."

"I suppose."

"Today, somebody's going to lose."

He flicked her a quick look. But of course she was right. What happens when an irresistible force meets an immovable object is that you find out which of them was all mouth and no trousers.

What Mickey Argyle didn't understand was that his threats were meaningless to the man at his feet.

Gabriel Ash had no fear of dying. If the God botherers were right, he might find his family again. Even if they were wrong, it would end his torment. He had nothing left to live for, only the remote chance that one day he might learn what had happened and find those responsible. For four years, not much more than habit had kept him breathing in and out.

It wasn't that he wanted to die, more that staying alive barely seemed worth the effort. If he'd wanted to die, he could have killed himself. He'd had time and opportunity enough. But if someone was prepared to do the job for him. . . . It was like clearing out your cupboards because your neighbor has hired a Dumpster. It seemed a waste not to make use of it.

Except . . . except . . . there was the dog. Six months ago he hadn't had a friend in the world, and no one would have mourned his passing. No one except Laura Fry would have noticed, and she'd have filled his slot within the week. (This assessment was both unfair and inaccurate. Laura Fry would not only have grieved for him; she'd have lost sleep wondering if she could have helped him more.) But now there was Patience, and Ash knew she would miss him. She might never find another owner who could hear her.

On top of that, there was Alice. If he died, no barrier remained between Alice Argyle and her father's self-interest. Argyle wouldn't harm his daughter until he'd removed every other threat to his safety. But when he realized that the only one left who could bring him down was a young girl—a strong, purposeful girl—grieving for her murdered lover, Mickey Argyle would begin to contemplate the unthinkable.

Gabriel Ash wasn't afraid of death. He wasn't afraid of being dead. He wasn't even afraid of dying. A bit of him thought he deserved to suffer. A bit of him believed, like the witch finders of old, in the redemptive power of pain. He thought—and he knew he could be wrong about this—he could take the worst Argyle could do to him because it still wouldn't make up for what in his single-minded arrogance Ash had done to his family.

That was the part Argyle couldn't understand—would never understand. That there were people who had more to worry about than annoying him.

But Mickey Argyle hadn't got where he was today by quitting at the first hurdle. He looked at Ash angrily, as if the man was being deliberately difficult. "What the blue blinding blazes is *wrong* with you?" he demanded. "Why are you doing this to yourself?"

"I'm not doing it to myself," mumbled Ash.

His eyes were swollen shut and his lips were broken, the blood sticky on his chin. He was half lying, half propped against the anvil, its iron horns thrust through his bent arms. From the start—and he was no longer sure whether that was minutes or hours ago—he'd been able to do nothing to protect himself. Now he couldn't even see the blows coming. Sometimes they used fists, sometimes boots, sometimes iron bars. They'd broken several of his fingers—he'd lost count now, though he'd been acutely aware of each as the bone snapped. He'd yelled, but he'd given Argyle nothing. Nothing to make him think there was no point continuing. Somewhere in the cool center of his brain where a fragment of pure personality remained aloof from the pain, Ash was quite proud of that. Less so of the yelling.

"You can stop it."

"*You* can stop it."

Argyle scowled. This wasn't going the way it should. His first instinct was always to blame someone, but in all fairness he couldn't fault either Fletcher or the Rat for lack of effort. Any more enthusiasm for the job and they'd kill the dummy stone-dead, and before that Argyle needed to know how much Ash knew. How he'd worked it out. Who he'd told, and if any of them were still alive. So he kept asking. He just wasn't getting any answers.

Soon, Ash wouldn't be capable of giving him answers even if he wanted to. Argyle needed another approach before it was too late. More leverage.

Unfortunately the girl was dead. Fletcher had described how they'd smashed her into a tree. If they'd grabbed her instead and brought her with them, Ash would have talked. Argyle had shouted at them for that, but his heart wasn't really in it. He couldn't have imagined that the dummy would need this much persuasion, either.

The girl . . . the ghost of an idea crossed Argyle's angry, murky, conscienceless mind. Suppose he told Ash he'd sent men back to the cottage and his friend was still alive. Suppose he fetched Alice from the blacksmith's cottage and told her to pretend to be the woman constable. To beg and scream a lot. If Ash could still see, it couldn't be much, not enough to tell one distraught young woman from another. If he thought they were going to do to her what they'd been doing to him, his resolve would break.

It was getting increasingly difficult to tell Alice what to do.

Then forget the deceit. If Ash was so worried about Alice, Alice would do. Argyle wouldn't have to hurt his daughter, just frighten her. Just make the dummy think he was hurting her. He'd talk then. He'd answer any questions Argyle could think of.

His hot, angry eyes never leaving the human wreckage at his feet, Argyle growled, "Go get her."

Pausing, noticeably breathless, Fletcher frowned. "I told you, she's dead."

"Not *her.* Alice. Go get Alice."

The big man's eyes widened. Stillness held him. "Boss—are you sure?"

For only the second time in this whole violent day, Mickey Argyle struck out. His forearm swung up, knotted fist at its end, until it rapped his lieutenant across the chest. The blow was inconsequential to a man of Fletcher's scale and profession, but it shocked him nonetheless. If anyone else had hit him, they'd be picking teeth out of their lip by now. He wasn't going to hit Argyle. But he wasn't going to forget, either.

He said in a low voice, "All right. Just remember whose idea it was."

Which made Argyle blink. Fletcher never talked back to him. No one did. He'd have done something about it if he hadn't had more urgent matters on his mind. And if Fletcher hadn't already left the forge by the back door.

Argyle nudged Ash with his foot. Even the most scrupulous wouldn't have described it as a kick. "This is your fault. You remember that. Your fault, not mine."

"What is?" It wasn't that he hadn't been paying attention, or that information was leaking out of his battered brain. He wanted to make Argyle say it.

"What happens next."

"Which is?"

"That we stop hurting you and start hurting her."

"Alice. Your daughter." He said the words as clearly as his broken mouth would allow and gave them time to sink in. "You're willing to hurt your own child in order to get what you want from me."

"That's right." Argyle leaned forward, the bubble of viciousness he moved in encompassing the man on the floor. "You want to be the tough guy? Let's see how tough you are with a teenage girl screaming for your help."

Gabriel Ash said quietly, "So this is how it begins."

Argyle didn't understand. "How what begins?"

"How a man sets about killing his own child. To start with, it's a act. You don't have to hurt her; you just have to convince me you're prepared to hurt her. But what if it isn't enough? Then maybe you do hurt her, just a little bit. A slap or two. Just enough to startle that first scream out of her.

"But what if I still don't talk?" Ash asked the blurred shape bending over him. "You're committed now, aren't you? If slapping her about a bit doesn't make me want to protect her, maybe cutting her will. Not badly, nothing that won't heal—just enough to up the ante. Add a bit of blood to the screams. That should do the job, surely?

"But what if it doesn't, Mr. Argyle? What if it doesn't? Will you admit defeat? Or will you keep ratcheting up the punishment until the screams stop and there's no more left of Alice than there was of Jerome Cardy after you'd finished with him?"

The door behind them opened again as Fletcher returned, his arms around Alice Argyle in a manner as ambiguous as the situation, half protection, half restraint.

Lashed to the anvil, Ash could not turn to look at her, and anyway his vision was all but gone. Which was a pity. If he'd been able to see her, he'd have known that what he'd been through had been worth it.

She was tall and fine. She had a cap of short fair hair that had been cut well and then left to do pretty much its own thing. She had long, straight limbs, strong, like a distance runner's. She had haughty green eyes that refused absolutely to acknowledge the fear knotting her innards.

The funny thing was, anyone seeing Mickey and Alice together would have known they were father and daughter, and also that everything that mattered she'd taken from her mother's side of the family. He'd given her life, and that firmness of jaw, and the strength of purpose to take what she wanted from life, and nothing else. There was a luminosity to her that owed nothing to Argyle. In better days it had been a joy in living that radiated from her so much, it brightened the days of people who didn't even know her, who just saw her in the street. It was why she'd loved Jerome Cardy, and why he'd loved her.

It was why she'd lost him. And it was why she, too, was now facing death. The haughty green eyes that refused to acknowledge the fear were too intelligent not to acknowledge the danger.

She was also dirty, as if she'd been locked in a dusty room for several days, and her hands were tied with cord in front of her. She saw Ash hanging from the anvil and her heart skipped beats. She rounded on her father in disgust. "*Now* what have you done, you frigging madman?"

Argyle was struggling to clear his head of the images Ash had planted there. "Do you recognize him?"

"His own mother wouldn't recognize him!"

"It's Sir Lancelot."

Alice stared at him as if genuinely doubting his sanity. But a real madman would have had some kind of an excuse. Argyle's only excuse was that there were things that he wanted and hadn't got yet. Alice refused him the compliment of an answer.

Argyle went on regardless, his voice spiteful. "Your knight in shining armor. He's been worried about you. He was afraid something bad might have happened to you."

He still had the power to take her breath away. She kept her silence because the only possible alternative was to howl like a dog.

Argyle turned to Ash, nudged him again with the side of his foot. "See? She's fine. Don't worry about her. Just tell me what I need to know."

If Ash had been as groggy as he looked, it might have worked. Unable to hold on to the line of his reasoning, he might have thought this was what he'd been hanging on for. That he'd absorbed the punishment for Alice, but now that he knew she was unhurt, he didn't need to absorb any more. But in fact most of his injuries were superficial. Fletcher knew his job well enough to avoid inflicting the kind of head trauma that would make nonsense of anything a man said.

Ash considered for a moment. Then he whispered, "Alice?"

Alice Argyle stayed where she was. An appalled tremor shook her voice. "Who *are* you?"

"Gabriel Ash. That doesn't matter. Listen to me. I've got something to tell you. Something important."

"What?"

"Listen . . ."

At a nod from Argyle, Fletcher took her closer. Alice bent to catch the words trickling from the broken lips. "I'm listening."

Ash sucked in enough breath to say everything he had to, because he knew he wouldn't get a second chance. "If you want to live, get away from here right now. It doesn't matter what you have to do or who you have to hurt—just do it and go and don't look back."

It was instructive how everyone in the forge reacted. The Rat looked at Fletcher. Fletcher shot a fast look at Argyle. Argyle moved almost like a ballet dancer to finally deliver the kick he'd been toying with for half an hour, not to Ash's cracked ribs or broken hands to punish him, but to his jaw to shut him up.

Alice recognized good advice when she got it and acted on it immediately, with courage and determination. She made no attempt to free her hands but drove one elbow as hard as she could into Fletcher's belly, picked up the length of rebar they'd been using on Ash, and bent it round the Rat's head. Then she used the leftover momentum to hurl it at her father and was on her way out of the door before any of them had time to grab her.

And there she stopped dead. Which would have been a bad mistake except that she'd run up against the sudden unexpected presence of Chief Superintendent Johnny Fountain, and it was like running into a small outhouse that someone had parked in the way.

CHAPTER 28

THE MEN BEHIND her were all picking themselves up, except for Ash, who stayed where he was, bleeding, so it took them a few moments to recognize that the situation had changed not once but twice. A stillness grew in the forge as one after another they noticed the new arrival and weighed what his presence here meant.

At last Mickey said guardedly, "Mr. Fountain."

"Mr. Argyle."

"What are you doing here?"

Fountain looked past him to the man on the floor. "What are *you* doing here?"

Argyle straightened up. "Nothing to concern you."

Fountain sighed. "Mickey, *everything* you do concerns me. It has done for the last ten years. Now I'm going to make you an offer that you really shouldn't refuse, because it's the best chance you have of still being a free man tomorrow morning. Get in your car, go home, pack. Use your contacts, your money, and your initiative to get out of the country some way that no one will see you going. If you're really lucky, we may never find you."

Argyle's thin lip curled. "I'm not going anywhere, Mr. Fountain. Why should I? Nothing has changed."

"Nothing's *changed*?" Suddenly Fountain was roaring like a cannon. "*Everything* has changed. You had a twenty-year-old boy beaten to death in my cells! How dare you, you arrogant little bastard!"

"He was fucking my daughter!" snarled the gangster. "What was I supposed to do—hold his coat? I warned him off. I told him what would happen if he didn't get back to whatever monkey jungle he came from. He thought he could give me the finger! *Nobody* gives me the finger, Mr. Fountain—nobody."

Alice had been following the exchange like someone at an increasingly tense tennis match, head turning first one way, then the other. None of it was exactly news to her—she knew what had happened and why—but this was the first time Argyle had admitted in front of her what he'd done. Finally she could contain herself no longer.

"He loved me, you mindless thug!" she yelled, her voice soaring—with pain, with distress, most of all with fury. "And I loved him. You've ruined my *life*. What are you going to do now—kill me as well? Everyone here knows you're capable of it. Only he"—she indicated Ash—"will even be shocked. So if you're going to do it, *Daddy*"—she filled the word with infinite vitriol—"do it here and do it now. If you ask him nicely, I bet Mr. Fountain will hold *your* coat."

If she'd spent hours studying to insult the chief superintendent, she could hardly have done any better. A dull flush the color of brickwork spread up Fountain's craggy cheeks. Men of his rank don't often hear exactly what other people think of them.

Until that moment, he'd thought Constable Best's fears for Alice were exaggerated. But the girl knew the situation she was in. She knew her father needed her dead. If Argyle hadn't realized it yet, he would soon. The scenario dreamed up by his newest constable and her strange new friend was no longer hypothetical.

Fountain's voice dropped low again. "What about it, Mickey? Are you going to take your chances—grab what you can and run?"

Argyle shook his head. He said, with a finality that was like the sound of a vault door shutting, "I'm not going anywhere."

The policeman nodded, unsurprised. He wasn't sure how this was going to end now. But he knew how it wasn't going to end, not if he could stop it. He half turned toward Alice. "There's a constable in my car outside. Go and get in, and lock the door."

As Fletcher extended an uncertain hand to bar her way, Fountain's voice hardened. "And you two get the same choice I gave your boss. Stay, or go. Choose now, because you won't get another chance."

Again, the Rat looked at Fletcher and Fletcher looked at Argyle. For what felt like a long time, no one said anything. Then Argyle growled, "You don't really need me to tell you, do you?" But it spoke volumes that he felt he had to say it.

The big man gave a little sigh that sounded almost like despair. But Argyle was right: for a hired thug it was no choice at all. "We're with you, boss."

"So I should bloody well think. Go outside. Stop Mr. Fountain's muscle from interfering. Or leaving."

Fletcher nodded, and he and the Rat went out.

They expected to find Alice Argyle being comforted by an enormous rugby-playing hulk who might need subduing. When they saw it was just another girl, not very much older, they relaxed.

This may have been a mistake.

"They're sorting things out," Fletcher told his corporal confidently, indicating the forge with a jerk of the head. "We're to wait out here."

That suited Hazel fine. She'd no intentions of going anywhere, not without Ash, or at least without knowing what had become of him. The girl complicated matters, because professional instinct said she should get the civilian out of harm's way at the first opportunity. But Hazel Best knew herself well enough to know that the big man standing by the car door was an excuse for not leaving; he wasn't really the reason.

Fountain always carried a penknife. It was about all that a man in a suit could have without being accused of carrying a concealed weapon. He went to cut Ash free.

Argyle stood in his way. "You know he isn't leaving here, don't you, John?"

"Mickey—you don't make the rules anymore. You don't get to say how this ends."

"It doesn't have to end," snarled Argyle impatiently. "Not for either of us." He looked at Ash. "And what's he? Does he even have a name? No one will miss him, no one will come looking for him. It's like putting down a mad dog—really, you're doing it a favor."

"And Constable Best?"

Misunderstanding, Argyle shrugged. "A road accident. These country lanes are a lot more dangerous than they look. When she's found, the local plods will interview the local farmers, learn nothing, and give up. Hit-and-run. Stranger to the area, vanished back to where he came from."

"She isn't dead."

That did alter things. If Argyle had known she was sitting

in the car outside, he might have thought it didn't alter them very much. But Fountain didn't tell him that.

"How much does she know?"

"She's a smart girl. I think what she hasn't worked out already, she *will* work out."

Argyle's narrow eyebrows soared. "Well, that decides it. There's no point wasting any more time on this idiot. I'll put a bullet in his brain now, and the boys can dump him in a reservoir somewhere. Then we'll round up the girl. With both of them out of the picture, we're safe enough."

Fountain shook his head. "You're wrong, Mickey. It *does* have to end, and this is where. Ten years late, maybe, but better late than never."

Argyle was regarding him quizzically. "John—what exactly is it that you think you're going to do? That you think I'm going to *let* you do?"

"My job," said Johnny Fountain simply. "Michael Argyle, I'm arresting you on suspicion of—well, actually, because I know you're guilty of—just about every crime in the book. You do not have to say anything. But it may harm your defense—assuming you can find a brief imaginative enough to come up with one—"

He got no further with his hand-knit caution. Argyle took a step backward, reached behind him, and drew a gun.

Fountain looked at his penknife and felt underdressed.

Here," said Fletcher, looking at Hazel in some alarm, "you're dead!"

"That's right," Hazel said evenly. "I've come back to haunt you."

She'd moved into the driver's seat after Fountain got out of the car. The key was in the ignition, so she had a weapon of a kind, albeit one she couldn't pull as quickly as Fletcher could pull his gun. He wore it under his jacket, a hard, unmistakable lump that would have made a tailor cry. Only the possibility that they might need to leave in a hurry kept her behind the wheel. Because Alice Argyle, stubborn as always, had refused to get in beside her and was standing by the wing, her hands still tied, staring at the big man with undisguised contempt.

"Why do you do everything he tells you?" she asked.

To Fletcher the answer was obvious. "He pays my wages."

"Then why do you work for him?"

He thought for a moment it was a trick question, but it wasn't, just another easy one to answer. He said it again, with slightly increased emphasis. "Because he pays my wages."

"Did you kill him?"

That was harder. She'd need to be more specific. "Him who?"

Her voice dripped acid. "Jerome. Jerome Cardy. The man I was going to marry."

Fletcher shook his head. "Barking Mad Barclay. I thought you knew that."

"I know who got Jerome's blood on his shirt! I want to know who's got blood on his hands. Apart from my father, of course. Was it you? Was it you who fixed things so Jerome would be put in a cell with a homicidal racist?"

"No," said Fletcher, and from the way his eyes flared it may have been the truth. "I just do the heavy lifting. The boss doesn't trust me with the clever stuff."

"He never did anyone any harm." Alice's gaze raked his cheek like claws. "Jerome. All he wanted to do was help people. The only thing he did wrong was love me."

"I know." There was the least hesitation in his voice. "It

was . . . rough. But come on, girl, you know how the boss feels. He was never going to take that on the chin!"

If simple hatred killed people, he'd have been lying on the ground now. Smoking. "I remember you from when I was a child," Alice said. "You used to carry me on your shoulders. You said it was because I could see farther from your shoulders than from my father's, but that wasn't the reason. He never wanted to carry me. He didn't want to wrinkle his suit.

"You carried me on your shoulders. I think you taught me to ride a bike?" Fletcher dipped his gaze in a nod. "Then you stood by and let him kill the man I loved, and now you're going to stand by and watch him kill me."

"I . . ." She'd touched him somewhere unexpected, left him floundering. "I . . . no. That's not—"

"Of course that's what he intends to do! He has no choice. It's him or me now." She glanced back at the forge door. "That man in there, the one you've been kicking nine bells out of, he knows it. So does she"—a nod at Hazel. "I've known for days. I've known since he brought me here. He was never going to be able to let me go. Now you know, too. So I'm going to give *you* a choice. My father or me. Choose me, and we take him down. Choose him, and he's still going down, but you'll have a hell of a lot more to answer for when he does."

The big man made no reply. Hazel, her heart thudding in her ears, thought he couldn't, was literally unable to, reach a decision.

Alice thrust her hands at him. "Untie me."

"Alice, pet . . ."

"*Untie me!*" she shouted. "Right now!"

After another, infinitely long pause he did.

Now she held her right hand out. “Gun.”

“No way!”

She didn’t take the hand back. Unyielding, she said it again. “Gun.”

“No.”

CHAPTER 29

"THIS DOESN'T HAVE to end with one of us dead, John," said Mickey Argyle.

"No, it doesn't," agreed Fountain.

"I'm not going to prison."

"You could still make a dash for the Harwich ferry."

"And leave everything I've worked for? When hell freezes over!"

Johnny Fountain sniffed reflectively. "The night this all started I was getting the Freedom of the Borough."

He had a penknife against Argyle's automatic pistol. That wasn't a great situation to be in, although there was an upside. An armed man facing an unarmed man thinks he's invulnerable. He thinks he has time. He thinks no one would be stupid enough to take him on. That was how Argyle was feeling now. That he'd already won. That the chunk of steel in his hand was heavy enough to outweigh everything else.

Fountain bent over deliberately and finished cutting Ash free. He didn't think Argyle would shoot him for it, and he was right. Nor did he think Ash would leap to his feet, arm himself with some leftover horseshoes, and change fundamentally the balance of the standoff, and he was right about that, too. Gabriel Ash couldn't have got to his feet to save his own life or anyone else's. All the same, he was glad to be free. There's no pride in being lashed to a lump of iron while people hit you.

Argyle watched with impatience and disbelief. He couldn't see the dilemma. From where he was standing, the way ahead was clear. "Okay. I know this hasn't been easy for you. It hasn't been easy for me—it was my daughter fell for that black buck. None of it would have been necessary if it wasn't for her. But let's be sensible now. All we need to do is tidy up and no one will be any the wiser. I'll deal with the loose ends"—he waved the gun casually at Ash—"and pack Alice off to some associates overseas until she's prepared to be reasonable, and that's it: problem solved.

"All you have to do is walk away. Go to the funerals, say how sorry you are, say you've got your best people on it. We both know they'll get no further than they have before. I don't mind being suspected of all sorts as long as there's no proof. Okay? Two bullets is all it's going to take." He looked at Ash disapprovingly. "I doubt this one even needs a bullet. Bursting a paper bag should see him off."

"And Constable Best?"

Mickey grinned. "Best you don't ask."

Half of Chief Superintendent Fountain was appalled and half was actually tempted. Appalled, because however much he understood the theory of people like Argyle, in practice the complete disregard for human life still had the power to stagger him. Tempted, because when Argyle could lay it out in a couple of sentences, he had to acknowledge that it was possible. Simple, even. He didn't have to put his life on the line. Life could go on pretty much the same, except for Gabriel Ash and Hazel Best.

"No," said Johnny Fountain.

Argyle's narrow brows lowered. "I could always make it three bullets."

"You want to shoot me, Mickey? You really want to shoot me? Not a probationer Whoopsie who's already out of the picture, but a senior police officer? You know what happens to people who kill cops. They never get away with it. They might think they have, for a while. But every cop in the world has a vested interest in catching them, and the odds are just too great. One day in Vienna or Venezuela you run a red light and it's game over. That's why, as a general rule of thumb, your people leave my people alone. You *know* this, Mickey. I'm not telling you anything you don't already know."

Silence confirmed this.

"Take what I'm offering and go," said Fountain. "There's no other game in town."

Finally Argyle seemed to be thinking about it. About getting out with what he could carry before even that door closed. It would mean leaving behind a lifestyle he'd spent ten years perfecting. But if he could take the profits with him, he could start again somewhere. Somewhere nicer than Norbold. Somewhere ripe for the picking.

It wasn't what he wanted. If he'd been ready to retire, he could have done it at any time, and—crucially—at a time of his choosing. But you can't always have everything you want, even if your name is Mickey Argyle. Sometimes you have to settle for second prize. If he stayed, he'd be risking it all. And there was no need. He'd already achieved everything he wanted, made as much money as he could spend, put the fear of God into as many people as any one man could hope to. He could go now and enjoy the fruits of his labors with, so to speak, a clear conscience.

Nobody told Mickey Argyle what to do. In one game-changing second his mouth twisted into an ugly shape and the gun came up. "Go to hell, Mr. Fountain."

Gunfire in an enclosed space fills the room, echoing off every hard surface. One shot can sound like a volley, two like a battlefield. Johnny Fountain's eyes opened wide in surprise. It had been a risky strategy; he'd known that. Still he never expected it to end this way.

On the floor, still leaning against the anvil, Ash flinched and squeezed his eyes tight. He didn't think he was the target this time, but he lacked the particular kind of courage to stare down the muzzle of a gun in order to see where it was pointing.

Mixed in with the gunfire was another bang as the door of the smithy hit the wall, and suddenly there were more people in the workshop than there had been and—what with the echoes still bouncing around and the smell of cordite—for a moment he couldn't work out who any of them were.

One of them was Alice Argyle, holding a handgun as though she'd been taught how, a dirty unkempt nineteen-year-old girl pointing a gun as if she meant it. Another was Hazel Best.

For three attenuated seconds nothing changed. Mickey Argyle kept his gun on Johnny Fountain; Alice Argyle kept hers on her father. Chief Superintendent Fountain stayed on his feet; Gabriel Ash stayed on the floor. Hazel looked from one to another of them, wondering who needed her help most, or most urgently, or was past benefitting from it, and whether—simply by moving—she'd break the spell and someone would die in front of her.

After three seconds Mickey Argyle let out an oddly gentle sigh, lowered his weapon, then slowly folded to the floor at Fountain's feet. There were two neat holes in his chest.

Alice Argyle kept pointing her gun at him, as if at the least provocation she would empty it into his dead body. "He killed Jerome." She spoke through clenched teeth.

"Yes," agreed Hazel. "Give me the gun. Alice—give me the gun."

Finally Fountain's brain accepted the evidence of his senses and understood that he hadn't been shot. He made a conscious effort to relax all the muscles holding him rigid. "All right. Is anyone hurt?" Then he looked at Argyle, at Ash, at Alice. He looked again at Hazel. "Okay, silly question. Was anyone else hit?"

By now Hazel had Fletcher's gun. He'd given it up because, bottom line, Alice was her father's daughter and Fletcher was trained to jump when an Argyle said "Jump." He hadn't known what she intended to do with it. He hadn't asked himself. The Rat had run at that point, but Fletcher was waiting out by the cars, ready to do what he was told by the first Argyle to emerge from the forge.

Hazel's left arm was around Alice, trying to still the shaking of her slender young body. She said tersely to Fountain, "We need an ambulance, and we need DI Gorman here right now. Get him on the phone, find out how long he'll be." It didn't strike either of them as odd, that she was issuing instructions to a man who outranked her by a whole career.

Gabriel Ash, beaten bloody, weak as a kitten and dizzy as a lush, mumbled through broken lips, "Detective Inspector Gorman isn't coming."

Fountain looked at him. Hazel passed him a tissue, though what good she expected him to do with it wasn't clear. "We called him from the cottage." She was keeping her voice very calm, very level, for fear of what would happen if she didn't. "He'll be here any moment."

"No," said Ash, "he won't."

Hazel thought he hadn't understood. She explained as simply as she could. "We talked to him before we left the cottage. Mr. Fountain knew about this place. He guessed Argyle would have you brought here. DI Gorman was going to get crewed up and meet us. Really," she added with a touch of asperity, "he should be here by now."

"Who called him?" asked Ash.

"Mr. Fountain." She looked at the big man standing very still in the middle of the concrete floor. When she said it again, there was a slightly different inflection in her voice. "Chief Superintendent Fountain did."

Ash used the tissue to clear himself a little vision. He tried not to notice how much of his blood came away on it, concentrated on Fountain. "Do you want to tell her or shall I?"

Fountain said nothing. There was a slightly puzzled half smile on his big craggy face. Hazel looked at the pair of them over Alice's shoulder. "Tell me what?" Her voice didn't sound like her own. "Tell me what, sir?"

Fountain shook his head. He blew out a gusty breath of relief. "I'm not sure. I think he's a bit . . . disorientated. It's no wonder." He reached out. "I'll look after Alice. You see what you can do for Ram—Mr. Ash. And I'll call Dave Gorman. Maybe he's having trouble finding us. Or maybe he never got the message."

"Message?" echoed Hazel. She frowned. "I thought . . ."

Fountain took Alice from her and walked the girl to the open door, where she didn't have to look at what she'd done. "It's all right, you know," he was saying reassuringly. "What you did. You're not in any trouble. He was going to kill me. You saved my life."

Hazel crouched beside Ash, still looking uncertainly at her chief superintendent. "I thought . . ."

"You thought he'd spoken to DI Gorman?" Ash looked

terrible, and his damaged mouth slurred the words, but his mind was working better than hers. "He told you that?" She nodded. "He didn't call anyone. He wanted to sort it out himself. He *needed* to sort it out himself."

"Why?"

There was a longish pause. He seemed to be wondering if she had to know. But of course she did—it all had to come out now, and Hazel Best had more right to know than anyone. "Because Sergeant Murchison wasn't the one in Argyle's pocket. *He* was."

Hazel didn't tell him he was crazy, because she knew he wasn't, and didn't suggest that he was concussed, because he probably was, but she didn't think it was that, either. "Explain."

"They had a deal. Him and Argyle, going back years. Fountain would leave Argyle alone if Argyle would help him tidy up the rest of Norbold. Stop his own people moonlighting, I suppose, keep an iron hand on his end of town, pass on any information that came his way as long as it didn't impact on his own business.

"That's how Mr. Fountain made such an impact in a high-crime area. He turned it into a low-crime area within a couple of years, and he kept it that way until today. Except for the drugs. Didn't it strike anyone as odd that he could get on top of everything from mugging to murder but the drugs scene just seemed to go from strength to strength?"

"I . . . you can't . . . nobody's a hundred percent successful," managed Hazel.

"That's true. But it's a lot easier if your prime suspect is helping you on the sly."

Hazel straightened up slowly. She was looking at Fountain. "Is this true?"

The chief superintendent gave a disparaging sniff. "Hazel,

you know who he is. You know *what* he is. For pity's sake, recognize a fairy story when you hear one."

Her gaze turned back to Ash. "Gabriel, you do know what you're saying? That it wasn't Donald Murchison who helped Argyle to murder Jerome Cardy, it was Mr. Fountain."

"Yes," said Ash simply.

Fountain gave a snort that was half a chuckle. "Hazel, you *know* where I was that night! In the Town Hall, getting the Freedom of Norbold from the mayor with four hundred of the great and good looking on." As alibis go, it was a pretty good one.

"Were you in uniform?"

Fountain smiled. "Dinner jacket and black tie."

That wasn't a lie; it would be too easy to check. Ash stepped mentally around it. "It's two minutes' walk from the Town Hall to Meadowvale. If Constable Best asks your wife, will she be able to say you never left her sight all evening? Didn't go to the gents, didn't nip out for a cigar? Ten minutes was all it would take. Once Argyle got word that Jerome was in custody, he sent you a message to say Barclay would be on his way in shortly. All you had to do was make sure they were put in the same cell.

"It wasn't Sergeant Murchison I saw outside the cell door, it was you. You took off your dinner jacket and your tie, and you looked like every other officer on duty that night. I saw a white shirt, dark trousers, shiny shoes, and I heard you say a few words. The chances of my recognizing you were minuscule."

This time Fountain said nothing. And that wasn't right. Perhaps he didn't feel the need to explain himself to Ash, but he owed Hazel better than to leave her wondering if the man she'd admired all this time, the man she'd worried about letting down, had feet of clay all the way up to the armpits. Was corrupt to his soul, and responsible for the brutal death of a twenty-year-old boy. If he'd had anything to say to her, he'd have said it then.

She found herself speaking aloud the thoughts that were chasing one another's tails in her head. "Even alone, you could have done everything that Donald Murchison and a couple of mates could have done. You could have let yourself in the back way without anyone knowing you were on the premises. The CCTV would have picked you up, except that the geek"—she couldn't remember his name—"had told everyone not to fiddle with it or it would die. You fiddled, it died, and there was no record that you were ever there that night. Until Sergeant Murchison called to say there'd been a DIC and you hurried back to deal with it."

"He wanted you out of Meadowvale," Ash told her tiredly, "not because you were barking up the wrong tree but because you were too close to the truth. You knew *someone* at Meadowvale had a hand in Jerome's murder. If Sergeant Murchison had managed to clear himself, you'd have wondered who else it could be. You were still thinking about it after everyone else thought they knew what had happened. That made you dangerous."

Finally, terribly late if he'd been innocent of what he was accused of, Johnny Fountain turned—his whole big body pivoting—and met Hazel's stare. He spoke very deliberately. "You know this is nonsense, don't you? You *must* know better than to listen to a man who hasn't been on nodding terms with reality for the last four years."

But Hazel was still thinking, and the more she thought the more the facts slotted into place. "How did Argyle know we were at the cottage?"

Fountain shrugged. "You must have left a trail."

She shook her head, no doubt in her mind. "No. The only

people I spoke to before Argyle's crew turned up were Rossi and you. You think IPCC had my call traced? The only one with a reason to do that was Argyle's glove puppet, and I never spoke to Donald Murchison. Anyway, he doesn't have the authority. It was you. I asked you for help, and you told Mickey Argyle where to find us."

Still something didn't fit. "Is DI Gorman involved as well? Because even if you didn't talk to him, I know I did. After the gorillas arrived at the cottage and before they ran me down, I told him we were in trouble."

Fountain said nothing, left her to flounder.

Ash was looking at the chief superintendent. "You lied to Gorman as well. He called you after Hazel called him. You put him off—said you were closer and you'd get some local help to deal with it. That's why he never turned up at the cottage, and why he hasn't found this place. He doesn't know he should be looking."

CHAPTER 30

"You found me out cold in the lane," recalled Hazel. Her eyes were wide with shock, but now her brain was in gear. "You said you'd called DI Gorman, but it was him who called you. And you told him everything was under control. You didn't want him showing up at the cottage, any more than you want him showing up here. You're not here to save Ash, or Alice. You're here to make sure that no one who knows about your deal with Mickey Argyle is ever going to talk about it."

Another pregnant pause, then Johnny Fountain said, "That's right." He was looking at the penknife still gripped in his hand. "With this."

When he saw that none of them realized it was a joke, he let out a gruff, despairing little laugh. "Oh, God help us all! I'm a policeman, for pity's sake! I don't go around killing people."

Hazel found her voice first. "But people die because of the kind of policeman you are. Jerome Cardy died because the crime returns mattered more to you than the fate of an innocent individual. Nye Jackson died because he found out about Jerome and Alice Argyle."

She was still aching for him to deny it. Perhaps even now

they'd got it wrong. Perhaps when he'd finished teasing, he'd put Hazel, and the world, straight. She could bear for him to think her stupid if she could avoid knowing he was corrupt. This was a man she'd respected long before she met him, a copper's copper. And not a paper tiger, more style than substance, who wanted the accolades without the hard slog necessary to achieve them.

Fountain sighed. "I'm sorry about young Cardy." He looked at the girl in his arms, and didn't try to stop her when she—carefully, watching his face—moved away. "Truly. I'd no idea things would go that far. I thought he'd get away with a broken nose, maybe a cracked rib. Mickey told me about him and Alice, said he wanted to mark his card. That's all. That's all I agreed to, and I only agreed to that because I thought I could keep matters from escalating. All right, I was wrong, but give me credit for good intentions.

"Jackson came as a complete surprise. I didn't know his death *wasn't* an accident. I suppose you're sure?" No one dignified that with an answer, so he shrugged. "I'm sorry about him, too, although the man was becoming a nuisance. I suppose it's what you risk if you want to be an investigative journalist."

The sheer impertinence of that struck Hazel to the heart. "He was just doing his job! No, he was doing *your* job. He was trying to find out why a twenty-year-old boy . . ."

And there her voice petered out, foundered on the thing he'd just said. She felt the last of the color drain from her cheeks. He'd dashed all her hopes in a few words. She'd been right, and Ash had been right, and Fountain wasn't even going to deny it. Argyle had had a mole at Meadowvale since before Hazel came to Norbold, and it was the chief superintendent.

Ash reached a decision. It was time he got off the floor. He labored as far as his knees, clinging to the anvil; Fountain helped him the rest of the way. He stood swaying, his head low, his face a butcher's mask. "You realize, of course, you're going down for this."

There was something supercilious in Fountain's gaze. "You reckon?"

Hazel's voice was breathy, as if he'd knocked the wind out of her all over again. "You think there's some *doubt*? You think you can do what you've done, and people find out about it, and you can still get away with it?"

The broad shoulders shrugged. "Maybe."

"*How?*"

"If I can persuade you that what I did was right."

In moments of stress Hazel Best occasionally lapsed to the kind of coarseness her late mother had disapproved of. She'd called it "common." "Oh yeah, like that's going to happen!"

"I am not a bad man," said Chief Superintendent Fountain forcibly. "I am not a bad policeman. I did some things that weren't in the manual. I did them because they were the lesser of the evils I was facing."

Suddenly he seemed to run out of patience. "You're such a *child,* Hazel! Such an innocent. How do you *think* I keep a town like Norbold safe? I do deals all the time—with Division, with the council, with the support services, with the taxpayers. I can wrap them up in cotton wool, so no harm will ever befall them, at a price no one could ever pay; or I can give them what they can reasonably afford and accept that sometimes it won't be enough.

"So yes, I take shortcuts. Turning a blind eye to Mickey Argyle was one of them. I kept my end of town clean, and he looked after his. He kept the lowlifes under control, made sure they didn't bother the nice people of middle England who pay their rates and don't want to know what goes on at gutter level.

Look at the figures. It worked. It saved lives every year. It saved lives, and pain, and fear, and money."

He almost managed to make it sound reasonable. As if he'd held this debate with himself so often that he'd honed his argument until it sounded almost reasonable.

"You've no idea what Norbold was like ten years ago. Crime was out of control. People got hurt, or worse, for being on the wrong street at the wrong time. Even in broad daylight. Women saved their shopping till their husbands came home, so they'd have someone riding shotgun. Old people traveled in convoy to collect their pensions. Nobody was safe."

"Nobody was safe because of people like Mickey Argyle!" exclaimed Hazel.

"Perfectly true," agreed Fountain. "There were half a dozen major players at that time, probably twenty significant street gangs, and more one-man bands than you could shake a truncheon at. It would have taken the Met two years to clean it up. Nothing less would even have made an impact.

"When they told me to take a crack at it, I had three options. I could quail before the enormity of the task and take to drink, which is what my predecessor did. I could do my best with what I'd got, which meant throwing patrols at the center of town and never mind what went on in the rest of the manor. Or I could get myself some allies. I chose Mickey not because he was the best of a bad lot but because he was the biggest, meanest dog in town. When he barked, the other dogs cowered."

If he was honest with himself—and Fountain had never lost the ability to be honest with himself, in the middle of the night with Denis snoring companionably beside him—it wasn't just an act of desperation. There had been a kind of glory to it, too—a headiness, as of too much wine and brave talk. There's a saying in

India: "He who rides a tiger can never dismount." But then you have to ask why people would want to ride a tiger in the first place. And the answer is: for the glory. For the sheer intoxicating splendor of doing something most people couldn't do and wouldn't dare try. Even if the beast wasn't really tamed, even if you rode it only on its own terms, for a certain kind of man the admiration that earned was worth the price that deep inside himself he knew he would someday have to pay.

Except that Johnny Fountain still wasn't entirely convinced that payday had arrived. The biggest obstacle to finding a way through this lay dead on the floor. Nothing would have bought Argyle's silence if Fountain had broken their truce. The others were more of an unknown quantity. More honest, of course, appalled by what he'd done, but possibly also more open to reason. If he could find the key to each of them, he might yet secure their cooperation.

Paradoxically, Constable Best, whose snooping had brought him to this pass, might be the easiest to convince. "Hazel, try to see it from where I was sitting. Norbold was like a Wild West town after the sheriff's been lynched. Nothing I did, nothing I had the manpower or the budget to do, made any difference. We arrested gang leaders, and the next rank down took their place. There was no end to them. Kids of eight and nine were carrying lethal weapons."

He paused, remembering. Hazel watched him intently, and for the life of her she could not see a wicked man. "When I first thought of cutting a deal with Mickey, it was like a joke. But the idea wouldn't go away. Because I knew it could work. I could give the silent majority of Norbold what they'd been begging for—the right to feel safe in their own town. And it wasn't going to cost them anything, and all it was going to cost me was some self-respect. I'd tried to get Mickey and failed. Really, the only difference was that now I stopped trying.

"And credit where credit's due," said Fountain generously, "he kept his end of the bargain. He cleaned up the gangs by giving them a simple choice: line up behind him or quit. Once he'd tamed them, the only crime in town—if you leave out the odd drunken housebreaker and a bit of domestic violence—was *his* crime, and he kept it off my streets. Users and pushers still ended up dead sometimes. I'm not saying that's a good thing, but it's the life they chose—nobody forced them. Decent law-abiding people were off-limits. That's what I achieved: that the vast majority of Norbold's citizens could get on with their lives in peace and security."

The man still, somehow, commanded respect. His argument did not. "Jerome Cardy was a decent law-abiding person! Nye Jackson was a decent law-abiding person. And actually," snapped Hazel, "I am and so is Ash. Your friend Mickey was going to kill us both."

"I know it got out of hand," admitted Fountain. "Mickey took his eyes off the prize when it got personal. He said he wanted to drum young Cardy out of town and I agreed to help. Reluctantly. I thought it was better than having them deal with him in a dark alley some night."

Alice couldn't contain a peal of hysterical laughter. Fountain frowned his disapproval, as if she were a child cheeking her betters. "You don't have to believe me. But that's what I thought. That if it was going to happen, it was better happening at Meadowvale.

"Mickey set it up. Not the accident, which was nothing more than that. But when he heard that Jerome had been arrested, he made arrangements to have Barclay arrested, too. All he wanted from me was to make sure they ended up in the same cell. It didn't seem that big an ask. I saw to it after the speeches had finished. When I heard later that the boy was dead, I was as horrified as anyone." His scowl dared Hazel to call him a liar.

"So what should I have done? Owned up? Would that have made Norbold a better place? Mickey wouldn't have come quietly. He and his crew would have shot huge holes in the thin blue line. I'll tell you something else." Under its mane of white hair the craggy face leaned forward urgently. "We play this wrong now and there'll still be mayhem. With Mickey gone, there's a power vacuum that every dog he kept at heel will want to fill.

"What do you suppose will happen if I go, too? The *only* hope of keeping the lid on Norbold right now is me. You talk to IPCC and I guarantee you that tonight all hell will break loose. People will die—lots of people. And some of them will be little thugs taking on bigger thugs, but some of them will be ordinary citizens and some of them will be police officers. Hazel—do you really want that on your conscience?"

"You talk . . ." Her voice cracked and she had to try again. "You talk as if there's an alternative. As if we can go back to Meadowvale and carry on like nothing happened!"

"No," Fountain agreed candidly, "of course that's not an option. I'll resign. I'll take responsibility for what happened to Jerome—it's my station, it was always my responsibility—and I'll leave. But before that I'll make sure nobody takes over where Mickey left off. That can be my legacy. To put things right before I go. To leave a town at peace instead of under anarchy. Wouldn't that be better? Honestly?" It was a tribute to the sheer power of his personality that she found herself wondering if it wouldn't.

It was necessary to say something before he took her silence for consent. "What about Alice? What can you offer her to *begin* to make up for the harm you've done?"

Fountain pivoted slowly, his glance sweeping over the forge

like the beam of a lighthouse. "I can't bring her fiancé back. But I can make all this"—he indicated the dirty workshop and the dead man on the floor—"go away. Give me the gun. Nobody need ever know that Alice shot her father. *I* shot Mickey Argyle. He tried to kill me, I got him first. No one will even question it. And Alice doesn't have to go through the rest of her life with the gutter press haunting her every move."

No one said, "Yes, that would be best," but no one told him what he could do with his suggestion, either. The silence *had* to mean they were considering it. Against their better instincts perhaps, but considering it nonetheless. For Alice. For Alice who'd lost everything, who wasn't to blame for any of this but who was going to pay for it, one way or another.

Fountain wasn't thinking about Alice. Fountain was trying to see his way out of this mess with his reputation, and if possible his pension, intact. It was true what he'd told Hazel—he'd gone into it with good intentions. He'd climbed onto the tiger's back thinking it would take out the other tigers for him and then he could vanquish it. He still didn't feel that being unable to complete the task made him a bad man.

All Fountain could think about was Denis. How she would face up to his disgrace. Bravely, of course, but God, he'd have given anything to save her that. He'd have given his life. Widow's weeds at a police funeral would at least have left her some dignity, and she'd never have known that he let her down. If it all came out, Denis was going to be so disappointed. He thought she'd stand by him—in fact he knew she would—and he thought she'd speak her mind only once, only to him, and after that she'd be the dutiful, supportive wife for as long as necessary. But Fountain had no illusions about what it would do to her.

Unless these three people could be persuaded that there

were better ways for this to end than with him in the dock and photos of Alice Argyle all over the tabloids. He thought Constable Best was at least considering his proposition. Alice, he thought, would do what the others told her to. Which left Gabriel Ash. Rambles With Dogs.

Johnny Fountain smiled at the battered man. "You're thinking I've nothing to offer you. Nothing to set against the satisfaction of showing a town that humiliated you that you were cleverer than its senior police officer and its top gangster put together.

"But you're wrong. You see, Mr. Ash, I know things. I may know more about what happened to your family than anyone else. Some of it because I got a brief from Division when you came back here, and some because Mickey Argyle knew another side to the story. I doubt if anyone else in the country knows as much as I do, and that's only because I made a pact with the devil. How's that for poetic justice?

"What do you want most in the world, Mr. Ash? To know what happened to your wife? To know where your sons are? What I can do for you is tell you things nobody else can—"

In the confined space, and the breathless hush into which Fountain was dropping his serpent words, the last gunshot sounded like cannon fire.

CHAPTER 31

ONLY WHEN JOHNNY Fountain fell over, no surprise on his face this time, just a dreadful blankness, did Hazel see Argyle behind him, propped up on one elbow, still aiming his gun with infinite care as if, in the clouding mists of his mind, he couldn't be sure if he'd hit him the first time.

Ash let out a wail of terrible anguish, the howl of a tortured dog. Fountain was dead before he hit the floor, but Ash wouldn't believe it. Couldn't bring himself to believe it. For most of four years he'd had no hope. Then someone had dangled the promise of information in front of him, and before he'd even had a chance to respond, the promise had balloon-burst in front of him. If Fountain was dead, what he knew had died with him.

Ash fell on him and thumped frantically at his chest, numb to the pain of his broken fingers. "Breathe," he cried, half furious, half weeping. "Breathe, damn you!"

Hazel reacted with a combination of instinct and training that precluded the need for thought. Before the sound had finished echoing around the forge, she'd caught Alice by the elbow and swung her outside the door. Then she turned back.

In training college they'd taught her the art of triage. It

didn't matter that Ash was breaking apart in front of her. It didn't matter that Johnny Fountain was dead or dying on the floor. It mattered that Argyle was still somehow conscious and still pointing his gun, and where Fountain had been a moment earlier, now there was Ash.

Hazel had half a second's notice of what was going to happen next. She didn't hesitate. She brought up the hand holding Fletcher's gun from due south to due west and fired.

Police trainees tend to divide into two camps: those who dread having to make the life-and-death decision and those who can't wait. On the whole, the former make better police officers. Hazel had been one of the former. What astonished her now was how easy it was, how uncomplicated by morality or compassion or simple human reticence, to make that decision when the moment came. To shoot a bad man in order to protect a good one. There was no thought in her mind of disabling Argyle. He needed stopping, right now, and she aimed the gun that fortune had provided her with at the center of his forehead and blew his brains out.

Hazel, he knew! What happened to them. He knew what happened to them!"

Now that it was over, Hazel's hands were trembling. She tried to keep her voice steady. "Gabriel, calm down. I don't think he knew anything. Only how to play with your emotions. He needed you to think there was something he could offer you, that's all."

"He said he knew where the boys are! Not where they died, not where they're buried—where they are!" There was something deeply pathetic about his eagerness to believe. "Doesn't that mean they're alive?"

Hazel put the gun down carefully on the anvil and put her

arms around him, though whether for his comfort or her own, she could not have said. "All he knew was what came down to him from Division—that you were living in Norbold again, and why, and that you might need an eye kept on you. I'm sorry, Gabriel. I don't think he knew anything that *you* don't know. He was trying to use you."

"But . . ." He so wanted to argue with her. To convince her that Chief Superintendent Fountain had put together snippets of information garnered on both sides of the fence and come to an understanding that no one else had. But before he was a grieving husband and father and a broken man he was a security analyst, trained to know when he was hearing the truth, and what she said made sense. At the end, Johnny Fountain had used every weapon at his disposal to save his professional life. And sometimes you don't even need a weapon to make someone do what you want—you just have to make them think you have one. He thought Hazel was probably right. The tears flowed from his swollen eyes down his bloody cheeks.

With DI Gorman and an ambulance finally on the way, Hazel took her companions outside, away from the abattoir inside the forge, and settled them in Fountain's car.

Ash looked doubtfully at the cream leather upholstery. "I don't want to bleed on it."

"Who's going to care?" asked Hazel brutally. "Listen to me, both of you. We have maybe ten minutes to decide what we're going to say. And the only way it can be other than the unvarnished truth is if we all agree."

Ash looked as if he hadn't quite taken in anything that had happened since Johnny Fountain turned his world upside down again, and he wasn't doing any better with this. "*Other* than the truth? Why . . ."

Hazel breathed heavily at him. "You know why. *Fountain* knew why. Because if we tell how it happened, I'm going to walk away undamaged and you're going to walk away undamaged, and Alice is going to have to convince the authorities that the father who murdered her fiancé was prepared to murder her, too, so it was self-defense when she shot him. Even after that her story—her tragedy—is going to be tabloid fodder for months. She's nineteen years old, Ash! She's been through enough already. What I'm asking is, can we save her from going through any more?"

Finally his thought processes seemed to engage. "How? How would it work?"

Hazel nodded, relieved to have got through to him. "We change a few salient details. Mr. Fountain offered to say that he shot Argyle—well, we take him up on that. I think the old bastard owes us a favor. So everything happened exactly the way it did until Argyle pulled his gun. Then Fountain snatched Fletcher's gun from Alice and shot him. Then he gave it to me to preserve as evidence. I'll put his prints on it, then some more of mine over the top."

It wouldn't just mean manhandling the corpse; it would mean lying. "But you killed Argyle?" Ash was making sure.

"I *did* kill Argyle. We're editing Alice out, that's all. If we're agreed that we should, and that we can all stick to the amended version."

Alice said numbly, "I meant to kill him. When I shot him, I intended to kill him."

"I know," said Hazel softly. "And I don't blame you, and I don't think anyone else would, either. The fact remains, you didn't kill him—I did. I was doing my job, and I'll answer for it to anyone who asks. There's nothing to be gained by saying it was you, not Fountain, who fired the first shots."

"I don't want anyone else paying for what I did."

"It won't cost me a thing. And it won't cost Mr. Fountain anything, either, and it wouldn't even if he was alive."

"Then . . ." The girl wrestled her head around it. "All right. Mr. Fountain shot him. I took the gun off Andy Fletcher, and Mr. Fountain grabbed it when my father produced his." Hazel could hear the burden lightening in her voice; but also the uncertainty that remained. The hope that could still be taken away.

"Exactly." She turned to Ash. "Gabriel?"

Except for physically, Ash wasn't even in the car. He was back in the forge, with Johnny Fountain offering to tell him about his sons. Recalled by the sound of his name, his body jerked. "What?"

"A kind lie or a harsh truth? Where do you stand on this?"

Ash blinked the better of his eyes. "If we lie, where does the lie stop?"

"Right there," said Hazel with certainty. "If you're wondering if I'm prepared to perjure myself to protect Johnny Fountain's memory, the answer's no. I don't care who knows. IPCC can worry about it, Division can worry about it. If they want to sit on it, they can. If they want it out in the open, they can issue a press release. I don't care. I'm asking if you'll help me protect Alice. One lie, to protect a nineteen-year-old girl who's done nothing wrong."

"You're a police officer. I don't think you're supposed to tell even one lie."

"No," she agreed, "I'm not. But I'm going to, unless you tell me you can't."

He thought for a moment. "I didn't see who shot Mickey Argyle."

Hazel gave a tight smile. "Good man."

"No, really—I didn't see. A lot of what happened I didn't actually see."

"Okay," said Hazel. "Stick to that, and don't speculate, and we'll be fine. And if either of you finds yourself in difficulties, remember the magic words."

"M-magic words?" stammered Alice.

"*I don't know.* Stops an interview in its tracks every time. Don't speculate, don't answer questions you haven't been asked, don't try to be clever, and any time you find yourself on shaky ground the answer is *I don't know.* It leaves the investigator nowhere to go. He may think you're lying through your teeth, but in order to unpick your story you have to give him a story to unpick. *I don't know* gives him nothing."

Alice said hesitantly, "You don't have to do this. If you're going to get into trouble . . ."

"I'm not going to get into trouble," said Hazel firmly. "I'll tell Mr. Gorman that the old sparring partners ended up shooting each other and he'll believe me. Why wouldn't he? If I was going to lie about anything, it would be about the shot *I* fired, and I'll be quite candid about that. I had no choice, so I did it."

"I wouldn't want you sacrificing your career for me," insisted Alice, shy and stubborn at the same time. "I've nothing to hide. Not my relationship with Jerome, not how it ended, and not the fact that I shot the man responsible. I don't know if it was self-defense. I think he *was* a danger to me, but that's not why I killed him. I killed him for Jerome."

"You didn't kill him," Hazel reminded her. "I did."

"I did my level best," said Alice.

Hazel heard the police cars coming and walked to the gate to meet them. But before they arrived, something else caught her eye. A very weary, very footsore, very dirty white dog was limping up the lane toward her, its tongue hanging around its knees.

"Oh dear God," murmured Hazel, and hurrying forward she bent and gathered the dog up in her arms; staggering a little under the weight because although it was leggy, it was also muscular. "Gabriel! It's Patience. . . ."

Alice, of course, had no idea where the dog had come from. But she saw how Ash reacted, and she got out of the car and went to the front seat so Hazel could put the animal in beside him. Patience put her head on his knee, and Ash stroked her grimy fur with anxious, damaged hands and bowed his head over her. His tears invested her with fresh new spots.

"She's all right," Hazel stammered, trying to reassure him. "I mean, she's worn-out, of course she is, and her feet'll take time to heal, but she'll be all right. Gabriel, she'll be fine."

"She followed me," whispered Ash. "When they took me from the cottage. She followed me here."

"She must have run for twenty miles," said Hazel, scarcely able to credit it.

The first of the cars arrived and she tore herself away. After a moment Alice went, too. Ash was left cradling his exhausted dog, both of them bleeding gently on the expensive upholstery of a dead man's car. "Are you?" he whispered. "All right?"

No, said the dog, I'm knackered. My feet are killing me and I'd sit up and beg for a cold drink. How about you?

"Had better days," mumbled Ash.

I can see.

CHAPTER 32

THE FOLLOWING AFTERNOON, when she visited him in hospital, Hazel thought Ash looked both better and worse. Worse, because those bits of him that weren't bandaged were swollen beyond recognition and his bruises were at their Technicolor height; better, because he looked cleaner and more cared for than he usually did. He lay propped on hospital pillows, his curly dark hair freshly washed, his splinted hands on the sheet folded over his chest, and for a moment she wasn't sure if he was asleep or if his eyes had finally swollen shut.

Then he gave a slow smile. "Hi, Hazel."

She returned the smile, hooked up a chair. "Hi yourself. How're you doing?"

"Oh, you know. Okay."

"You look terrible."

"You should see the other guy."

"I did," said Hazel, baldly enough to stop further conversation for a few moments. Then she shook off the memory. "Patience sends her love."

For a second he looked surprised. "You heard . . . ?" Then he realized it was a figure of speech. "Oh. Yes. Is she all right?"

"She's fine," said Hazel. "I took her to the vet last night, just to make sure. Then she slept for twelve hours straight and woke up ready to bring down a moose. Her feet are a bit scabby, but I'm putting cream on them and she's on the mend."

"It's good of you to take care of her," Ash said quietly.

There had been four options, but it didn't take long for Hazel to dismiss three of them. The dog wasn't ill enough to stay at the vet's, and it would have been poor reward for her loyalty to book her into a kennel. Hazel's landlady could probably have been talked into taking a temporary boarder, but what the dog really needed were the familiar comforts of her own home. Hazel had packed a bag and moved in with her.

No, that wasn't right. She was starting to think like Ash. She'd packed a bag *and moved into Ash's house.* The dog was a dog, not a tenant.

Hazel shrugged. "No problem. I'll stay with her till you're back on your feet." She sniffed. "It's not like I've much else to do."

He frowned. At least, that extra twisting of his misshapen face was probably a frown. "You're not going back to work?"

"Not for now. I've talked to IPCC, and I'll be seeing them again, but nobody's willing to give me the okay to return to duty. I shot someone. Even if he deserved it, they're worried I might have some kind of a psychological reaction and they don't want me ripping my clothes off and singing 'Nellie Dean' in front of the courthouse." She vented a weary sigh. "I'm not sorry. I'd only put a dampener on the gossip in the canteen if I went back now."

"But you will do? When the dust has settled?"

"Yes, of course," she said, sounding more confident than in fact she felt. "I might look for a transfer at some point, but I should go back to Meadowvale first, just to show I'm not afraid to. That I'm not the bad guy here. That their old mate Johnny Fountain was."

"You *should* go back," Ash agreed softly, "but not yet. Give yourself time to heal."

"That's good, coming from you."

He tried to shrug without hurting himself. "Don't underestimate the effect all this will have had on you. You've been through the wringer, too. You ended up having to kill someone. If nothing else had happened—if you hadn't been hurt, and threatened, and cut adrift by your colleagues—you'd have needed time to come to terms with that. Don't rush the process. Take all the time you need before you start easing yourself back into the groove."

Hazel nodded slowly, touched by his concern. "What about you? What are you going to do with the rest of your life?"

For a moment she thought Ash was going to lie to her. His gaze slid off around the room. But then it came back and he met her eyes with the bruised, narrowed slits of his own. "I know what you think, and you're probably right. That Fountain was blowing smoke in my face. That he didn't know anything about my family that isn't a matter of record.

"But Hazel—what if it was true? He was on friendly terms with a target criminal: What if Mickey'd heard something that never made it into the official record? What if they talked about me, after it turned out I was in the cells that night? What if Argyle told Fountain what he'd heard?"

Hazel knew how much he wanted it to be true. But she didn't think it was, and anyway she didn't think it would make much difference. "Suppose for a moment that you're right. I don't think you are, but suppose. Whatever they knew died with them. Don't let it torment you when there's no way you can ever know what it was, or even if there was something."

Ash didn't accept that. He couldn't—it mattered too much. "There are things we can assume," he said stubbornly. "Why would

Mickey know anything about piracy? If Fountain knew something, and if he got it from Mickey, Mickey got it from somewhere much closer to home than where these munitions were hijacked. The attacks happened in Africa, but I don't imagine that's where Mickey got his information. So maybe these people don't just work out of Somalia. They work here, too."

"*Norbold?*" exclaimed Hazel, astonished.

"Well, England anyway," amended Ash. There was a light like coals burning in the slits of his eyes. "Somewhere Mickey Argyle might have bumped into them. And that means, somewhere they can be found. Some place where they can't just disappear into the desert."

Hazel thought for a minute. "Listen to me, Gabriel. We'll talk about this again. When you're better, and I'm feeling a bit more normal. I know I'm not going to talk you out of it, so if you want to try and follow it up, I'll help you. I'm going to have time on my hands for a while—we can go over what you know and what Argyle could possibly have found out."

Her voice hardened. "But promise me you won't get your hopes up. You're not going to find your wife and your sons. You may conceivably find out what happened to them, even who was responsible, but you're not going to find them. They're gone. Do you understand that?" She knew she was being cruel. She also knew that she owed him the truth.

He gave a long, sad sigh. "Yes."

"All right, then. We'll get you home, get our breath back, and then you can tell me what you want to do. Who we could talk to, what we could ask. Yes?"

"Yes," Ash said again. He managed a tiny, grateful smile.

"One thing you can do right now," said Hazel, changing the subject, "is tell me where you keep your can opener. You've got a cupboard full of dog food and no way of getting into it. I ended up making us stew for dinner."

Ash refrained from saying that the reason the cupboards were full of dog food was that he very often shared his own meals with Patience. It hadn't struck him as particularly odd. "Try the top drawer of the hall bureau. I was using the bottle opener bit."

Hazel made a mental note. "You do know that most dog food comes in ring-pull cans, don't you?" she asked tartly.

"Patience prefers the other sort."

"Why am I not surprised?" Hazel couldn't however stop herself from smiling. She got up to leave, then on an impulse leaned forward quickly and kissed his forehead. "Get better. She's missing you. Well—we both are."

He was so surprised at the kiss that she was at the door before he called after her. "Anything else you can't find, ask Patience. She knows where everything's kept."

Hazel paused and looked over her shoulder at him. "As a matter of fact," she said stiffly, "I *did* ask Patience. She was no help. She must have forgotten about the bottle opener."

"Either that," murmured Ash to her departing back, "or she fancied your stew."

Turn the page for a sneak peek at
Jo Bannister's next novel

Perfect Sins

Available December 2014

Copyright © 2014 by Jo Bannister

CHAPTER I

STEPHEN GRAVES REMEMBERED the name well enough. But he wouldn't have recognized Gabriel Ash if they'd passed in the street. He'd struck Graves as a big man when they first met: tall, big-boned, powerful of build and of intellect. The man before him now seemed entirely shrunken. He even seemed shorter, thanks to a slight apologetic stoop.

Graves ushered him to a chair, quickly, as if afraid he might fall down. But his anxiety was unwarranted. Ash was in better shape than he looked. He was in better shape than he'd been for years.

With his visitor safely seated, Graves called his PA and asked for coffee. Ash waited politely, aware that these days his host's time was more important, or certainly more expensive, than his own.

Finally Graves overcame his surprise enough to open the conversation. It wasn't difficult to guess why Ash was here—there was only one issue that concerned them both. "I imagine it's the same matter you want to discuss."

Ash nodded. Thick black curls fell in his eyes. Graves doubted he'd spent proper money on a haircut since they'd last met. Only the suit was the same, and though clean and pressed, it now hung from Ash's cadaverous frame. "Some things have come up. Queries. I hoped you could cast some light . . ." Graves didn't interrupt him. The sentence just petered out, as if he'd lost interest in it.

The CEO of Bertram Castings took a moment to realize he'd finished. "Yes," he said. Then, keenly, "Yes, of course. Anything. If I can. If there's anything I haven't already told you. But first"—he bit his lip—"can I say how sorry I am about what happened? When I heard . . . I couldn't help feeling . . . guilty, I suppose. If you hadn't been trying to help us, perhaps . . . none of it . . ." It was his turn to run out of words.

Ash smiled. It was an oddly innocent smile for a man of forty, apparently without bitterness. "I was just doing my job. If I hadn't been doing it here, I'd have been doing it somewhere else. The consequences would very probably have been the same."

Whether or not it was true, the manufacturer appreciated him saying it. He'd assumed that Ash had been hating his guts for the last four years. It would have been understandable. "Has there been some news?"

"No," said Ash quickly. "At least, nothing"—he sought an appropriate adjective—"reliable. But someone said something, in a different context, and he was probably just winding me up, but I didn't feel I could let it go without at least trying to be sure."

"Who?" asked Graves, almost holding his breath. "Said what?"

"It was a policeman. A senior policeman, who might well

have heard things that weren't public knowledge. But who also had a good reason for wanting me to think he could help me." Ash swallowed. "He said—he gave me to understand—that he knew what had happened to my family. And I think—I *think*—he was saying that my sons are still alive."

Graves took a steadying breath and let it out slowly. "That would be wonderful."

"Yes, it would," agreed Ash. His voice was gossamer-thin. "If it's true."

"You said a policeman?"

"But not a very good one."

"You mean, you think he's lying?"

"He could have lied."

Graves frowned. "How can I help? Surely the one you need to be talking to, or someone needs to be talking to, is this policeman—to establish whether he actually knows anything or not."

"You're right, of course." Ash nodded. "Unfortunately, he's dead."

The man across the desk froze. "Who killed him?"

"A criminal. It's a long story," said Ash tiredly. "Before he died, when he was anxious for my help, he said he knew where my boys are. He might have meant where they were buried, but that's not what he said. Before I could ask him to explain, he died in front of me. And now I don't know, and don't know how to find out, if he was telling the truth."

It was a much abbreviated version of that desperate day's events, but it was accurate and it was as full an account as a peripheral player like Graves would need. Being a weapons manufacturer didn't make him an expert on gang culture. The whole of the arms trade is so ringed about by regulations that he couldn't have sold weapons to gangsters if he'd wanted to. He was an engineer by training, a businessman by choice, a pen pusher by necessity. The government inspectors cast such long shadows over his trade that he'd once found himself photocopying his wife's birthday card, just in case.

"Gabriel, I don't know what to say." The use of his visitor's first name didn't come naturally—they'd never been on first name terms—but it felt more awkward still to call him Mr. Ash when the man had stripped his soul in front of him. "Tell me how you think I can help."

Ash smiled again, gratefully. "In all honesty, I'm not sure you can. I just couldn't think where else to go. The thing is, this policeman had been working in Norbold, where I live, for the last eight years. Before that he was up north somewhere. He was never in Africa. If he knew anything about Somali piracy, he heard about it while living and working in England. And that's what he said—that he heard it from a local criminal. In fact, the one who shot him.

"And if he really did know something, if it wasn't just a bait he was dangling in front of me, I think that had to be true. I'm pretty sure he didn't get it from an official source. I've been to Whitehall—I still know people there—and what they told me is that they've learned nothing new about my family in the last four years. I believe them. If there'd been anything to report, my old boss would have told me, with or without his minister's approval."

Ash had worked for Philip Welbeck for five years. He'd known he was a good boss. He hadn't known how good a friend he was until his world fell apart. Admittedly, Ash had broken

Welbeck's nose in a highly public brawl in Parliament Street, and Welbeck had had him committed to a psychiatric institution, but both these acts had long ago been forgiven. Ash had been far from rational when he took a swing at his superior. And Welbeck had been absolutely rational, as cool and clinical as always, and totally focused on the safety of Ash's family, when he called the men in white coats.

There was no knowing if Cathy and the boys were still alive when Ash, insane with worry, stormed down to London, demanding to know what was being done to find them. But if they were alive, it was to keep Ash from returning to his job in national security and hunting down those responsible for the hijacking of British-made munitions. This was what he was good at, what he was perhaps better at than anyone else. It had taken the pirates some time to recognize the fact. But when they did, they had moved quickly to neutralize the threat he posed. Holding his family hostage gave them control of Gabriel Ash.

After the scene in Parliament Street it was impossible to pretend he hadn't disobeyed Welbeck's instructions by returning to London. All Welbeck could do to salvage the situation was make it clear that Ash wasn't working, on his family's abduction or the acts of piracy that preceded it, because he wasn't fit to work, and quite possibly never would be again.

That was then. This was now. Ash couldn't use official channels to pursue the search anymore. This was what he was doing instead: picking up the threads of the investigation that had cost him everything and trying to find out if they still led anywhere.

He was grateful Graves had agreed to see him. Ash wanted him to understand that, though he had little in the way of new evidence, he wasn't just raking over the same old coals. "If this policeman was telling the truth, he learned what happened to my family from a Norbold drug dealer. And that means that everyone involved in these hijackings isn't half a world away in Somalia. There's a local dimension. Someone here is involved."

"Here?" Graves's eyebrows shot toward his hairline. Although he was no older than Ash, his hair was gray and he kept it clipped short to teach it a lesson. He did spend proper money on haircuts.

"Sorry," said Ash hastily, "I don't mean here at Bertrams. I mean here in England. And I found myself wondering—you're going to think I'm crazy," Ash interjected with the painful wryness of someone who knew what it was like to be thought crazy—"if there was any chance that someone you work with could be selling information on your shipments. Not necessarily one of your employees—it could be an auditor or a tax inspector, or someone from Health & Safety, someone who comes and goes without exciting much interest. But someone who has access to your shipping details, so the pirates know when you're sending munitions in their direction, what aircraft you'll be using, and which airfields you'll be putting down at."

Graves was obviously taken aback. His company had lost a small fortune in goods hijacked en route to their end users in Africa, but the general understanding had been that that was where the problem lay—in Africa, with the customers' security arrangements. Five times in four years it had happened, and it wasn't just the munitions that had disappeared each time but also the aircraft and the crew. People had died trying to deliver his goods, and the only consolation was that the British police had looked at Bertrams's security protocols and told the CEO there was nothing more he could have done to protect them.

Now Gabriel Ash seemed to be telling him something different. "How would I know?" he asked, concerned.

"Maybe you wouldn't. Maybe there was nothing to notice. But maybe there was someone who showed just a bit more interest in your shipping arrangements than seemed natural. Who asked where aircraft would be refueled, or which carrier was carrying which shipment, or how crew were recruited. Something like that. Or something quite different, but still not quite what you'd expect. Not quite right."

Graves was trying to think, but this had been sprung on him. He'd had a couple of hours' notice that Ash wanted to call, none at all that this was the reason. His face creased with the effort to remember. Finally, regretfully, he shook his head. "I'm sorry, nothing's coming to mind. But can I have some time to think about it? I'll go through the records, see who was in the office in the days before each hijacking. See if any pattern emerges. Give me your number. I'll call you if I come up with anything."

Ash gave him the number of his new mobile. "Call me anyway. It doesn't need to be a concrete suspicion. If you think of anyone with access to the relevant information, I'll talk to the other firms that lost shipments and see if the same name comes up again."

Graves pulled over a notebook and wrote some names and numbers from memory. "Talk to Bob Simpson at Gaskins. I know they lost a shipment of assault rifles not long ago. And Sandy Pierson at Viking. That's Ms. Pierson, incidentally," he added with a nervous grin, "don't get off on the wrong foot by asking for

Mr. Pierson. They've both become involved since you . . ." Another unfinished sentence. This time the missing words were *Went doolally.*

Ash nodded his thanks and folded the paper carefully into his breast pocket. "I suppose it's a pretty small world, arms manufacture—that you all know one another?"

"In some ways," agreed Graves. "In others, of course, it's global. But anyone in the industry will help you if they can. We need to get on top of these hijackings. Somali pirates are making a quarter of the world almost a no-go area for weapons exports."

"Which begs the question why you continue selling a sensitive product to such a volatile region."

Graves shrugged. "Because it's our business. Because volatile regions are where arms are needed. We couldn't stay solvent by selling what we make to the Isle of Man. And then, don't we have an obligation to support Third World countries that are trying to make a go of the democratic model? They wouldn't get far if all the demagogues and tyrants around them could march over their undefended borders."

It was a valid point. Besides, Ash wasn't here to do battle with the arms industry. His mission was much more tightly focused than that. "I need to be candid with you, Mr. Graves. Tackling piracy against British citizens, British carriers, and British goods is the job of the British government. It used to be my job, but it isn't anymore. My only interest now is in finding out what happened to my wife and my sons.

"They disappeared because, when I *was* part of the government investigation, I got close enough to the pirates to worry them." Ash's deep, dark eyes were hot with the memory: at how clever he'd been, and how stupid. "For four years I believed my family were dead. Now there seems just a small chance that they aren't—that if I can work it out, I can find them. I may be fooling myself. But I don't want to mislead you. If finding my family means destroying these people—in Somalia, in England, wherever they are—then I will if I can. But that's not my priority. If you help me, you have to understand that I may not be able to help you much in return. If the pirates offer to buy my silence with the only currency I'm interested in, nothing—not honor, not duty, *nothing*—will stop me from taking it. Nothing matters to me as much as finding my wife and sons."

"I understand that," said Graves, rising and offering his hand. "Bertrams will help in any way we can."

Jo Bannister began her career as a journalist after leaving school at sixteen to work on a weekly newspaper. She was short-listed for several prestigious awards and worked as an editor for some years before leaving to pursue her writing full-time. She lives in Northern Ireland, and spends most of her spare time with her horse and dog, or clambering over archaeological sites.

FICTION BANNISTER

Bannister, Jo.
Deadly virtues

SEAST

R4001635507

SOUTHEAST
Atlanta-Fulton Public Library